Until You FORGIVE

An Until You Novel

Book Five

D.M. DAVIS

www.dmckdavis.com
Cover Design by Hang Le
Cover Photo by Wander Aguiar Photography LLC
Cover Model is Andrew Biernat
Editing by Tamara Mataya
Proofreading by Mountains Wanted Publishing & Indie Author Services
Formatting by Champagne Book Design

This book is a work of fiction. Names, characters, places, and incidents are either the product of the author's imagination or are used fictitiously.

This story contains mature themes, strong language, and sexual situations. It is intended for adult readers.

About This Book

D.M. Davis' *Until You Forgive* is a heart-wrenching, second-chance romance with a love triangle between a playboy millionaire, a celebrity athlete, and the loyal best friend.

I'm two people: the man I was *before* her and the man I am *after* her.

It's been seven years since I've laid eyes on my heart, my Gabby.
The girl I hurt in one devastatingly thoughtless act.
The girl who broke my heart after I broke hers.
My chest is full of shame and missteps.
I wear regret like the suit I don every day as VP of Marketing
for my family's tech company—my number one regret being
Gabby, the girl who got away.

You may know me as the middle McIntyre brother—the
playboy millionaire who spends his days in the boardroom and
his nights in any bedroom he chooses.
She's the reason for my manwhore ways… *She* drove me to it.

But I'm not *that*. Not anymore.

**When destiny puts her in my path again, can I convince the
only girl I've ever loved I'm worth forgiving, worth a second
chance, or will I lose her to a man I can't stand, who warms
her heart but not her bed?**

Note to Reader

Until You Forgive runs concurrent to Until You Books
1-4 and beyond.
Therefore, I highly recommended you read the previous books before
jumping into Matt and Gabby's story to avoid spoilers and missing out
on getting to know the whole cast from word one.

You won't be disappointed. I promise.

XOXO, Dana

Playlist

Love Me Now by John Legend

I'm Never Getting Over You by Gone West Gone West

Bad Habit by Ben Platt

Takeaway by The Chainsmokers, ILLENIUM Ft. Lennon Stella

You Broke Me First by Tate McRae

Half a Man by Dean Lewis

But We Lost It by P!nk

Words Ain't Enough by Tessa Violet

Cold At The Alter by Chris Klafford

Patience by Chris Cornel

Lonely by Justin Bieber & Benny Blanco

Let's Hurt Tonight by OneRepublic

Talking to The Moon by Bruno Mars

Falling by Harry Styles

Walk Me Home by P!nk

Helium by Sia

I Love Me by Megan Trainor

Carry You by Ruelle

This I Promise You by Richard Marx

Strong Enough by Sheryl Crow

Always by Francois Klark

Dedication

For all the women who break boundaries every day by just being you.

For my daughter who's starting her first season of football.
May it not be her last.

For every woman who dreams of *more* and goes for it.

This is for you.

Until You FORGIVE

One

THEN

THE WIND WHIPS MY HAIR INTO A CHAOTIC MESS. I struggle to tame it, pulling a few strands out of my mouth and lashes while simultaneously trying to remember if I have a hidden hair tie somewhere on my body. I curse myself for not putting my hair in a ponytail before I was dragged to the practice field.

Okay, maybe not dragged. *Coerced*, most definitely. The blonde nymph wouldn't take no for an answer. I figure what's the harm. It's just a little flag football between dorms. There aren't even real coaches just other students, coming together for some fun.

Yet, I feel stupid. I shouldn't be here. I don't even know what I'm doing.

I've never played flag football. Soccer is my sport. It came naturally. Barely even had to try. But it's been… a while. A long while.

Life took the wind out of that sail.

My mom…

"Hey. You're Gabby, right?" The thin, perfect-bone-structure, making-me-feel-like-a-fat-cow blonde points at me.

"Yeah." I'm not sure I want to admit that as she motions over my shoulder.

"You're with him."

"*Him?*" My question falls limp as I turn to face the dark-haired, you've-got-to-be-kidding-me,   aren't-there-any-fat-people-at-this-school god behind me. His smirking gaze is already on me like he's been waiting for me, setting off tingles down my spine and fireworks in my brain.

A flashback to a paper I did on Greek mythology has Priapus, the god of virility, coming to mind.

I think I could get pregnant from here.

Down, girl. You're not even in his league. He doesn't look like the kinda guy who likes girls with meat on their bones and junk in their trunk.

A few guys shuffle over to him as per the blonde's directions. Other groups gather with their designated "coach" who are students like me except with experience.

"Come on, Gorgeous," the god waves me over, "I don't bite." His grin deepens to reveal dimples.

Kill me now.

"Not without a proper introduction at least." He sticks his hand out.

I stare at it far too long without moving in his direction.

He steps away from the guys at his side, takes my hand in his, emerald eyes shining, entirely too confident. "I'm Matt. It's a pleasure to meet you, Gabby."

Damn, he was paying attention, cared enough to learn my name.

Heartbreakingly handsome, attentive, with devilish charm. A lethal combination.

"Are you going to bite me now?" I'm going for funny and lighthearted, but the little shake in my voice has it falling just shy of tentative.

Gah, I hate tentative Gabby. I thought I left her behind—at home—where she dwelled all too comfortably in the timid zone. *Go away, timid Gabby. There's no room for you here in my new life. My new life in college where I get to be whoever I please. No parent or older brothers reminding me I'm not skinny enough to be a proper woman and not big or tough enough to be considered one of the guys.* I was just me. Always just me. Never enough and yet entirely too much.

Matt's laugh zips me back to him, my hand in his, his head shaking. Amused at me, or maybe himself. It's undetermined. Before I consider it further, he leads me to the group of guys waiting on him. It's not until we're in a circle that he drops my hand and winks.

Yep, he's an expert flirt. He could give lessons, offer a seminar to dorky college guys. He'd make a killing.

Introductions all around. Matt nods; he doesn't try to shake their hands or mention biting them.

Is it just me he's being a bit nicer to?

No. It would never be just you, Gabriella Two Ton, my oldest brother's tease whispers in my ear.

Yeah, I know. Thanks for the reminder.

"Gabby?" Matt eyes me expectantly as the others look on… waiting. Shit. "I'm sorry. What?"

His smirk is delectable as he beats a rhythm on his clipboard with his pen. "Name. Phone number. Position."

"Oh, um—" I rattle off my details until I get to the position part. "I've no idea. I've never played before." I glance around and wonder why I'm the only girl in his group when all the other groups look to be evenly balanced. Maybe I could switch?

Maybe I could leave. This is voluntary, right? I can't be locked into anything yet. It's just an intermural league between the dorms. They wouldn't miss me—

"Have you played any sports?" he continues, undaunted by my lack of experience.

"Soccer. Volleyball. A little softball."

"Can you throw? Catch? Run? Ki—"

"I can kick," I interject, wanting everyone's focus off me. Not *his,* but it's not… He would never. Gah, I can feel their eyes judging me, trying to figure out why he's so focused on me. I want to melt into the field and disappear. But maybe take him with me.

He nods and makes a note. The rest of the guys give their details and preferred position. I look around, anywhere but at him. *Don't stare.*

It's not long before we're back with the rest of the group, stretching, warming up, then running a few laps—my favorite. Not. Running and me have never been the best of friends, hence why I played goalie in soccer.

How translatable are those skills in football?

I get lost in the mix and move farther and farther away from my group as we return to the sidelines.

"Trying to escape?" Mr. Sexy Pants' road-worn, radio-ready voice tickles up my neck.

I shiver and catch his smirk as I pivot to face him. "If I say *yes*, would you let me off the hook and remove my name from the roster?"

He chuckles. "Not a chance, Gorgeous."

I stifle my shock. Is he teasing me? Making fun? The god of virility wouldn't think I'm *gorgeous*. He wouldn't even notice me at all. I shrug, playing it off. "It was worth a shot."

I heard some of the girls giggling over him. He's a freshman like me, but he seems to know everyone, feel comfortable here, whereas I feel like a fish out of water—on this field and on this campus.

"Come on." Ushering me forward, he pulls two other guys from the bunch as we make our way to the end of the field. He tosses the first guy a football. "Show me what you got." He points down the field. "Aim for the goalposts."

"Just punt it?" the lanky dark-haired guy asks.

"Yep." Matt folds his arms and tips his chin down the field.

The guy steps back, takes a few steps, releases the ball and misses. "Shit."

"No worries. No pressure. Try again," Matt calmly instructs with no judgment, pretense, or expectations.

Lanky kicks it the second time, making it about forty yards.

The next guy kicks it a little farther.

Then it's my turn.

All eyes on me, I take the ball, get a feel for it. It's different than a soccer ball, but the motion is the same—or looks to be based on what the two previous guys did and what I've seen on TV. I might have even kicked a football with my brothers when I was little, but honestly, I don't remember.

I step back a little more, eye the goalpost, then the ball, point it to where I want it to go, take two steps and dropkick it on the third. My foot makes perfect contact at the desired angle; my leg follows through as the ball soars in the air with a sweet spin, picking up speed and arch.

That felt good. It's been too long.

"Damn," from Matt.

"Holy shit," from Lanky.

Second Best just scowls. I shrug and glance back just in time to see the ball bounce in the endzone. I didn't quite make the goalpost, but it was close.

A whistle from the sidelines has me flashing to a beefy guy talking with his buddies. If I were to guess, it's about me.

"Move along." Matt waves them off. "She's ours."

Ours? He doesn't even know me, and he's claiming me? I want to hug him *and* run in equal measure. "Who are they?" I ask as the big guy smiles, giving us a chin nod, his eyes lingering on me before he turns and saunters off with confidence I'll never be able to muster.

"That's our school's quarterback, wide receiver, and center." He circles me, his gaze assessing as I turn to face him. "That had to be a six-ty-yard kick."

"Is that good?" I'm sure I can kick farther, but it was my first attempt in years.

"Is it good?!" Lanky chuckles.

Second Best shakes his head. "Forty-five yards is an average punt. The NFL field goal record is currently sixty-four yards. I'd say your kick was pretty damn good."

Huh, maybe there *is* something I'm good at. Though I doubt my dad would be proud. He wants a daughter, not a tomboy, or a wannabe. I never wanted to be his son, and he certainly never treated me like a princess. I only wanted to fit in, and doing traditionally boy-type things seemed to be the way to his heart… His approval. Or so I thought.

Turns out, he only wants grandbabies from me. Someday. That's all I'm good for.

"Hey, Gorgeous." Matt grazes my arm. "You with me?"

No. And please stop calling me that. You're messing with my head. "Yeah."

Some guy runs over, giving me a nod before handing a tee to Matt, whose gaze flashes to me. He licks his lips, then places the tee on the grass and sets the football on it with a slight lean. Coming to his full height, which is still at least five inches taller than my 5'10" frame, he eyes me speculatively. "You good?"

"Um, yeah. You just want me to kick it?"

"Yep. Give it your best. We can work on form later."

Form. The idea of his hands on me getting me into position the way he moved the ball flashes before me. I turn my focus to the football as my cheeks heat up. Yep, my dirty mind is going full-on Girls Gone Wild—Spring Break Edition.

Focus. People are watching. *He's* watching.

I line up behind it, stepping back.

"A little more," Lanky urges.

So, I step back until he nods, then to the left two steps. "I've seen this on TV. I've just never done it."

He nods again. "Natural stride, no stuttered steps, then kick the hell out of that ball, darlin." Lanky winks.

Natural steps. No stutter. Pulverize ball.

Natural steps. No stutter. Pulverize ball.

Ignore them. Ignore *him.*

Natural steps. No stutter. Pulverize ball.

A couple of deep breaths, I rock back and forth on my feet, walk, then quicken my last few steps—a run but not quite. Hips open, leg swinging, foot pointed and locked, I make contact, loving the *thwap* and *whoosh* as the ball takes flight. I concentrate on my follow through, a small hop to keep the momentum going, kicking leg swings up and quickly down. A few more steps, I come to a halt and track the ball, counting in my head the hang time.

I'm sure I'm counting too fast, but look at that baby fly.

I shake out my leg. I should have stretched more. My hips are tighter than they used to be. I need to work on that.

But, you know. Cardio.

"You okay?" Matt motions to my leg.

"Yeah, I'm good." I'll be sore later.

He smirks, shaking his head as the ball flies through the goalposts. "Yeah, you are, Gorgeous." His hand presses to my back. "Damn good."

I keep Gabby in sight for as long as I can before she disappears around a building. Whatever Jen is saying is going in one ear and out the other. I keep nodding, a bit in shock of what just happened. I don't think these guys have any idea of the magic we just witnessed on this practice field. Magic in the form of a striking brunette with killer blue eyes and a million-dollar leg.

Mark my words—she's pure magic.

I'm not the only one who noticed. Deke, our quarterback; Trent, our wide receiver; and Nate, our center; all noticed. Nate in particular. They might have moved along when I told them Gabby was all ours—I really meant *mine*. I didn't miss them hanging back, watching her make that field goal.

She said she can kick.

She wasn't lying.

But I don't think she realized what an anomaly she is. A female kicker. A female *football* kicker.

The glint in Nate's eyes was unmistakable. It won't be the last time we'll be seeing him.

I need to stake my claim before he does.

Before *any* of these other assholes do. Afterall, she's here because

I asked Jen to invite her, and I only agreed to help out because it was a chance to meet the long-legged beauty I spotted a few days ago.

"You heading home?" Jen draws my attention with a hand on my left pec.

"Yeah." I've thought of taken all Jen has to offer, but… she's a little too easy for my taste.

She bites her lip, moving in closer, her tits rubbing against my chest as she shimmies. "Sure I can't entice you to join me for lunch and *dessert?*"

She'd make a savory snack, but a brunette with killer legs has my attention. I'm not good with multitasking. "I can't. Raincheck?" No reason to burn this bridge. Never know when I might feel like crossing.

"Sure." She hides her disappointment behind a fake smile. "Thanks for helping out today."

"Not a problem." My pleasure, actually.

After helping her load up all the equipment in her car, I head home. I'm not sure I'll tell Fin about my discovery today, but I do know I'll be thinking a whole hell of a lot about my kicker.

Two

THEN

AS OF THIS MOMENT, I DON'T HAVE A ROOMMATE. I didn't ask for a single dorm room, but that's what I have. Though I'm not sad about it, I was kinda looking forward to the whole college dorm experience, and that requires a roommate or two. Maybe that's why I let myself be convinced to play on the dorm's co-ed flag football team—to meet people.

People who don't know me, don't know my hang-ups or my family. Here I can be whoever I want, and I definitely want to be the *new* Gabby.

But at the moment, I'm feeling like the *old* Gabby. Went to dinner by myself, ate by myself, and returned to the dorm in the same manner.

Lonely is just a word, but it's a horrible way to feel.

So much life all around me, and yet here I sit, getting ready for class tomorrow, no roommate to bond with, to conspire with, to get into normal college-kid trouble with.

Early childhood education is my major, but how am I ever going to convince a shy child to step out and take a chance if I never do?

It feels hypocritical at worst, letting myself down at best.

It's time to make a list. Decide what I want. Set goals and steps to achieve them. I open my Notes app and create a new one.

Gabby's Wants

1. A best friend
2. A boyfriend
3. Lose my virginity
4. Find a group where I belong
5. Ignore the doubt (silence the voice in my head)

Yeah, I don't sound crazy at all!

6. Lose 50 pounds

Okay maybe thirty...

6. Lose 20 pounds
7. Forget Dad/brothers (don't let them hold me back)
8. Mom... forgive? Forget?
9. Give up Diet Coke and sugar

Maybe just cake. For starters.

10. Be lovable

A knock at my door has me jumping to attention. Do I answer or ignore it?

New Gabby. Remember?

With renewed determination, I open the door to the blonde goddess from practice. To say I'm surprised to see her at *my* door is an understatement. I wouldn't expect her to even speak to me, much less seek me out.

"Hey…" Gah, what's her name?

"Hi!" She waves like I'd expect a girl like her would—friendly and with pep. "I don't know if you remember, but I'm Jen." She motions down the hall. "A bunch of us are heading out to a party. Wanna come?"

"P-party? Me?"

"Yeah, of course." She shrugs in a bouncy sorta way. "You're cool. I thought you might like to meet some people and… I don't know… have fun." This chick has to be a cheerleader. She's entirely too enthusiastic.

Stunned, I just stare.

Her smile only grows. "We'll be leaving in like an hour. Come. It'll be awesome." She points across the hall. "I'm 210. Door will be open. Just come in when you're ready."

"Ready?" Am I not ready? Shit, what do I wear to a college party? I'd ask to borrow something, but there's no way her clothes would fit my ass.

"Yeah, nothing fancy." She eyes my yoga shorts and t-shirt. "Just maybe not workout clothes. It's hot out, so dress cool… We're walking."

With that, she turns and skips—no joke, skips—down the hall, waving before slipping inside her room.

Wow. I put it out there that I needed to make friends, and the universe answered.

Or so I hope. She seems genuine, but I know no one is friendly without a reason, a motive. What's hers? Am I her charity case?

Forty-five minutes later I knock on her door. I was ready in about fifteen minutes, then paced, changed clothes three times, only to put back on my original stonewashed cutoff shorts and pale floral blouse that hugs my breasts and hangs off the shoulders. It's a little see-through in the light of day but should be all good at night. Then, of course, I paced some more psyching myself up for this. New Gabby wouldn't be afraid.

Jen beams when she opens her door. "Yay, you made it!" She waves me in. "This is Stacy, Nikki, and Teri." She points around the room. Each of the girls are in a different state of readiness. "Ladies, this is Gabby."

Greetings exchanged, I hold up the wall while they finish getting ready.

"I love your hair," Teri—or it might be Nikki—says as she fusses with her naturally curly hair before deciding to clip it up.

"Thanks." I'm glad I decided to wear mine down. I put some loose curls in it and have a hair tie in my pocket in case I get hot and need to put it up. I double-check I have my license, cash, debit card, room key, gloss, and phone in my pockets. I don't like to carry a purse when I don't have to, and a college party seems like a no-purse zone.

It's not too long before a few more people join us as we exit our dorm and head out across campus. I'm not all that comfortable with the campus layout just yet. I know how to get from my dorm to my classes, administration, bookstore, student union and back. But I have yet to explore campus to find those hidden gems, best coffee spot, study escape or even simple shortcuts. Hopefully, in a few weeks I'll be an old pro.

Like a pied piper of parties, Jen pulls more people into our group as we go. She doesn't even have to try. She just smiles and sashays, and *boom*, they follow her. How easy it must be to be her, golden girl with all the charm. She's the blonde version of Matt, all allure and charisma, backed by a confidence I can't even comprehend. The urge to cower and slink away is strong, but I fight it. She invited me. She thinks I belong here. Maybe I do.

Or I'll pretend I do until I believe it. *Fake it until you make it.*

By the time we get to a house just off campus, we've amassed a group of twenty or more. I stopped counting around fifteen.

The cottage-style house is vibrant with life, music, and cheer. People mill around the front yard, come and go around the sides, so I assume most of the action is in the backyard, as there's no way all these people could fit inside the tiny house—or maybe it's bigger than it appears. At the moment, it appears like a clown car, more people coming and going than it could possibly hold.

Jen turns to the group, eyeing me and a few others I believe are freshmen too. "For you newbies, don't drink anything you didn't open or pour yourself. Other than that, have fun. Be safe." Her PSA complete, she sashays away with her close group of girls like the cheerleader I'm sure she is.

She brought us to the party, but she has no intention of partying *with* us.

I'm actually relieved. I'm working on New Gabby, but I don't think I have the energy to keep up with Jen and her friends. They shine a little too bright for me.

"Whose house is this?" I ask no one in particular.

The guy next to me tips his head with a wide smile. "No idea, but I think we should find out." He prompts me forward as he steps ahead.

Operation Make Friends, Be A College Student awaits me through those doors. I guess it's now or never.

I was right about one thing, well, maybe two things. The house is bigger than it appears, and it *is* teeming with life—college life. Wow.

We only make it a few feet in the door before a huge guy with a messy brown mop of curls eyes us. Stepping closer, he squints at me. "Are you her?"

He's looking right at me, but I've never seen him before.

"Who?" I glance behind me to see if he's really talking to someone over my head, but no, no one behind me seems to have his focus.

"You are," Mop of Curls hollers across the room, "Hey, get Nate. Tell him she's here." Another big guy nods and disappears through one of three doorways. Is this like a fun house? How many rooms could this clown-car house have?

My attention falls back to Mr. Mop of Curls. "You have me confused with someone else. I don't know who you're looking for, but I'm quite sure it's not me." I move to step around him, but he hooks my elbow.

"Hold on a sec. Nate'll be pissed if I let you go."

"Let me go? I don't even know you or Nate."

His brows rise into his hairline. "You don't know me?" He motions to his body as if that's any help. "I'm famous. Infamous, actually."

I think he's serious. In disbelief, I eye him up and down. "For what?"

"For being an ass," a baritone voice answers beside us. "Let her go, Dwight."

Mop of Curls, apparently named Dwight, holds his hands up. "I was just making sure she didn't slip away."

"You did your job. I've got her now." Firm jaw and hazel eyes loom over me, topped by floppy light-brown hair. "I was hoping you'd show up tonight."

My brows pinch. "That's a crock. You don't even know me."

He fights a smile and crosses his arms over his massive chest.

What's up with all these muscly guys?

"I'm Nate." Like that's any help.

"Yeah, I gathered that from your henchman." I thumb to the other even *bigger* guy.

Nate's lips twitch. "And I do know you."

Not possible. "How?"

He unfolds his arms and motions across the room. "Come on, Firecracker. Let me explain over drinks."

"And then you're going to kill me and bury me in the backyard? No thanks." I reverse but hit something solid, and it's not a wall. I look back into the inquisitive stare of Dwight.

"If he hurts you, I'll kill him. Promise, he doesn't mean you any harm," Moppy, err Dwight, assures me.

"From one serial killer to another," I grumble.

They both laugh.

I'm glad they find this funny. It's just weird.

"I like her, Nate. Don't ruin it." Moppy urges me toward Nate with a meaty paw on my hip.

"Don't plan to." Nate chin nods to him then pins me with his heated gaze I feel everywhere. "I knew I liked you the second I spotted you on that field holding a football like it was precious." He leans in, stealing a feel of one of my dark curls. "Let me show you I'm one of the good guys. There's no murder here tonight unless you deem it necessary on some poor sap who steps out of line, then it's my honor to oblige."

Damn, be still my heart. "One drink. I open it or pour it."

He smirks. "Yes, ma'am. You're the boss."

Bottle of beer in each of our hands—he twisted off the top while I watched, such a gentleman—we make our way to the basement, where guys bigger than him sit on couches watching a game on a massive screen. A few girls are chilling with them, on them, but mostly is seems to be a guys-only room.

"Whose house is this?" I ask in passing as he continues to guide me out the back sliding door to a secluded deck below the upper deck. "Is this where the murder happens?" I mean seriously. "No one knows where I am."

"Hey." He stops in his tracks, moving into my space. "You're safe here. You're safe wherever I am, and once everyone knows you're with me, you'll be safe wherever you go."

Is he serious?

"With you? I'm not *with* you."

"You're kinda lucky you *are* with me. Don't ever tell a strange guy no one knows where you are." He shudders.

Stalker or Samaritan? "Are you for real?"

Ignoring my comments completely, he holds out his hand. "Give me your phone."

Like the trusting person I'm typically not, I hand my unlocked phone over. He did have a point.

He messes with it a minute and hands it back when his phone dings. He smiles at his screen, his striking features lighting up as he types before sliding it into his pocket.

My phone chimes with a text message.

Nate (BFWB) Sinclair: *Now you have my number. You'll always have someone to call.*

Damn, that's sweet. "Cute." I pocket my phone. "What's BFWB?"

"Best Friends With Benefits. BFWB." He throws out like it's nothing, like I'm not shocked that he wants to be my friend, much less my *best* friend, and *benefits*… Jesus. *Yes, please.*

"Sit." He pulls two chairs till they're angled nearly facing each other.

I take the one facing the yard, back to the wall. A girl can never be too safe… says the girl who followed a complete stranger to a secluded, dark location.

"You're with me in all the ways that matter," he answers my earlier comment. "You're one of ours now."

"*Ours?* Yeah, that doesn't sound creepy at all." I chuckle in disbelief. Ten minutes ago I didn't know anyone except Jen—who abandoned me *before* the door—and now I've seen the mancave, been sequestered away, and claimed by the Hulk and his buddies.

This. Escalated. Quickly.

"You really don't know who we are? Who I am?"

"No clue." I should feel scared or unsettled, right? So, why does this guy feel safe?

Safe-ish.

"Hmm…" He takes a long pull from his beer.

I do the same.

"I don't know whether to be offended or impressed." He points his bottle at me. "Jen brought you here because I asked her to."

Ah, so she wasn't just being nice. Noted. "And why's that?"

"Because I saw you kick. Because there's something about you besides a killer body and a powerhouse of a leg."

Killer body? Powerhouse? I take another drink to hide my frown. He asked for me and now all the compliments. And BFWB. It feels like a set up. This kinda stuff doesn't happen to me.

"And what do you want from me?" There's got to be a catch.

"Two things." He holds up two fingers around the bottle he has resting on his knee.

This should be interesting. "I'm listening."

"I want you on our football team."

I nearly choke on my last sip. Coughing, I manage a quick, "I'm sorry, what?"

"I want you to join the Longhorns."

All these big, muscley guys make sense now. They're football players.

My smile can't get any bigger. "You're joking, right?" I start to stand, but he positions himself over me, not entirely, but close enough to prevent me from getting up unless I push him out of my way or rub up against him. And let's be honest, hot guy alert. And let's not forget number three on my Wants List: *lose my virginity*. Maybe Nate could help me with that.

"You've got a solid leg with great potential. We need a kicker. You're a natural."

But then he goes and reminds me of my kicking skills. SO much for "killer body." He doesn't *want* want me. He wants my leg.

I visually trace the broad lines of his shoulders up to his eyes. Damn, he's got an amazing body and hazel eyes that scream kindness despite my wariness. "You realize I'm missing a key ingredient, right?"

His smile messes with my head. "I'm quite aware you're a girl." He winks, moving in closer, whispering, "I'll try not to hold that against you, Firecracker." His gaze moves up my legs, stopping where they join before caressing up to my breasts. He bites his lip and tips my chin. "On second thought, I might like to hold it against you, over and over again."

Damn, this guy has fiery sexuality locked down. He oozes confidence and promises of yummy stuff between the sheets, table, or wall. Not that I know about such things, but I read… and, well, movies. If I wasn't turned on before, I am now.

A deep throat clearing, "Ahem," has me flashing to the space where you can walk into the backyard. "I told you she was taken." Matt approaches, jaw clenched and his hand extended. "Gabby. Let's go."

Go? I flash between the hot mess standing before me and the hot mess sitting next to me. Taken? Man, what did I do to find myself in this hot-man sandwich? I heat up from the inside out, my cream filling ready to be tasted by one or both of these hotties. What would that even feel like to have two guys fixated on me and my pleasure? Damn good, I imagine. But, hello, virgin. What the hell do I know about being with two guys, much less one? I gulp, swallowing my moan. Yeah, that visual will be hanging around my brain for a long while.

"She looks pretty free to me, Matt," Nate grits out as he sits back in his seat, releasing me from his potent yet invisible hold.

"Gabby." The command in Matt's voice has me popping to my feet and smashing into reality. He grabs my hand and pulls me away, into the lit backyard.

"You have my number, Firecracker. Talk soon." Nate's deep chuckle tingles up my back as we make our way through the crowd.

"Where are we going?" My gaze lands on Jen with her arms crossed, glaring between Matt and me. What did I do to piss her off?

"Lose my number," Matt all but spits at her as we pass.

Dang, guess I won't be calling her a friend anytime soon. Not that she genuinely offered. She invited me because Nate asked her to, not because she wanted to be friendly. She said I was cool but then dumped me once we arrived. She didn't have any intention of hanging out with me. She did it for Nate, and by the looks of it, she was hoping to *hang* with Matt.

I know girls lose friendships over boyfriends sometimes, but Jen and I aren't even friends… And I *so* do not have a boyfriend.

I might, in fact, have a caveman.

Once we're in the front yard, I plant my feet and pull on his hold. "Stop dragging me."

He doesn't release me but spins. His hard lines clash with my lush curves, taking my breath. "I know I'm being unreasonable. I need distance between you and *him*. Can you give me this, Gorgeous?"

The way he calls me *gorgeous* and the tenderness behind the fire in his eyes melts my resolve. "Under one condition."

His hard features soften with his dimpled smile.

Gah, sexy god of virility has made an appearance.

"Anything." He exudes with certainty… Whatever I ask, he'll give.

"Feed me." Not sexy, but I'm not trying to play on their field. I'm playing on mine, and my rumbling tummy says food is a must if I'm going to survive the god pressed against me.

His smile turns to smolder as his heated lips press to my forehead and he mumbles, "Done."

Three

THEN

IT'S ONLY THE SECOND WEEK OF SCHOOL, AND I finally feel like I have a handle on my schedule. Taking a breather, I grab lunch at the student union between classes. I have Econ next, so I'm reading ahead when a familiar figure catches my eye. I hide behind my book to scope out Matt as he grabs a table with a few friends.

Only… it's not Matt.

I squint, tilting my head. It's his doppelganger. And he's hot. Not Matt hot, but… hot, hot.

A few pages later, I look up to the Matt twins. The original and the copy. Brothers? Cousins? The one I know to be Matt snags a fry off his twin's plate and sits next to him. The twin pushes his plate toward Matt and gives him half his sandwich.

So sweet.

Sliding down in my chair, book perched on the table in front of me, I watch their interaction. I can't take my eyes off either of them as they laugh and interact with their friends. Not an ugly guy in the bunch. Kinda reminds me of my brothers and their friends. They always seem to fit so nicely. Not an odd one among them. No one left out. No third or fifth wheel. They're loyal to each other through thick and thin. A bond I've witnessed but can't relate to.

I'm always the odd one out. Round peg trying to fit into a smaller myriagon-shaped hole.

Now that I've totally bummed myself out, I toss my trash in the nearest receptacle. I still have a half hour before class, but my lack of social life is screaming at me to run far away from this place, which is holding a mirror up, forcing me to acknowledge my loner status. I throw my book in my bag and start to slide my phone in my back pocket when it chimes with a text.

Matt god of virility: *Don't move.*

Without lifting my head, I glance up to find Matt stalking in my direction. He's in faded jeans and a light green t-shirt that looks worn and so soft, but it's the words across the front that get my attention: Beaver Wrangler.

Jesus, he's hot and so damn adorable. I'm sure he *wrangles* all the beavers with skill and single-minded focus.

We've been texting since he stole me away from Nate's party, fed me, then brought me home. He's asked to see me a few times, but I brush him off each time. He's one of *those* people. He shines too bright for me. I'm a shadow walker. Even *new* Gabby can't escape the dark completely.

I swing my bag over my shoulder as I stand, figuring he can walk me out so no one sees us. Except he's not stopping. He keeps coming, pushing chairs out of his way, making a scene. I glance around and move back, hiding, until my back hits the corner of the glass wall.

"I said don't move," he growls.

"Your mother know you wear that shirt?" I speak over him.

He settles against me, his hand cupping my neck and sinking into my hair. "You were staring."

Mortified he noticed, I look away and count the sets of eyes watching us. "People are staring at *us*."

He forces my gaze back to him with a gentle brush of his thumb to my jaw. "Don't care. You've been avoiding me." His lips graze my cheek as he whispers, "You're not invisible. You know that, right?"

My breath catches; my heart hammers two times faster than it already was, and my eyes close. *How? How does he know?*

"I usually am," I whisper as my blue eyes lock with his potent green ones again.

His hand on my hip, teasing the skin just under my shirt, squeezes. "Baby, I'm staring right at you, and I'm damn sure you're not invisible."

I swear I'm trembling, and my knees are about to give. I guess swooning is a real thing. I never thought *I'd* experience it. "Matt?"

"Yeah, Gorgeous?"

"I don't want to be invisi—"

Before I can finish, his mouth crashes against mine, searing my lips and coaxing them open.

"Fuck," he breathes against my mouth before diving in, his tongue sweeping mine up in a seductive dance that has me panting and melting into his hold. "So fucking not invisible." He leans into me, kissing harder, deeper. He squeezes my ass, urging me forward, closer.

Is this really happening? Is the god of virility kissing me for all to see? Isn't he embarrassed to be seen with someone less goddess-like than he deserves?

I gasp when he presses his hard length against my stomach as if he's trying to shove those negative thoughts out of my body to make room for him. I whimper at the thought, need crawling up my spine, wrapping around to my core. I press into him, making him groan and my own pleasure surge.

Pulling away seconds later, he rests his forehead on mine. His haggard breaths mixing with mine. "I'm gonna walk you to class. I'm gonna ask to see you later, and I'm gonna need you to say *yes*."

I think I'd agree to anything if he'd just kiss me like that one more time.

I'm still buzzing from the gravitational pull of Matt when a familiar shadow drops in the seat next to me, halfway up the lecture hall for my Econ class.

"Hey, Firecracker." Nate is all smiles and cockiness, yet I catch the slight hesitation in his eyes.

My brows rise. "You're not in my class." Okay, maybe my tone was a little too accusatory.

"I am now." He opens his MacBook, side-eyeing me. "You noticed I wasn't in your class before? Miss me?"

"Hardly," I huff. "I would have noticed if the Hulk was in my class, though."

"Hulk?" He stops mid-reach into his bag. "You're calling *me* the Hulk?" Nate chuckles. "Dwight will get a kick out of that. His panties are still in a twist you didn't know who he was. You know, he's known for his size."

"He shouldn't take it personally. I don't know anybody." It's a sad fact. Not a reflection on him or his buddy's prowess on the football field.

Sitting back, he nudges my arm. "You know me."

"Hmm." I don't know why he's here, in my class, but I've no intention of falling into the belief he's truly here for me or is someone I can rely on.

His gaze warms the side of my face as I make a new note for today's lecture on my iPad using the keyboard on my case. I continue to ignore him as the professor enters the room with his TA in tow. The lights dim, and the projector comes to life. It's only been a few weeks, but I've learned Prof Graph likes visual aids. He doesn't want all your focus on him as he lectures, but on the pictures, graphs, examples he shows on the screen, which I love, but I do wish he'd post them online so I'd have a copy to go along with my notes. He talks pretty fast, and it's hard to capture it all before he switches to the next slide or topic.

When the chat app on my iPad lights up with a silent notification, I click on it just to verify it's not urgent.

Nate (BFWB) Sinclair: *You're ignoring me.*

I bite my lip to hide my smile. My fingers fly across the keyboard before I switch back to my notes and continue to type and listen to the professor.

Me: *No, I'm paying attention to the lecture. TRYING to take notes. You should too.*

Beside me, Hulk messes with his phone, keeping it hidden behind his laptop.

Another notification.

Nate (BFWB) Sinclair: *Damn, you even type like a firecracker. Fast and fierce. I don't need to take notes. I have you. You wouldn't let a guy fail for typing too slowly! *blow kiss emoji**

I nearly laugh out loud. Instead, I flash him a frown and continue to take notes. He may have a whole football team backing him up. I only have me. I can't afford to fall behind or lose focus.

I ignore all the texts that come in until the professor takes a quick break while his TA hands out our next assignment.

Nate (BFWB) Sinclair: *You're ignoring me again.*
Nate (BFWB) Sinclair: *Come on. I'm fun. I'm worth getting to know.*
Nate (BFWB) Sinclair: *Okay, I can see you're serious about this notes business. So, I'll let you in on a little secret. I already had this class before switching to this time/day. I'll email you my notes and the presentation.*

What?!

Me: *You have the presentation?*

He leans in, watching me type, and whispers, "I do. I have contacts." His gaze locks on mine. "Have dinner with me, and I'll share."

"You're bribing me?" I whisper back.

"No, I'm giving you incentive to get to know me. I promise I'm worth your time."

Gah, that damn cocky grin of his. I either want to slap it or kiss it right off his face. It's a tossup.

"When?"

Lord, I regret even considering by how satisfied his expression turns. "Tonight."

"Can't. I have plans."

"Tomorrow then?"

I could use a friend, especially one with contacts and access to class. presentations. I nod. It's just dinner. It's not a date.

When the papers for the assignment make it to our row, Nate quickly fills out the last page and passes it back to the TA as he comes down the aisle.

"You're my partner."

"For what?"

He flicks my paper. "For this assignment." He grins like a Cheshire cat. "It's a partner assignment."

"Is that the reason you're in my class today?"

He shakes it off. "I'm here because I want to get to know you. The assignment is just a bonus. I'd forgotten about it until Graph started handing out the assignment."

"Why is it I don't believe you?"

"Because the men in your life have let you down." He hits entirely too close to home with his insightfulness.

I try not to flinch.

His eyes gentle. "I'm not going to be one of them. I promise." He says it with such sincerity, I have trouble doubting him.

"You'd be the first." But it's not just the men in my life.

No one will ever love you the way you are. My mother's voice rings in my head.

The words that happen to be the last she ever said to me.

She was dead only hours later.

I shut my iPad, pack my stuff, and slip away before Nate can stop me or say another word that will hit deeper than I'm willing to feel.

My phone pings with more texts. I don't read them until later. I don't reply. I don't know him. He doesn't know me. He wants to, but he won't once he forgets I can kick and *sees* the real me—the old Gabby. I'm trying so hard to be *new*, but it feels like the world loves to remind me I'm lesser than, and I'm most definitely lesser than Nate. He shines too, like Jen and Matt. He's on *their* spectrum and far, far from mine.

Nate (BFWB) Sinclair: *I'm sorry if I upset you. Not my intent.*
Nate (BFWB) Sinclair: *Have a good evening, Firecracker.*
Nate (BFWB) Sinclair: *I'll pick you up at 6p tomorrow for dinner.*
Nate (BFWB) Sinclair: *Call if you need anything. I mean it. I'm here.*

Four

THEN

MY GIRL HAS GONE RADIO SILENT. I CALLED AND texted her after class, but there was no answer or reply. I'm hoping she hasn't changed her mind about dinner... About me. The way she kissed me back, melted into me after she practically begged me to show her she's not invisible, I'm sure she feels this thing between us. She was *there*. All in.

I'm sure of it.

Yet my confidence falters the closer I get to her dorm room.

If she's changed her mind, I'm only out the cost of the food and a bruising footprint on my ego.

My heart.

Yeah, my heart has never felt this invested before. I've dated... a bit. Nothing serious. I've had a few one-night stands. I'm not a fan. I prefer to know the person I'm sleeping with. Call me crazy, but I want what my mom and dad have. A deep, feel-it-in-your-bones kind of connection. I want my *person*. I may not be the force my brothers are, but if I had my other half, it wouldn't matter. I'd be her world just like she'd be mine. I want *that*—and I think I've found it.

Gabby is different. In all the right—intoxicating—ways.

Her raven hair and pale blue eyes might not be that unusual, but the way they draw me in, I lose all sanity. I'm still the charming McIntyre, but with her I want to be *more*. I want her to dig in, clear out the rubble, make a home for herself inside my chest and know me for who I am. Not who my family is or what my money can do for her.

She's not like that. I know it. She's so much more than the shy, unassuming girl she projects. She has fight. A backbone. A gleam in her eyes that stokes the fire I feel when I'm near or lucky enough to find her gaze locked on me.

Invisible? She could never be. Never.

I pocket my phone, switch the bag of food to my other hand, take a deep breath and knock.

Please be here.

Please be happy to see me.

Please don't break my heart.

Jeez, I'm a pussy. A pussy for her. Never felt this type of connection before. When her eyes stray, I want to move to find myself in her line of sight, her eyes on me, focused on me. I sure as fuck am focused on her. It scares the shit out of me, and yet I can't stop myself from wanting more, needing more, receiving *everything*.

When she opens the door, I catch a full breath for the first time since we parted ways. Who knew she was essential to my blood oxygen level? I didn't even realize I was running low until she filled me up. I'm lightheaded. Elated, until I take in the stress in her brow and the red of her eyes.

I rush forward, dropping the food, and pull her close with a soft tug on her nape and hip. "What's wrong?" Did someone hurt her? Has she been in here crying alone? "Who do I need to maim?"

Her brows pinch on a soft laugh.

That sound. I want more of *that*.

"No one. Well, me… My family? Maybe." She frowns. "It's family drama."

She dismisses it like family drama is nothing. I know for a fact family drama can be the only drama that matters. But I don't want to push.

"I brought Italian." I kiss her forehead, deeming it my spot, and snag the food off the floor. But before she can pull back any further, I caress her cheek and speak my truth, "I don't like that they made you cry."

Her smile is indulgent as she closes the door, locking us in her little room—her home for the next year or so.

"Where were you while I was growing up? I could have used that kind of protection then. Now, it's just old news, old wounds that never quite heal."

"Still, family or not, I will take them out." A little heavy-handed, yeah, but she gets my drift. I don't like the idea of anyone hurting her. If she's mine or not, she deserves better than what I'm sensing she's gotten.

She presses a kiss to my jaw, scorching my skin and stoking the fire burning for her. I never want her to stop touching me.

Sadly, she does.

Fin gave me shit for making such a spectacle of kissing Gabby—for the first time—in such a public display.

The guys razzed me, but not in the same way.

Fin only cared about me embarrassing Gabby. I've told him how shy she is. I've told him everything. He knows…

"What? You're a chubby chaser now?" Dick #1 spouts off.

"Yeah, man, so much more to hold on to." Dick #2 simulates holding hips and ramming in from behind.

Fuckers. I want to kill 'em.

"Jesus, grow the fuck up," Fin growls as he reaches for two beers. "And get the fuck out of my house." He glares at me as he stomps off—he's got company of his own waiting for him in his room.

I should have been the one to say it.

Guilt has me hugging Gabby from behind as she sets out the food on her desk. "You're perfect," I whisper into her raspberry-scented hair. So fucking perfect I could eat her for breakfast, lunch, and dinner.

He tickles my ear as he kisses up my neck, squeezing my ass, urging me closer. "Can I have you for dessert?"

Gah, this guy. He's been an octopus since we finished dinner. Not complaining. He's got my insecurities wrapped in sexual knots, my panties soaked, my mind mush, and my heart hammering to get to his, feeling things I never thought I'd be comfortable enough to feel with a guy, a hot-as-fuck guy, like Matt. He's touched all my soft places, and I'm not squirming to get away or moving his hand to places that aren't so *extra*.

I heard things would be different in college, but I never dreamed my first week here I'd meet a guy like Matt, much less have him all over me like I'm the prize he's dying to unwrap.

This would never have happened—never did happen—in high school.

If it weren't for the sincerity in his eyes and the raw ache in his voice, I'd think this was a cruel joke.

"Baby," he growls when my nails dig into his back. His hips press forward, grinding his unmistakable hardness against my core.

I shudder on a desperate mewl, "Matt." Fully dressed, I've no doubt I could come if he'd just do that a few more times.

"Let me touch you," he breathes across my lips, kissing and licking me into submission.

…wanting to submit.

He'll see me. Panic rises.

"Hey." He caresses my cheek, our hooded gazes locked. "Nothing happens you don't want to happen." He rubs his nose along mine. "I could dry-hump you into eternity if that's as far as you want to go."

His crassness makes me laugh, easing my nerves.

Kissing me softly, he pulls back. "I can sit here and hold your hand and be content." He rises to his knees, offering his hand to help me sit up.

But I don't want to sit. I want him pressed to me like he's desperate for more—for everything—the same way I feel for him.

I grip his shirt and yank him down till we're nose to nose. "Take your shirt and jeans off," I bolden. "If you're going to touch me, I'm going to touch you." And I can't wait.

New Gabby happy-dances, high-fiving old Gabby.

Five

THEN

THE ONLY WAY I'M GOING TO MAKE IT THROUGH the day, and not have my dick precede me in every room, is to relive every lush curve and wanton cry my girl shared with me last night while I rub one out in the shower.

It's quick, hard, and oh-so-needed.

Finally able to think a non-sexual thought, I dry off and dress, grab my backpack and dart for the kitchen to fill my travel mug with much-needed caffeine.

Fin holds up the counter, munching on a bagel. He motions to the plate on the table. "That one's for you."

Damn, love this guy. He takes care of me like a parent, but… less parental and more brotherly. "Thanks, Brother."

"Course." He cocks his head as I take a bite and pour my coffee. "You good?"

I don't even try to hide my smile. "I'm great." I nod, biting my lips thinking of Gabby. "I'm awesome."

His eyes widen on a laugh. "This thing with Gabby. Serious already?"

I make a sandwich out of my bagel, wrap it in a paper towel to go. "Yeah, I want it to be. It's serious to me."

I'm sure it's serious for her too. She let me touch her, and damn, if I don't want to spend every day doing just that.

"Good. Remember you're not some little teenage shit any more. You're a man. Treat her like one."

"Treat her like a man?" I joke, then cough after taking a sip of my too-hot-to-drink coffee.

"No, numbnuts. Treat her like a man would, not a teenage boy, happy just see a boob."

I've seen plenty, probably not as much as my two-years-older brother, but enough to know Gabby's are spectacular. And I respected the hell out of her last night, not acting a bit like a kid. She makes me feel like I'm all man, and damn, if I didn't love her hands on me too.

I hide my preen as I remember how her breasts feel, how they taste, and how hard she came when I bit her dusky nipple just right.

Fuck, I may need another shower.

"Like a man. Got it." I sling my bag over my shoulder, grab my mug and bagel, holding both up. "Thanks for breakfast, bro. Don't wait up."

"Shit head," he mumbles.

"Love you too."

"Yeah, yeah, love you like a brother."

"From the same mother!" I holler as I shut the door leading to the garage.

Love my brothers. I wouldn't want to live anywhere else than with Fin and, in two years, my younger brother Joe. I'm trying to talk Fin into staying one more year so the three of us can live in the house together, but he's not hearing it. He's on the CEO path, the one he wants, and the one my dad is waiting to hand over as soon as he feels Fin is ready to take over the family business, McIntyre Corporate Industries.

Fin's been ready for years. Schools is just a formality… A last hurrah before getting serious about the real world and all that entails.

As for me, I'm heading to the role of VP of Marketing. I'm using my God-given charisma to its fullest. I may not be as gung-ho as Fin or my younger brother, but I'll be ready by the time graduation comes… in four years.

For now, I've got class to get to and my girl to lay a good-morning kiss on and make my day even brighter.

I stretch through a yawn and relish every sore muscle—inside and out— that aches from Matt's touch, or me straining, flexing to be touched by his hands or gloriously pouty mouth.

The thought of him in only his black boxer briefs, cut abs, broad shoulders, and tapered vee have me groaning and wishing he'd never left last night.

It was there in his eyes, the wish to stay.

On the tip of his wicked tongue, the unasked question.

In his greedy hands, the need for more.

As much as my body was saying yes, my mind still has doubts, reservations, fears that he doesn't really see me, and after we have sex, he'll realize he doesn't like junk in the trunk and 5'10" brunettes. Then there's that stupid part of my heart, believing it needs to be in love before I have sex for the first time.

I would have given if he'd asked. I'm so glad he didn't. Regrets suck. And I have no regrets today.

New Gabby. I like her so very much.

I rush through my shower, no time to waste if I'm going to make breakfast before my first class.

With my bag over my shoulder, ID and phone in my pockets, I jump, race, maneuver down four flights of stairs, popping out into the lobby only to run smack dab into the man himself.

"Jesus, Gorgeous, I'm anxious to see you too, but slow your roll before you hurt yourself." His dimples on full display, he steadies me by the shoulders as he scours me inch by inch—or at least what he can see with me pressed to his chest.

"I'm late," I offer entirely too breathily.

Matt turns us and heads toward the door I was aiming for. He steals my bag and slings his arm around my shoulder as we exit. "You can't be that late. You have an hour before your first class."

"How do you know?"

He only smirks. "Breakfast?"

I nod. "That was my plan."

"Then let's go." There's no question if he'll join me. He just does.

Oh, to be that confident, to assume I'm wanted wherever I go. Which, of course, he is—by me and the myriad of onlookers who can't seem to get their fill of him. Me, they sneer and whisper about.

Ignore them, new Gabby reminds me.

"That's all you're eating?" He eyes my plate with fruit and a miniscule amount of scrambled eggs.

"I—"

"Nope." He takes my tray, hands me his. "Find us a seat. I'll be right there."

"But—"

"You don't want to be late, right?" He kisses my forehead. He seems to like doing that. Like he's reapplying his invisible lip-mark that faded or washed away since the last time he did it.

I don't mind it either.

Before I can scan the room for a table, someone bumps me from behind. I turn with an apology on my lips only to freeze when I come face to face with a sneering Jen.

"Watch it, cow." She laughs at my shock. "You think *he* really likes *you*? That *Nate* likes you too?" Her friends circle at her sides as she stops in front of me.

My face pounds as the blood rushes to my head, fear and shame slashing through my heart. Was it all a sick prank? She and Matt set me up? I glance around, looking for the bucket of pig's blood about to be dumped on my head. How stupid am I? So easily deceived. Desperate to be loved.

"Please." She rolls her eyes. "They only want you because the other wants you."

"What?" Wait. They *want* me? So, not a set up…? My head is whirling. She's just jealous?

Of me.

Shiny Jen is jealous of *me* because *two* guys she likes… like me?

"Don't get used to it. They'll fuck you and move on like they always do." She leans in. "You're just a game to them. Everyone thinks cows are cute, but they're only good for their milk."

What?! "That doesn't make any sense. People like to eat cows too." I look her up and down, finding her skinny ass lacking and pissed she made me doubt him. "Matt is all carnivore." The old Gabby cheers for new Gabby.

A warm, familiar hand slides up my back to rest on my neck, possessive and comforting. "Trust me. I couldn't get enough last night, and I tried. Hard." Matt lays a heated kiss on my mouth, releasing my bottom lip with a *pop*. "Come on, Gorgeous. We don't want to be late." He winks at me then side-eyes Jen. "It smells like yesterday's trash over here. Let's find somewhere to *eat* in private."

If they say anything further, I don't hear it or even care. I'm lost in the giant of a man—in spirit and stature—as he guides me away with his soothing hand on my lower back, nearly touching my ass.

Sequestered in a corner, he sets down our trays and pulls out a chair, waiting on me to sit. When I do, he leans in, hands on the arms of my chair, his gaze eating me up. "I want to keep kissing you, if only to preserve the look of contentment on your perfect face."

I swoon a bit more, falling, falling for this man.

Before I can reply, he sweeps in, groaning his pleasure when his tongue meets mine, tasting, savoring, delving deep and oh so thoroughly. By the time he sits, breaking our kiss, I've melted into my chair.

"Eat, baby." He places my plate he filled with more eggs, adding bacon and toast, in front of me and takes his. He moves in closer, his arm around my back, and nuzzles my cheek before spearing a bite, encouraging me to do the same.

We don't talk about Jen and what she said or how much he heard. I don't have to address the elephant in the room—my beefier size—or why he likes me when he can have a million Jens ready to drop at his feet to worship him like the god he is. Or Jen's claim that all he wants is to compete with his frenemy for me, then bail once he's had it.

It's the most sensual meal I've ever experienced. Warm kisses between bites. Playful glances that have me feeling naked and heat my blood. Sexual groans of satisfaction from the tastes of our food, both on our forks and in each other's mouths.

I'm a sweltering mess by the time we have to leave.

He's sporting a boner that he shamefully rubs against my belly as he kisses me goodbye outside my first class. First my lips, then my forehead… Leaving his mark.

"You need to go before I fuck you right here." He turns me and swats my ass, sending me on my way. "Text me your schedule."

All I can do is nod and jelly-leg it to my seat. Sink down and miss every word the teacher says for the next fifty-five minutes.

Six

THEN

THIS MORNING'S BARELY COLD INCIDENT LINGERS on the periphery of my mind, reminding me how cruel the world can be. Though Matt's response and heated kisses did wonders to soften the blow, I'm still hoping to avoid Jen and her CREWellas for a few days at least. One confrontation was plenty.

The fates have other ideas.

Nearly out the door to meet Nate for dinner, my phone chimes with a text. I check it in case it's him changing our plans.

Matt god of virility: *I'll be there in thirty to pick you up for the game.*

Game? "Shit."

I plop down on my bed, kicking my shoes off. I obviously won't be needing my cute sandals for a stupid flag football game. I totally forgot or blocked it out.

Me: *Can we just pretend that's not happening?*

I really wished I'd never answered my door that first day they were looking for players. If I hadn't answered, I wouldn't be on the team and feel my nerves creeping up my spine. The need to run and hide, and avoid all things Jen, not be a spectacle like this is guaranteed to be. But truly, it'd be antsy no matter what. Being a team player never bothered me before. This feels different. Like I'm on display and have something to prove to her and the world—not that the world is watching—and maybe myself too. I've become entirely too good at hiding, old Gabby reminds me.

> **Matt god of virility:** *No. Your team needs you.*
> **Matt god of virility:** *I'm on my way. I'll get you pumped up.*
> **Matt god of virility:** *No shirt. I have your jersey.*

His enthusiasm has my heart calming and my stomach flipping in anticipation of seeing him again so soon. I didn't even get a chance to tell him about my dinner plans. *Shit. Nate.*

I quickly reply to Matt.

> **Me:** *You're entirely too gung-ho. I'm feeling a cold coming on. *cough, cough**
> **Matt god of virility:** *Gungho about seeing you. 10 min.*
> **Matt god of virility:** *I'll kiss you till you're feeling better.*

I can't wait for all the *kissing*. But… Nate. I send him a text:

> **Me:** *Something's come up. I can't make dinner. Sorry. Another time?*

Another time? Should I be going out with Nate now that things have heated up so fast with Matt? Nate and I are just friends. Right?

> **Nate (BFWB) Sinclair:** *You're skipping out on me at the last minute? Really? I thought we'd come so far too.*
> **Me:** *It's not like that. Honest. I forgot I have a prior commitment. Believe me, I'd rather go to dinner.*

But I wouldn't rather see him over Matt. Right?

Nate (BFWB) Sinclair: *Tell me about this prior commitment, and I'll consider forgiving you.*
Nate (BFWB) Sinclair: *And yes. I want a raincheck.*

Do I tell him why?

Me: *I'll only tell you if you promise not to show up.*
Nate (BFWB) Sinclair: *Well, now I want to be there for sure.*
Me: *No! Please. It's embarrassing.*
Nate (BFWB) Sinclair: *Now I want to be there to support you.*

Jeez, where were these guys when I needed support growing up? Why couldn't I have grown up with a Nate or a Matt making me feel good about myself instead of always feeling like there was something wrong with me… The odd man—girl—out?

Me: *I appreciate that, but no. I'll see you in class tomorrow.*

A few minutes pass. He doesn't reply, and the message doesn't show as read. He must be busy. Which is good. Hopefully it means he's forgotten all about me.

I rush to change and re-brush my teeth because, well, Matt, the god of virility, is on his way, and he promised kisses. I intend to hold him to that.

I've barely knocked before her door swings open. Bent over, hopping to get a sock on, she glances up through a mess of bangs, smiling and flushed. "Hey," she rushes out as she pulls up her sock, shuffling backwards. "Come in."

I step inside, close and lock her door. Lust crashes into me, the sight of her in cropped workout pants, tube socks and a black tank that does nothing but accentuate her curves. She's out of breath, and all I want to do is make her pant some more.

"Hey, you." I brush a hair from her lips, stepping closer, inspecting her rosy cheeks, shimmering blue eyes, and tempting lips that match her cheeks… All natural and begging to be devoured. I glance at the clock on her desk, sighing in relief. We have time.

Moving closer, I drop her jersey to the floor and peel mine off just as fast.

"What are—"

"I promised you kisses till you felt better."

She backs up as I press into her, not giving an inch of space until she hits her bed and rocks back. I keep her upright with a tight grip on her hips.

She chuckles. "I'm not really sick." She grips my shoulders. "I just don't want to go."

Yeah, I gathered that. My shy girl doesn't like to be the center of attention. It's too bad. She's about to be the center of *my* attention. I nudge her nose with mine, skimming her cheek and pressing a kiss to her neck. "Lie down, Gorgeous." I soften her fall with a hand on her back as I follow her down.

"I thought—"

"Shh…" I silence her protest with a slow, lingering kiss. "Close your eyes and don't open, or I stop."

"Stop?" Her brows curve, and her tongue dashes out, wetting her lips. "No, don't stop."

I've no intention to, even if she opens her eyes, but her keeping her eyes closed is more for her than me. "Close them." I nibble her ear. "Or maybe you prefer a blindfold."

"Blindfold?" Her brows now pinch.

I soothe them with my fingers, kissing softly along her forehead, and work my way down, relishing her intake of air and small gasps. "I promised you kisses. I didn't specify where."

I swallow her gasp, savoring and pushing through till our tongues meet, and I devour her mouth like I intend on devouring her pussy as soon as I can get her naked. I touched the promised land last time. This time, I'll taste and consume until she's loose and all hints of nerves are shattered.

But first, this mouth deserves its due attention, then her breasts, then heaven.

Seven

THEN

H
E GRIPS MY HIP, KEEPING ME CLOSE AND STEADY as we make it back to the bench. Despite my flush and jelly legs, I managed the kick-off without issue. It was pretty decent, if I do say so myself, considering I had my legs wrapped around Matt's head, coming like the world was ending, not fifteen minutes ago. A small shudder has me sinking into his hold a little deeper.

Defense takes the field as the other team lines up to try for a first down. I suck in my cheek to keep from smiling. Maybe I do know more about football than I thought. It was a sport nearly always on in my house with my dad and four brothers. My mom was never much of a fan, but she put up with it, knowing her men loved it. She lived to feed them on game days—whatever they wanted. No counting calories. I hung around, but I can't say I'm a huge fan of watching sports on TV. I'd rather see them in person.

I plop down on the bench farthest from everyone else. Matt squeezes my knee and slaps a bottle of water in my hand. "You did great." His knowing gaze locks on mine. "Love you all sexed up." His finger runs down my cheek when I lay my head on his shoulder.

"Maybe too sexed up." Is that even a thing? I yawn behind my hand, wishing we were still in my bed, his hands and mouth still on me—in me. I shiver, and Matt's eyes flash to mine.

His eyebrow quirks, and a single dimple appears when he sees whatever he sees when he looks at me. "Maybe we should have stayed in bed."

Blushing, I hide my face in his shoulder. "It's not too late."

He groans what I think is his response to my bedroom suggestion, but when he tenses, I sit up, tracking his gaze across the field just past the bleachers. Nate, Dwight, and a few other guys I assume are football players stand there, watching.

I don't have time to dwell on why they're here or ask why he dislikes Nate. Our team makes a touchdown on a fumble, and I'm in for the extra point. As the game progresses, I relax into it, feeling the groove I used to feel when I played soccer, ready to do my part and cheer my team on when it's their turn to shine. And shine we do, winning 35-6.

I didn't even mind being around Jen. She ignored me and Matt, focusing on the game and flirting with anyone within earshot.

Busy being congratulated by Matt via warm kisses and needy hands, I miss the celebration going on around us until a deep voice breaches our bubble.

"Congratulations. That was a good game." Nate isn't close, but he's definitely not across the field where I last spotted him and the group of football players whose numbers only seemed to grow as the game progressed. They never did make it to the bleachers. Instead, they hung out under the trees, some sitting, some standing, some laughing and having a good time. But Nate just stood with his arms crossed, glaring and talking to the older guy next to him, not taking his eyes off me when I took to the field. Maybe he's pissed about dinner. If he was mad, why stick around?

Matt's chest rumbles with irritation as he breaks our kiss and comes to stand behind me, hands on my hips, squeezing as Nate's eyes meets mine over Jen's head. She continues to talk, not even noticing he's already checked out of their conversation.

"Why are they here?" I catch Matt's perturbed gaze over my head.

He presses closer, kissing my forehead. Marking. "One guess, Gorgeous."

Me? He can't mean—

"That's quite a leg you got there, Ms. Chisholm." The older man who was talking to Nate is now in front of me, offering his hand. "Coach Eaton."

"Thanks—" I shake his hand that dwarfs mine, and that's saying something. At 5'10", no part of me is small. "And it's Gabby, Coach."

"Gabby." His smile is warm, inviting. "Mr. McIntyre." He nods to the man behind me.

"Coach." Matt reaches around me to shake his hand. His smile is genuine but strained, reluctant even.

"Tell your brother hello for me." Not a request.

"Sure. Of course." The tension in Matt's body leads me to believe being cordial is the furthest thing he wants to be.

Coach's attention returns to me. "You should come see me in the morning."

"See you?"

"She has class," Matt speaks before I can.

"After class then," Coach offers. Again, not a question. He's a man used to getting what he wants. Football programs rule in Texas, like they probably do in many other states. The programs bring in the money, the fans. I don't think this man has been told *no* often.

"She'll be there," Nate's baritone voice and piercing hazel eyes steal my focus.

"What?" Why would I meet with Coach? What could he possibly want with me?

"No." Matt steps forward, his glare solely on Nate.

Chuckling, Coach pats Matt's shoulder, but his eyes are on me. "Good. See you then." He steps away as Matt presses between me and Nate, his hand on my hip, keeping me behind him.

"You need to back off." Anger rolls off Matt in waves. He's done playing nice.

"Oh, lawd. You two need to stop fighting over *her*." Jen stands next to them with her hands on her hips, disdain dripping from her eye sockets.

She's got it all wrong. "They're not—"

"You need to back the fuck off, Jen." Nate puts himself between her and us. He steps forward, causing her to step back or fall on her ass. "Don't. Ever. Talk. About. Gabby like that."

"You've been warned now, twice." Matt moves to Nate's side. "There won't be a third."

"What?!" she shrieks. "You—you *both*—" She points between them and me, struggling to find her words, her sanity. Her cheeks redden, and she sighs, "Gah!" and throws her arms up. "The world's gone crazy." She air-pokes at Matt and Nate. "You two are insane if you think—"

"Go!" Nate barks.

She and I both jump. She stumbles back. Matt pulls me closer, then presses his lips to my temple.

"Oh, and," Nate moves toward her again, forcing her to retreat, "find a new kicker. She's taken."

"Completely insane," she mumbles before walking away.

When Nate turns, his smile is big and endearing, his anger completely forgotten. "Now—" he rubs his hands together, wiggling his brow, "—how about that dinner you owe me?"

Shit.

"Dinner?" How the fuck did I get roped into agreeing we'd have dinner with Nate and his football buddies?

She's been silent since the game and the run-in with Jen... and Coach Eaton. I know what he wants. She's clueless and confused by the attention.

I just want *her*.

Nate wants her *and* her not-so-hidden talent.

Coach definitely wants her golden foot. I didn't miss the gleam in his eyes. Fucker. I know Coach through Fin, who couldn't be a bigger fan or supporter of UT football. He bought a box at the stadium, for God's sake. I'm surprised the stadium isn't named after him or at least called McIntyre Athletic Complex for how much money he's donated. And I don't mean MCI. I mean, Fin directly. Dad is a huge supporter as well.

I squeeze her leg after grabbing a parking spot at the Hole in the

Wall, a local college dive. Her perfect pale blue eyes slowly rise to mine. "Tell me about you *owing* Nate dinner."

She sighs as her head falls back against the buttery soft passenger seat of my Mercedes Maybach SUV, my baby—my *other* baby. Her head rolls my way. "I was supposed to have dinner with him tonight. He asked me a few days ago. We have an econ project together." She shrugs. "It was no big deal. But I cancelled when you reminded me we had a game tonight."

No big deal. I grip the steering wheel till my knuckles are white. "I think it's a big deal to *him*." And to me.

"We're just friends." She turns in her seat to face me. "I barely know him, Matt. He only noticed me because of that first day I met you, kicking." Her gaze seeps back out the window. "I guess that's why you noticed me too."

"No." I bring her eyes back to me with a soft nudge of her chin. "I noticed your beautiful eyes, long legs, and luscious ass first."

She scoffs, dismissing my words.

I pinch her chin, keeping her eyes on me. "I called you *gorgeous*, Gorgeous. Didn't I? I may be a flirt too, but I'm no liar. I noticed *you* long before you laid eyes on me, and long before I could see what that leg of yours could do."

"Yeah?" Her hopeful gaze has me wanting to turn around and show her again just how much I think of *her* and every delectable inch of her killing-me-softly body.

"Yeah." I pop my seatbelt, get out and round to her side before she can get the door open. Helping her out, I push her against the door as it closes. "You're still on my tongue, Gabby." I lock her gasp between our mouths, sucking and licking her lips until she opens, then consume and mark what's mine before we head into a room full of football players who want her to be *theirs*.

Eight

THEN

MATT MIGHT NOT BE GREAT FOR A GOOD NIGHT'S rest, but he's amazing for my ego, or lack thereof.

He kissed me goodnight—and I mean all night.

He kissed me good morning—again and again.

He kissed me goodbye at my first class. This time, only on my mouth unlike all the other *kisses* he gave me *everywhere*.

I've been tripping over thoughts of him all day. I'm deliciously exhausted and keenly aware of his absence, my body, achy and needy. How that's even possible, I don't know. I've never been so sexed up without actually having sex. How can I miss what I'm getting so much of? It's only been hours, yet my body shamelessly acts like it's been weeks… years.

Last class of the day. I yawn my way to my seat, convinced I smell like sex I haven't had, yet the proof coats my panties. Wanton. So, so very wanton. I'm grateful for the scent of my triple mocha latte I picked up on my way in. It's full of calories I don't need and caffeine I would mainline if it wasn't frowned upon.

"Late night?" Nate falls into the seat next to me, his frame entirely too large to land so gracefully.

"You've no idea," I say through another yawn. I shrink under his scrutiny, hiding behind my grande caffeine as I take another sip.

He leans closer, his nose nearly touching my cheek as he takes a deep breath. "Jesus, you smell good enough to lick."

My eyes fly open as I sink further into my chair. He can't possibly know that we… that I'm still so wet…

His gaze moves lower. "Stop that."

"What?" I freeze.

"Gyrating your hips." His eyes lock with mine. "He's got you primed, ready to blow, Firecracker." He winks. "I'm a bit envious."

"Of him or me?" *Oh, fuck.* I slap my hand over my mouth. I can't believe I said that much, less *thought* it.

His left brow quirks. He leans in further, close enough to kiss if I were so inclined to take my state of *primedness* out on him. "Would you be surprised if I said both?"

Both? "Matt is crazy hot. I wouldn't blame you." But… something in his eyes. "You're serious?"

"Don't dismiss the hottie sitting next to me." He pulls out his Mac, getting ready for class as I sit here like a bump on a log, sipping caffeine like it's oxygen.

I look to the seat next to him, fully expecting to see a hot chick… or hot guy. Empty.

His eyes slide to my lips and settle on my eyes. "I mean you, Gabby. Jesus, has no one ever told you you're attractive?"

"You mean before you and Matt?" I whisper low enough he might feel the vibrations more than hear my words.

The corners of his eyes soften. "Babe, tell me that's not true."

I screw up my lips, fighting the prickling behind my eyes and shrug, not willing to voice my lameness.

"Fuck." He laces his hand with mine on my lap. "I gotta be gentle with you, don't I?" His smile is sweet as he brushes a rogue tear before it slides down my cheek. "You're an Amazonian warrior on the outside, but tender, unappreciated goo on the inside." He kisses my cheek. "I got you, Firecracker."

Dang, he makes me want to cry all over his shoulder for all the gentle treatment I've missed out on. This man's a keeper. He'll make someone beyond happy one day. For now, I close my eyes and take a steaming sip of glorious caffeine, and relish his kindness.

Though he releases my hand and urges me to pull my tablet out, his leg stays pressed to mine, nudging me when my caffeine fails and my eyelids grow heavy. Then he hides me behind his folder when my head falls to his shoulder and I doze through the rest of class.

"How did I let you talk me into this?" I screech to a halt just outside the athletic complex where the football team trains and practices, and where the coaches have offices.

His laugh is quick and full. "By letting you sleep on my shoulder and sharing my class notes with you." He steps closer, a seriousness falling over his demeanor. "I promise, Gabby, if, in the end, this is not something you want, I'll back off. But I won't leave you hanging. You don't know it yet, but we're going to be lifelong best friends. You'll see."

I don't know what he sees when he looks at me, or why he'd want me as a friend, much less a *lifelong best* friend. But new Gabby preens and smiles, totally up for the idea of that. "I think you're crazy, but okay." Maybe the reason I've never found a best friend was that I never tried it with a guy. Okay to besties, and okay to talking to his coach.

He grunts his approval and opens the door.

I step past him.

Barely five feet inside the locker room, Nate cusses and blocks me. "Ugh, I didn't think this through. Close your eyes."

"Why, so you can murder me?"

He frowns and pushes me against the wall. "What is it with you and murder?" The tender richness of his voice makes my shoulders slope—so much for my fake confidence.

"Guys don't ask me to come places with them, and if they did, it must be for nefarious reasons. 'Cause—" I motion to my abundant size.

"Why else?" I bite my lip to quell the tremble before I admit, "It's hard to accept you actually like me and want me around."

He's a star athlete, a year older than me. What the hell is he doing with me? What do I have to offer no one else in his life is giving him?

His features soften as he leans in. "Firecracker, you are loaded with unrealized potential and a skewed opinion of yourself. I'm a little rusty on my Freud, so let's skip the psych assessment and jump to the part where I tell you you're sexy as fuck, and any guy would be lucky to have you follow him anywhere. But if any fucker tries to lay an unwanted hand on you, much less murder you, they'll have me to contend with."

The air rushes out of my body in one long exhale. I'm speechless and a little light-headed.

His brow rises, earnest arrogance directed at me—a look I'm coming to adore. "Got me?"

I nod.

"Good. Now, close your blue peepers. We got swinging dicks in here, and I don't want to scar you for life."

I close my eyes on a laugh, covering my mouth to stop a full-blown giggle.

He places his hand over my eyes, an arm around my back, and grips my hip, sequestering me against his side. "Woman on deck!" he grumbles as we move forward. "Put some fucking clothes on."

All I hear is laughter and whistles as we move through the room.

"Hey, Gabby, didn't know you were coming today."

"Dwight, Jesus, put your python away," Nate barks, his hand on my hip tightening.

Instinctively, I pull back, wanting to *see* and also, seems rude to not say *hi*. I mean, *python…*

"No fucking way, Gabby Elizabeth," he chastises.

Damn, he middle-named me.

"Keep your eyes closed," he growls.

His protectiveness has me laughing harder. "I don't want to be rude."

"Be rude. These assholes don't deserve your curiosity."

I grip the wrist of his hand over my eyes when we make an unannounced turn and stop abruptly.

"Coach." He knocks on his door, removing his hand from my eyes.

A scrape of chair and then, "Son."

"Can I open my eyes?"

"Yeah, sorry," Nate softly replies.

I blink open, focusing on Nate before sliding my gaze to Coach Eaton.

"I'm going to wrangle these assholes into decency while you two chat." His steely gaze meets mine. "Don't leave his office till I get back." And with that he closes the door as he backs out. Leaving me alone. With his coach.

My heart picks up speed, reminding me I don't like to be taken out of my comfort zone, and talking to a college coach is definitely not in my wheelhouse.

Coach comes around his desk, pointing to the chair in front of it. "Sorry about that—" He motions behind him. "Well, have to figure this thing out as we go." He moves to a small fridge. "Water?"

"Uh, sure." I meet his gaze as he breaks the seal on a bottled water and hands it to me. "Figure out what, exactly?"

He takes a drink of whatever is in his coffee cup as he sits.

Coffee. I could use more of that if I have any hope of making it to bedtime without a nap.

"I'm getting ahead of myself." He leans forward, his fingers laced and resting on his desk. "You've got a leg on you. I've no doubt we could turn you into a right good kicker—punter—if you're interested."

"Interested in…?" He needs to spell it out for me, as there is no way he wants me on his college football team—all *male* college football team. Maybe he coaches the girls' soccer team too.

"Playing football for me." He looks through a stack of papers. "I lost my star kicker. I've got a few backups, but none of them as promising as you." He finds what he's looking for and slides the paper toward me. "I'm offering you a full athletic scholarship, Chisholm."

"But you haven't even seen—"

"I saw you kick and punt at the flag football game. I've experience enough to know talent when I see it. You played soccer, right?" He pulls out another folder, flipping it open. "Ah, yeah, goalie." He looks up, impressed. "I'm surprised you didn't come on a soccer scholarship."

"I, uh, don't play anymore." *Please, don't ask why.*

He merely nods. "Lucky for me."

"You know I'm a girl, right?" I mean, just to put it out there for transparency's sake.

He belly-laughs and sits back. "Yeah, Chisholm, I'm well aware. You come with challenges. I'm willing to tackle them if you are."

I glance at the paper set before me. "What all does a football scholarship entail?"

"Everything."

Everything. Wow.

I'd be stupid not to consider it, right? A full ride. I wouldn't have to take my dad's money or the guilt associated with it. I wouldn't have to get a job I've been considering for extra cash.

"I'll think about it." Playing football wouldn't change my Early Education degree, and accepting his offer would let me cut off my dad completely. But… the *only* female in a male sport? Do I want that heartache?

"That's all I can ask." He shakes my hand and steps around his desk, glancing out his door for Nate, I assume.

I stand, fold the piece of paper and slide it in a backpack pocket.

"Gabby—" He waits for my eyes to meet his. "We could make history together." He steps closer. "That's not why I'm offering you a place on my team. I need a kicker, and you're the best natural talent I've seen in a long while. And I don't have anyone else as good as you. This could be your chance to be part of something. I want to work with you and see where this thing takes us."

I nod and shake his hand again as Nate steps inside. "I appreciate the offer, but I need to think on it."

"I wouldn't expect less." He motions to my pack. "My cell is on that piece of paper. You call me if you have any questions."

Our exit through the locker room is far less eventful than our entry. The few guys left give us a chin nods and skeptical looks. I'm sorry we rush out because the locker room is spectacular, padded bench seats in front of a large station that holds their gear, personal items, and it's backlit. I've never seen a locker room so nice or tricked out. I'd expect something like this in the pros, not at the college level. But then again, what do I know? I've never been in a college locker room. Maybe they all look like this.

"How would they feel about a woman on the team?" I ask Nate as we exit the building.

"I won't lie. Some will be happy for the wrong reasons. Some will be assholes. Some will be enlightened, like me, and know it's the best move for our team. Some will bask in the edginess. You're our best bet."

"No pressure?"

He chuckles. "No, Firecracker. There will be lots of pressure, but I'll be right there with you the whole way. I've got you."

Nine

THEN

IT'S BEEN WEEKS OF GABBY BLISS. NO MORE RUN-INS with Jen. We've reached a middle ground where Gabby is friends with Nate, and he's stopped trying to get in her panties. No decision on the football front. In fact, she's avoiding the topic altogether. I'm not pushing. It's a great opportunity but not one she's all that thrilled with. I don't believe it's playing that concerns her—though *I'm* concerned with her getting tackled—but the notoriety being the first female on a college football team will bring her. Center of attention is not something my girl craves. Except being the center of *my* attention. Something I'm totally down with.

I finally convinced her to come over so I can cook her dinner. Actually cook, not order in. Fin promises to make himself scarce. It's Friday night. I'm sure he's got a date or a hookup lined up. I didn't ask. I don't really care. I love the guy. I just need him gone. I'm hoping tonight is the night Gabby lets me in—I mean *all the way* in.

If it turns out she's not ready, I'm cool. I'm happy just being with her, but damn if I don't want to show her how much she means to me, and it feels like my cock inside her pussy is the deepest way to demonstrate it.

I know. A total guy thing.

She feels it too. I'm sure of it. She's needy for me in the best damn possible way.

A soft rap on the front door has my heart racing like a virgin princess on her wedding night.

Calm the fuck down.

Thank God Fin isn't here to witness my bout of nerves. I bounce on my feet, shake my arms out, crack my neck, and let out a deep exhale.

You got this.

I open the door, and my future is standing in front of me, looking completely edible and more nervous than me. My shoulders fall and a smile breaks free.

Pulling her inside before she can change her mind, I press my lips to hers—soft, gentle, no tongue—and touch our foreheads. I squeeze her hand, caress her cheek, and, finally, sink into her hair. "Hey, Gorgeous. I've missed you."

Her melting into me is the biggest confidence boost, not that I really need it, but getting this level of trust from her means everything. I don't know her history. She doesn't like to talk about her family. There's stuff she's not ready to share or deal with. I just know her dad is paying for college, and it comes with a toll. I have no idea where her mom is. I get the impression she's not a part of my girl's life. Her mom's loss as far as I'm concerned.

My family is everything to me. I have great parents and amazing brothers. I rarely make it a day without talking to all or one of them, not counting Fin, since we live together. My past doesn't haunt me, and my future is one I'm looking forward to all because of my remarkable family. I'm damn lucky, I know.

She sighs and presses her lips to my neck, resting there. "It's crazy; I just saw you a few hours ago, and yet I've missed your face, your voice, and sexy-as-all-get-out way you look at me."

I cup her face and pull her gaze to mine. "Oh yeah, and how's that?" I brush her lips with mine.

"Like you lo—" She cuts herself off with a sheepish smile.

"Hey." I squeeze her hip, calling her eyes back to me.

She pats my chest and shrugs. "You just shine brighter when your eyes are on me." Her eyes glisten like it's a painful thing to admit.

"You're not wrong. My whole body lights up when you're near." I kiss up her neck, needing the contact if I'm going to be brave. "And when I look at you… You know what you see?"

She gives the slightest of nods and whispers, "My love shining back at me?"

Damn, my brave girl. "Yeah, baby. It's my love raking you in, eating you up, dying to pull you closer, lay you out, take you out, hold you close, and let every asshole out there know you're mine. All. Damn. Day. Every. Day."

Her eyes widen; her brow furrows. She leans back, but I grip her tighter. "Did you… did we—"

"Yeah, Gabby, I just told you I love you, and you did the same."

"I… wow." She wraps her arms around me, her hands digging into my back and hair. "I do. I'm so scared to admit it, but I do love you, Matt."

I chuckle, picking her up as I walk us to the kitchen. "That's good, Gorgeous." I set her ass on the kitchen counter and step between her longer-than-sin legs, running my hands up her thighs to rest on her hips. "That's damn good, 'cause I've fallen so damn hard for you, it scares the fuck out of me."

She grips my shirt and tugs me closer. "I won't hurt you." She giggles across my lips.

"Even when I fuck this up?" I grip the back of her head, keeping her close. "Cause I'm bound to at some point. Say the wrong thing. *Do* the wrong thing. I've never… This is a first for me. Never felt this way before, Gabriella, and it's scaring the hell out of me."

"Gabriella?" She beams.

"Yeah." I kiss her nose then find relief when our lips touch, so warm and soft. The knot in my chest lessens. "Full name seemed appropriate. Such heavy feelings and all."

"Just don't hurt me," she breathes into our kiss.

"Never."

Never.

Never.

Fuck, please, God, never let me hurt my girl.

Matt made tacos. It's nothing fancy compared to what he probably has every night. It's endearing he didn't try to go for something more impressive. But this is Matt. He's about as down to Earth as a guy can get despite the car he drives, the house he lives in, and the family money he comes from. Tacos seem appropriate and, honestly, quite delicious.

Plus, it's my fav. He went to the trouble of making a taco bar, everything laid out in individual dishes, meat and shells kept warm in separate casseroles. He even left out cilantro since I'm allergic. He remembered, gah! He accompanied it with refried beans and chips and queso. The delicious homemade margaritas are an added bonus.

Never has anyone cooked for me, much less gone to so much trouble to make me feel welcome, safe, and cherished. And if I drink any more, I might just cry. And nobody wants that.

"You get enough?" He scans my empty plate, licking his fingers as his eyes roam my body, locking me in his heated embrace.

Even if I wanted more, could eat fifteen more tacos, stuff my face until I'm on the ground in a food coma, I can barely breathe under his focus, much less swallow another bite. "Yep," my sad excuse for control has me squeaking my response.

"You wanna watch a movie?" He starts to clear our dishes, his hand rubbing my arm as he passes.

"Sure." I'd watch paint dry with him.

I grab my plate to scrape in the trash, but he stops me. "Why don't you go relax?" He motions with his chin. "My room is the last door on the left. There's an attached bathroom if you need it. Get comfortable. This will only take me a few minutes." He kisses my cheek, lingering a second, giving me a nose full of him. Yummy and tantalizing. "I got this."

I've never not cleaned up from a meal. I'm the one left in the kitchen while my dad and brothers crash on the couch or hit the local pub. It feels wrong not to help. But I wouldn't mind a minute to freshen up, finger brush my teeth, change my panties, take a shower, shave my legs… again, lose thirty pounds.

You know, the usual stuff when the guy you're dating tells you he loves you for the first time and you want to go all the way, but you need to feel pristinely clean before he touches you, even though he's done nothing but touch you for the past month or so. And now you're stuffed with tacos. Yeah, all that stuff.

Backing away slowly, I watch him load the dishwasher, catching his eyes. He winks and licks his lips. "I wouldn't mind finding you naked in my bed." He tips his head, a dimple popping free from his crooked smile before I disappear from sight. "Just sayin'."

Holy cannoli. Yeah, I'm totally going for the shower.

When I emerge from his adjoining bathroom, Matt is sitting on the bed, his eyes already on me. His nostrils flare seconds before he stands and is in front of me before I can catch a breath.

He grips my waist through the towel I've wrapped around me. "Fuck, baby. I was half joking and half praying about you being in my bed. But coming in here and hearing my shower on, I about broke down my door to get to you."

Oh my. "I was just—"

"Nuh uh. You don't have to explain or apologize for using my shower, my stuff. Whatever I have is yours." He runs his nose down my neck. "You smell so fucking good. Like me, only better." He chins over his shoulder. "I brought you a water." He swivels us so his back is to the bathroom door. "My turn."

I release my grip on his shoulders as he steps back, turning sideways to step inside. At the last second, he reaches out, tugging my towel free. "You won't be needing this."

I freeze, holding my breath as he takes me in, all of me. He's seen me naked up close, lying down, but never standing in front of him completely bare in every way.

"Fuck, you're killing me, Gorgeous." His head falls forward, shaking from side to side on a chuckle as he closes the door. "Killing. Me."

Ten

THEN

H E STALKS FROM THE BATHROOM LIKE A GOD ON a mission, his sights narrowing in on me. I didn't climb in bed. Too nervous. Instead, I borrowed one of his t-shirts and paced like a caged lion until he came out.

I suck in all the air when he grips my waist—one of his favorite places to hold me—kneading my flesh like he can't draw me close enough or touch me deep enough for his liking. His greedy hands make me feel wanted, desired—nothing I've ever felt before him.

Green eyes nearly glow as he takes me in. "Whatever happens or doesn't happen tonight is completely up to you. There's no pressure, Gabby. I'm happy just holding you and making out until we can't see straight."

My man. "How'd I get so lucky?"

His tender smile has me sinking into his chest. "I'm the lucky one." He slowly scans my face, heating me in all the right places. "Never thought I'd fall so fast." Resting his forehead to mine, he caresses down my sides to my bare thighs and up. "Fall so fucking hard."

Our breath hitches when he finds me sans panties. He kneads my ass, separating and squeezing me tight, exploring lower and lower. My head spins when he finds me wet. His growl of pleasure has me seeking his mouth and hitching my leg around his hip, so friggin' needy.

"Matt," I beg for his touch, for his everything.

He nibbles my bottom lip, then licks the sting away. "What do you need, baby? All you have to do is ask, and it's yours."

New Gabby fists his towel, pulling till it falls to the floor, then rubs against his impressive length standing at attention between us. "You."

His hand on my ass moves lower, teasing my opening with skilled fingers. I nearly die from my heart tripping over itself to catch air and climb him at the same time.

"Need you inside me, Matthew. So hard, so deep that I'll feel you for weeks afterwards," I pant, my mouth hardly leaving his before diving back in.

"Jesus, fuck, Gabby." He captures my chin with his teeth, biting, then sucking. "Where have you been hiding that dirty mouth?" He sinks a finger inside me, pumping slowly.

When I tighten my leg around him, he grinds against me in just the right exquisite place. "Oh, fuck." I grip his shoulders, riding his finger, rising on tiptoe to feel his shaft… Right. Fucking. *There*. "Matt," I beg and beg and beg.

"Like that, baby, just like that." He encourages me with his wicked tongue, fucking my mouth, matching his finger's in and out movement, his hardness rubbing my clit with each flex of our hips. "So fucking gorgeous."

It's a slow ride, a frenzied need to get him closer, to feel him everywhere, deeper, harder, yet more tender and caring than I've felt before. The knowledge of his love tingles across my skin and roots in my core, bringing me closer and closer to the end, and closer and closer to the beginning.

My orgasm hits me hard, convulsing around his fingers and spasming in his arms. He holds tight, praising and kissing me through wave after wave of aftershocks.

"Fuck that was hot." His heated breath tickles my neck as he lifts me off my feet and lays me down on the bed, ripping his t-shirt from my body and settling between my thighs. "Promise me you'll always ride my fingers like that." He smiles, sucking my mouth, stealing my already shortened breaths, pressing his hips to mine, ensuring I'll never get a full breath again.

"Matt?"

"Yeah, Gorgeous."

"Inside me. Now."

He swallows his chuckle when I open my legs more and his cock hits my wetness. I rub against him. His head hits my shoulder. "Gabby," he pleads. "You're killing me here."

I cup his face, bringing his eyes to me. "Not trying to kill you. I'm trying to get you to fuck me."

His growl is instantaneous. I feel its bite deep inside, only making me want him more.

"Not fucking. Making love." He tweaks my nipples, presses forward, his mouth finally taking mine in the kiss I've longed for, and he's been dying to give. It's deep, soul-sucking, life-affirming and apparently tied to my hips. With each drag of his tongue in and out, my hips follow, tethered in a dance I didn't know I knew, coming to life, with need only for him.

"You sure?" Suited up, he rubs his entirely-too-big-for-my-virgin-pussy cock against me, just nudging my opening, testing, teasing.

Despite my fear of pain, I nod, and I wonder for a split second when he lost his virginity. Did she love him like I love him? Did she make it good for him? Was she a virgin too? Did he love her?

"Hey." He tips my chin. "We don't have to do—"

"I want to." Running my fingers through his hair, I bring my mouth to his. "I want you." *I want you to be my first.* My eyes prick with the idea that we might not be each other's last. But I brush it away, diving in and encouraging him to do the same.

Oh, fuck. Fuck. Fuck. Fuck. Don't fucking come.
    She needs to come first.
    I need to last more than two seconds.

I push in farther, my eyes never leaving hers. When she winces, I stop. "Fuck, I hate hurting you."

She shakes her head and tries to catch some air.

I grind against her clit, not going deeper, play with her nipples until she gasps and her pussy walls clench and then pull me in a little deeper. "Ah, fuck, that's amazing."

Jesus Christ, how am I not going to come?

I've had sex before, lost my virginity at sixteen to a college chick one weekend visiting Fin. He wasn't too thrilled to hear that. I was ecstatic and couldn't wait to do it again. I did. Many more times that weekend. But I quickly realized I prefer a connection to random sex with strangers. Okay, that realization may have taken me six months of hookups and an extensive number of orgasms, but I got there.

And now, here I am with the love of my life, deep inside her no-longer-a-virgin pussy, praying I can make this good for her and last longer than my first jerk-off session because she feels so fucking good. I've never been with a virgin. I've never been someone's first choice. The fact that she's trusting me with this gift is enough to send me over the edge. Then add on the fact she's so tight and enduring even a little pain so we can move to the next level is near torture—in the best fucking way.

When she moans and arches into me, I sink deeper. She gasps and moves her hips, taking me further until I'm fully seated. Her breaths are choppy, more gasps with exhaled mews, but there's no pain on her face—only pleasure.

"You okay, baby?" *Please, fucking be okay.*

"Yes, oh, yes," my girl moans.

Damn, loving hearing that. "Okay if I move?"

"Yeah." She bites her lip.

"That's mine." I suck her lip free and take her mouth as I pull out and slowly sink back in.

She shakes and sucks in air each time. Her trembling below me, arching to take me into herself and complaining when I pull back, is the most special gift I've ever received and the most amazing sex of my life. I haven't even come, and I'm already satisfied. I could live in this moment forever and be completely content. Both of us on the verge, but not quite there, living in the now, because, damn…

"I love you, Gabriella. So fucking much." My voice cracks. I bury my face in her neck to stop her from seeing the mist in my eyes.

Who cries during sex? Apparently, I'm about to.

She gasps and clenches around me. "I love you too, Matthew." *Please, please, please* she begs in my ear.

Ah, damn, my balls tighten.

I go deeper, faster, lock one arm below her shoulders to hold my weight, while gripping her ass with the other, grinding her clit against me with every forward drive. "I'm close, baby."

"Yes," she breathes against my lips. "I want to feel you come."

Fuck, if only I could spill inside her without a condom. Feel her bare. Then fill her up again and again. Have her smelling like me and dripping down her thighs.

"Oh, fuck," I growl. "Baby." I can't hold off.

"Ohmygod! Yes, please." She grabs my ass and claws my back.

Just. Fucking. Like. That.

I come so fucking hard, I barely register she's squeezing me until her cries of pleasure have me grinding harder, deeper, and sucking and playing with her nipples until she comes once more. Then I'm hard again, needing to ravish her until she's as sated and happy as I am that she saved this *first* for me.

Then we start… again.

Eleven

THEN

I CAN FEEL HIM—THE SORENESS, THE WANT TO BE filled again—with every step that takes me farther away from him.

I couldn't convince him to come with me. His brother is going but not Matt.

It wasn't a fight. We disagreed on how to spend our Saturday night. Usually, we do what he wants—hang with *his* friends. But I'm not feeling it tonight. The closeness, the bond we built, the intimacy shared all night and most of the morning and afternoon, all left me a bit buzzed. I'm unwilling to dampen it by putting up with the looks and whispers from his friends they think I don't see or hear. I'd have to be deaf and blind to miss the sneers from the women and the scrutiny from the guys.

Yes, I know I'm not in Matt's league.

I know I'm not his normal type.

No need to rub it in.

Plus, I promised Nate I'd come to the football game. I've been avoiding all things football since I met with his coach a few weeks ago. I said I'd think about it. I'm not sure I'm up to that type of commitment. It's not the game, really. It's all the stuff that will come with it. If I could join the team under the radar, hide behind the pads and helmet, I might be swayed.

Nate also guilted me a bit. I've become *that* girl who changes her life for a guy. I do love Matt, but I still need to have friends and pursue my own interests. And Nate hit a nerve when he said, "What? Now that you're all coupled up, are you just going to lay back and spit out babies? Come to my fucking game. Be *my* friend and not just Matt's girlfriend."

Damn, it was harsh but a good reminder that I came to college for a degree and to find myself—my new self—and not prove my father right… that I'm only good for making babies.

So, here I am at the football game without Matt… to support Nate and my own interests.

I get my ticket from Will Call, buy a drink from concession, and make my way to my seat. The team is already on the field warming up. I look for Nate but get sidetracked by the kicker and punter warming up. I could do that. Nothing they're doing looks too difficult, nothing I haven't done before. The punting technique is a little different than soccer, in that you hold the football with both hands. In soccer you hold the ball with the opposite hand than your kicking foot. In my case, I hold the ball left and kick right.

A loud whistle gets my attention. I scan the field and zone in on Nate standing there with his helmet hanging by his side, his eyes on me. I give a small wave, which grants me a chin lift and a big smile.

Damn, he's cute. And those football pants. Strong, muscular legs, tight bum. They show it all off nicely.

Matt's butt would look great in those pants. Even better out of them.

Gah, where's my brain going?

We stare for a few more seconds before his coach calls him over. I get a quick wave as he pulls his helmet on and runs toward Coach Eaton. They talk for a minute, each taking turns talking while the other listens, which impresses me. I thought coaches only want you to listen, not talk back. Coach pats his shoulder, and as Nate runs off to join his team still warming up, Coach looks my way, giving me a wave with his clipboard. I wave back and quickly look away.

Were they talking about me?

I sink down in my seat—front row, smack dab on the fifty-yard line—putting my feet up on the railing in front of me. They're damn good seats. Now I wonder if the seat was from Nate or Coach. I don't look around. I don't want to know if anyone noticed the interaction between me and a player and the head football coach.

Under the radar, that's my motto.

A part of me wants to slink away, but the friend part wants to stay and support Nate and his team. Maybe it's *my* team. I'm a student here. I get to claim them too, don't I?

We win the coin toss and decide to receive. Get the ball and hit it hard. I'm all for that. I'm fascinated by the kick off, watching the layout, how the kicker sets the ball and systematically steps backwards and then to the side a few steps. He looks to be lined up perfectly. Not that I know. I've seen it a hundred times but never watched it from the perspective that it could be me out there doing it on this very field.

A chill shoots up my spine. I shimmy in my seat, my skin prickling with goosebumps.

Do I want that?

Yeah, maybe I do. Just a little bit. Maybe a bit more than a little.

On deep exhale, I ignore the knot in my stomach at that realization and focus on the game, taking it in from a new perspective of being a player on the field with skin in the game instead of a spectator. It's an opportunity a lot of guys get, but how many women get asked to join an all-male sports team?

Asked. I was *asked*. I didn't push my way through the door, insisting they give me the same shot as any other male player. Coach—Nate—invited me in. *Willingly.*

Oh, shit. A flood of nerves has me popping to my feet, the need to pace or run overwhelming. After a quick glance around, I sit back down. I don't want to make a scene, and I'm blocking views. What am I saying? It's a football game—everyone's on their feet!

I need to calm down and think this through. Be rational. Logical. Not driven by emotion. I need to talk to Matt.

He'd get it, right? Or maybe not. He didn't seem too keen on me hanging out with the players, or Nate's interest in me. Though, I think that's more about Nate than football.

I drink my Coke, wishing it were a beer, but I'm not a fan of the taste. The buzz, I'd welcome, though. But… underage.

I set my me-thoughts aside and watch the game, cheering on Nate, Dwight, and the team as a whole. When halftime comes, we're winning by twenty-two points. *Go Longhorns!*

As the team starts to run off the field, one splits off, and I nearly die when I realize it's Nate… and he's coming to me. His helmet is in one hand and something orange in the other, his hazel eyes shining nearly as bright as his smile. He gets close, his breath heavy. "You came."

I lean close enough to touch his hand on the railing. "I said I would."

"You did." He plops the orange thing on my lap. "Put this on. Be my fan."

I hold up his jersey, the one they sell in the team's shop. I slip it over my head as he watches in amusement.

"My number looks good on you."

I laugh. "Of course you'd think that."

He nods. "It could be your number, you know." When I just stare and don't answer, he pushes over the barrier between us, kissing my cheek. "Meet me afterwards. Tony will let you through."

Tony is the security guard I met a few weeks ago. I want to see what behind-the-scenes looks like now, even just a few weeks later.

Someone down the field calls Nate. He waves them off, waiting for me to reply.

"Okay." I won't tell him now that I don't want to party afterwards. I don't want to dampen the high he's riding.

He winks and backs away. "Hey," he stops, garnering my eyes. "I'm glad you're here."

"Me too." My smile is genuine. I'm happy to be here, and it's an added bonus that *he's* so happy I'm here. He takes a few more backward steps before turning around and trotting off the field.

I watch. I mean, football pants.

After the game, I congratulate Nate on the win but don't stick around. He didn't seem surprised I wasn't going to party with the team, though he asked me more than once to go with him. In the end, he kisses my cheek and leaves me with, "Be safe," before I make my way out of the stadium to my car. The congestion in the parking lot has died down enough for me to exit quickly, making my way across campus to the house Matt and his friends are partying in. I texted him to let him know I'm on my way, but I don't get a response by the time I'm parking a few houses down.

The windows shake from the driving pulse of "Let's Hurt Tonight" by OneRepublic. It all reminds me of the first party I attended when school had barely started. That was the night Matt escorted me home after feeding me.

I look down at the jersey I'm still wearing, pull it off, and toss it back in the car. It's like an orange neon sign announcing my arrival and ties me to the team I'm still not quite sure I want to be a part of… yet. No need to look like a team stalker in the meantime. I can do without that. Plus, no reason to remind Matt I chose to go watch Nate play over hanging out with him and his friends. Though, he did the same. Didn't he?

I put on a brave face and make my way through the front door, acting like I belong, like I know where I'm going, when really, I have no idea where Matt could be. I check my phone again and send him another text.

Me: *I'm here. Where are you?*

I clench my lips, scanning the room, waiting to see if the text shows read, or if he'll even reply.

A few more minutes and nothing. My first text doesn't even show read.

With a sigh, I push through the spacious but packed room, navigate around large groups and dancing partiers only to find myself backed up in a line to get through the kitchen to outside. This is exactly the time I didn't want to have tonight. I wanted friends, but this feels so empty. Nameless drunken strangers looking for a good time isn't *my* good time.

Maybe joining the team would give me a healthier community? Maybe not.

I need to talk to Matt about it. I rest against the wall, waiting to see if the sea of bodies will dissipate, or if I should give up and go back the way I came and walk around the house to the backyard.

I let my head fall back and stare at the ceiling, thinking of all the places I'd rather be than at a party full of strangers.

The dentist? *Yes*, and that's saying something considering how much I hate having my teeth cleaned. The smell, the sounds, the tastes… yuck. Not my favorite.

The gynecologist? *Maybe, yes?* Being probed and swabbed seems just a little less invasive than standing here like an outsider among a sea of beautiful, happy people looking at me as though I don't belong with my boyfriend. Which reminds me… Matt. I scan the room again, getting closer to the kitchen. I check my phone again. Still no response, no incoming texts.

Over the music, Matt's laugh resonates in my ears. He's here, and he's happy. But of course, he's found someone to laugh with and talk to. He's one of the *most* beautiful people. Never alone or lacking for company.

I tilt my head, listening closer, trying to figure out where it's coming from, so I know where to go once I get into the kitchen.

"I don't know how you do it," some guy says.

"What?" my man asks.

-Make the best homemade guac I've ever tasted?

-Stay grounded when his family name means there's no ceiling?

-Shine like a lighthouse—my personal beacon of hope that love could happen for me, and light me up a bit too, somehow.

Would I even have the bravery to try for the football team and all the scrutiny if Matt hadn't been here, illuminating my worth these last few weeks?

I love him so much.

"Do you just climb on top and hold on?"

My feet stop before the stranger's sentence is finished.

"Ride her like a wild bull?" Another guy laughs.

"Nah, man, I get it. She's hot. I didn't know fat could be so beautiful," a fourth guy shares.

With each word, my head lowers. I sink into the wall as far as I can. *Are they talking about me? Of course they are.*

"Fuck off," Matt bites. I perk up, waiting, hope rising in me for the first time ever in the face of someone attacking me.

No one's insulted me like this in front of someone who loves me the way Matt does. It's protective and pure, and he is going to lose it! I don't want him to get in a fight, defending my honor like some old romance novel… but I want to hear him wipe the smiles from their faces when he tells them how much he loves me.

How real we are. How good our love feels.

Please don't get in a fist fight for my honor, but, yeah, you tell 'em. You tell them off.

"I guess. I mean, I'd do Gabby in a heartbeat. But it would be in the dark, and I sure as hell wouldn't bring her out in public," one of the original shamers says.

Okay, maybe one punch?

Like the one your silence is doing to my gut.

"Fuck, Matt. Keep that chubby-chasing fetish in private, man."

Stab. Tell them you love me!

"For real, bro, none of us need to see that."

Stab. Stab. Tell them about us. Please. Stand up for me.

"Raise your standards or take the kinky shit behind closed doors."

A punch right to the heart. Every word said and those *not* said by Matt defending me and protecting us.

Is that how he really feels?

Am I just a dirty little chubby-chasing game to him, a fetish? I'm not even a person to him? I'm a size he wants to fuck?

With tears looming and rage brewing, I rush out of the house faster than I made it in, knocking a few people over in my haste. I hear comments as I pass, but I'm already five feet out the door in my head.

I don't stop. I can't. Not until I'm safely away from their words I can never unhear.

Gabriella Two Ton, my brothers' voices push through my thoughts.

Come on, G2, don't hog the potatoes; pass 'em over.

No one will ever love you the way you are, my mother's parting words.

I didn't know fat could be so beautiful.

None of us need to see that.

Chubby Chaser.

"Stop. Stop. Stop," I yell and hit my steering wheel as my shame slides down my face one wretched tear at a time.

He doesn't really love me.

It was all a game.

A fetish.

I'll always be the fat girl.

No one will ever love you the way you are.

I thought… I thought he was different. I thought he and Nate were a special kind of different who saw past my size. Treated me like a person with thoughts and dreams of my own. I wasn't invisible any longer.

Nate. He said to call him if I ever need him. He didn't want me to leave him tonight after the game. He wanted me to party with him and his friends. He wanted me to join the team… Maybe…

Forgoing my phone, I tap my Apple watch as I screech away from the curb. "Call Nate, cell."

He answers on the first ring, "Firecracker."

"Where are you?" I bite my lip to squelch the tremble in my voice.

"Where do you need me to be?" The concern in his voice is instant, making more tears fall and the road blur.

"Here," I cry. "I need you here."

Twelve

THEN

SLIDING TO A STOP ONLY FEET AWAY, A STONE-faced Nate jumps out of the passenger side and runs around, wrenching my door open. "What the fuck happened?" He kneels beside me, turning my car off, unbuckling my seat belt, and pulling me out and into his arms.

I'm dying inside, near hysterics, crying so hard I can hardly breathe, much less talk.

I'm so fucking stupid.

He captures my face, swiping at my tears. "Babe, you gotta calm down enough to talk to me. Are you hurt? Did someone hurt you? Fucking… car crash? Gabs, if someone hurt you…" The urgency in his voice has him shaking, trying to reel himself in as he slides his gaze down my body, scanning for injuries.

All I can do is shake my head and try to tell him I'm okay, at least on the outside, I wasn't attacked like he's thinking. "Not phy…sic…al…ly." I hiccup and trip over my words, too short on air, too worked up like a friggin' toddler who just lost her favorite toy and can only babble through choppy sobs.

Relief blankets his face. "No one hurt you physically?" Back in his arms, he soothes me, his hand holding my head to his chest, petting my hair. "But someone sure as fuck hurt you emotionally, didn't they, Firecracker?" He kisses my head. "My Amazon got her gooey insides trampled on." He's not making fun. He's damn serious, and it only makes me cry harder. "It was Matt, wasn't it?" he grumbles. "I'll fucking kill him."

That thought is put aside as Dwight steps up, kisses my head and rubs my back. "It'll be okay, baby girl."

They have a low-octave discussion with grunts and few words, deciding to get me and my car to their place.

A little calmer, I dry my face and glance at Nate driving my car across campus. His jaw is clenched, his shoulders, tight. I can see visions of murder running through his thoughts. I touch his arm, and he quickly glances my way, squeezing my hand and giving me a soft smile. "You'll be fine, Gabby. I'll make sure of it."

Why couldn't I have fallen for Nate?

Matt. My heart hurts. My eyes sting as a new wave of sorrow rises.

"I need to talk to Coach," I rasp, clearing my throat, pushing the emotions down.

Nate studies me for a second before turning his focus back to the road. "Okay."

We pull into the athletic dorm. He parks and jumps out. "Stay here."

A minute, maybe two later, he opens my door, offering his hand. "Get whatever you need. We're taking my truck."

I love that he knows I need to talk to Coach in person and not just call him.

He nods to Dwight. "Only a handful of guys. I'll call. Be ready."

"On it." Dwight tips his invisible hat to me. "Be strong, baby girl."

It only takes a few minutes to pull outside a house I assume is Coach's. I check out my red makeup-cried-off face in the visor mirror and groan. "I look like I've been rode hard and put up wet."

A warm chuckle has me glancing at Nate. He chucks my chin. "Trust me, Coach has seen worse." He cocks his head, keeping my eyes on him. "For the record"—his brow arches—"you look beautiful, Firecracker." He swipes under my right eye and smiles. "Perfect."

"Liar." I don't give him time to respond. I close the visor and hop out, take a deep breath and steady my nerves.

I can do this.

I'm the new Gabby. I don't let other people's opinions keep me down, embarrassed, and hiding in the shadows.

Fuck Matt's narrow-minded, judgy friends.

Fuck Matt for not having the balls to stand up for me—if he cares. For not loving me more than his need to appear cool in the eyes of his friends.

That's not love.

And if Jen's a cheerleader, her skinny ass is going to cheer for me.

A concerned Coach Eaton greets us at the door. "You okay, Gabby?" He motions us inside, but I stop him with a wave of my hand.

"I'm good, Coach. I don't want to take up your time. It's late. I'm sorry about that."

He steps forward, closing the door behind him. His eyes slide to Nate before returning to me. "I hope you being here is good news, but even if it's not, you need something, you let me know."

Wow. The tension in my neck and shoulders lessens just a bit, surprised by his candor and willingness to help me even if I'm not one of his athletes. "I appreciate that." He has no idea how much it means. "I'd like to join the team, but I have two conditions."

Coach crosses his arms over his broad chest. I wonder what position he played in college. "Uh huh, and what's that?"

"I need to move into the athletic dorm—"

"Not a problem." He nods, his hands moving to his hips.

"—tonight," I finish.

His eyes widen; his head bobs, thinking. He runs his hand over his brow and pulls out his phone. "Give me a sec." He walks down the driveway, talking to whoever's on the other end.

He motions to Nate, who jogs over. They talk for a minute as I stand there feeling more like a silly, needy girl as the seconds pass. I need to make a knife-edge break between me and Matt. I can't stand the idea of him knocking on my door, finding me crying… over *him*. I shouldn't care. But just because he didn't really love me doesn't mean my love wasn't real.

Nate leaves Coach by his truck and walks back to squeeze my shoulder. "You doing okay?"

"Mm, yeah." I could use some food, coffee, and some sleep. Not necessarily in that order.

Nate's phone dings. He smiles, typing on his phone as Coach returns.

"Done," Coach advises like it was no big deal. "What's your other condition, Chisholm?"

I almost smile at his use of my last name, like I'm already one of the team. "I don't want a big deal made of me being on the team. No media."

He chuckles and steps closer, his eyes growing serious. "We can try to hide it as long as possible. But it will get out, and news will travel. You're breaking new ground here, kiddo. People will be curious, furious, supportive, and outspoken about it. I can put you down as Gabe on the roster, but *when*—not *if*—the news gets out that you are a woman and not a guy named Gabe, they will think you're hiding more than just a girl playing on a guy's team."

I frown. "You mean like I'm pretending to be a guy?" Ouch, my ego.

"Or hiding other facts." He looks between me and Nate. "It's better you use your real name so they'll dig less. You'll have days, maybe weeks before the news becomes public knowledge, but better it be the truth than lies that will only complicate things down the road and diminish the strides you're making as a woman in a male-dominated sport. Don't confuse it by making it a gender identity or sexual preference hot button by hiding behind a guy's name."

"It shouldn't matter—"

"No, it shouldn't. But it will. You want to fight for women's rights, or you want to fight for gay rights?"

"I'm not going to be the team's trans or lesbian Rachel Dolezal. Pretending to be something I'm not would undermine the cause and make me a shitty ally—and person." And is being me so bad?

"Exactly."

"Alright, my real name." It honestly hadn't even occurred to me that my name being on the roster would be the reason the news would get out. It's obvious now. Once it's published, *Gabriella Chisholm is a kicker on the Longhorns*, news will travel. I've no doubt.

"Good." He lets out a long sigh. "I promise we'll do everything to mitigate the impact this has on you, but playing a college sport, no matter which one, would bring you a certain level of notoriety. There's no way around that… and it is good for the team and school."

Yeah, I'm getting that.

He looks to Nate. "Get her settled. Let me know of any problems."

"Yes, Coach."

Coach squeezes my shoulder. "I'll see you on Monday, introduce you to the special teams' coaches. We'll go from there." He pats my arm. "It'll be okay, Gabby. We're making history." He winks. "No pressure."

As we walk away, Coach calls, "Hey, Chisholm?"

I pause and turn. "Yeah, Coach?"

"Welcome to the Longhorns. We're proud to have you."

And damn, if that doesn't spark a whole new wave of emotions, a sense of belonging, rightness, I've never felt.

He's happy to have me around.

He's not embarrassed by me.

And more, he thinks this could be the start of something important—largely because of me. I matter already.

It feels right. The way Matt made me feel when he kissed me for the first time. He claimed me in front of everyone in the student union. I felt seen and appreciated.

God, please let this be the right move and not just a knee-jerk reaction to Matt's betrayal. The catalyst for a good thing. *Please. Please. Please.*

"Thanks, Coach," I manage around the tightness in my throat.

"Come on, Firecracker." Nate helps me into the cab of his truck. "Let's get you settled in your new home."

Thirteen

THEN

INSTEAD OF HEADING TO MY DORM, NATE TAKES ME to get food.

Why couldn't I fall in love with Nate?

"Hamburgers or tacos?" he asks like there can't possibly any other choices.

"Either, as long as it's greasy, and I can get fries and a Coke."

"Done."

Less than fifteen minutes later, bags of food between us, parked in the burger place's back parking lot, we eat in the car. He eats two burgers and three tacos. I don't know where he puts it all, but when he goes for my fries, I nearly bite his hand off.

His bottom lip puckering, he practically begs, "Come on, Firecracker. One fry. Two max."

He hasn't pushed me to talk. It's a comforting silence that has me more thankful for this man sitting beside me with each passing second. I set the fries between us as I finish my last taco. "Don't eat them all."

"Deal." He swipes my cheek and bathes me in a brilliant smile.

I roll my eyes and drink my Coke, amazed at how at *home* I feel around him.

When we pull back into the athletic dorm parking lot, I assume we're getting my car before heading to my dorm. Instead, he motions to my car. "Do you need anything out of it tonight?"

"No, but aren't we—"

He slips his hand in mine. "Come on, they're waiting for us."

"They?"

He smiles and continues to walk, urging me along. "I got you, Firecracker."

On the top floor, we run into Dwight and a mess of athletes I assume are football players. Some I recognize; others I don't, but their size and fitness are formidable.

Dwight runs, whooping and hollering. I brace for impact, but instead of a flying tackle, he lifts me up and spins me around. "Baby girl, you ready for this?!"

In the background, the "Are You Ready For This" song starts playing. I can't help but laugh and hang on as he jumps and starts off down the hall with me still in his arms.

He stops at a room second from the end and sets me down. Nate is right there, his hand on my back shuffling me forward until we're standing a few feet inside.

A familiar object makes me feel like fate is smiling on this decision. "I have the same lamp!"

"No, you don't." He grins.

Confused, I look to him and around the room and stop on the bed in the corner. *Wait.* "That's my comforter. I have the exact same…"

Nate points to the closet on my left.

Holy… "Those are my clothes!" I spin and freeze at the sight of Dwight standing in the doorway, framed by faces I somewhat recognize. "You… you guys moved me in?"

Wow. It should irritate me that they were in my things, yet all I feel is grateful I didn't have to deal with packing tonight too. Or chance running into Matt, if he even noticed my text and came looking for me, or Jen, who would only gloat to know Matt is… Well, I don't know, whatever Matt is, but she would most definitely feel justice had been served.

Maybe she's there with him now, and they've been laughing about his fetish all along. Is there a jealousy fetish where they use me to get off?

I'm sure she felt I was breaking some cosmic law by stealing a man like Matt from her clutches. I guess she can have him now.

Damn, the idea of that rips at my heart. Beautiful people stick together...

Nate steps in front of me. "Yeah, Firecracker, I didn't want you going back there in case he showed up."

I lean into him, my hand on his chest, blinking up at him, fighting to hold it together. "Because I'm on the team?"

His forehead falls to mine. "Because we're going to be lifelong besties, remember?"

Damn, this sweet man.

Just as fast as it came, the tender moment is gone. "Alright you, assholes. It's late, get to bed. You can all say *hi* in the morning." Nate pushes them out, and after a quick word with Dwight, the door clicks shut.

"I can't believe you did this," I whisper as I take in my new room. My sanctuary.

"I'm next door. Dwight is my roommate. For now, you don't have one." He pushes on the door to my right. "The good news, this is your private bath. The bad news, you're responsible for cleaning it."

All I can do is nod in awe that he and Coach did all of this for me. I'll have to work hard to not let them down.

His soft hazel eyes meet mine when he tips my chin. "Shower. Then sleep. Deal with all of this tomorrow."

I bite my lip and nod. I seem to be doing a lot of that. "Okay."

Exhausted and dazed, I step out of the bathroom, freshly showered, and still at the sight of Nate in my new bed, propped on one elbow.

My heart slams against my chest. He doesn't think—

"Calm down, Firecracker. I'm not here to get in your panties. Though—" He quirks a brow and grins. "Another time, maybe."

"I thought we were besties?" I pop a hip.

He waves me over. "We are, I promise. Come on. You need sleep."

The bed is at least three feet off the ground with a dresser beneath it, but I don't use the end railing like a ladder, I simply lift a knee and climb in… The benefit of long legs and being tall.

"Damn, that's hot." Nate holds out the covers he's already under, granting me access to his large form in only black boxer briefs and a white V-neck t-shirt. The male version of what I'm wearing, panties and a tank top. I probably would have put on a larger t-shirt if I'd known I was having company.

I laugh off his comment as I lay next him, on my side facing away in a friggin' twin bed. *Where are all these legs and arms going to go?*

He covers us up. "Seriously, you just climbed in, like me, like the height is no big deal. That's hot, my Amazonian Princess."

Princess? Please.

"You're the only one who's ever seen my size as a plus," I murmur, situating my pillow, trying to get comfortable with a mammoth of a man behind me and not rub all against him. I thought *he* had too, but…

"Damn, that's just wrong." He pulls me back with a hand on my belly, kisses my neck and whispers all too tenderly, "You need to cry, you cry. Tomorrow, you'll tell me what that fucker did so I know why I'm kicking his ass. Then you buckle up and show the world the fierce warrior you are."

When my shoulders start to shake and the visions of what happened tonight crash around me, he turns me in his arms and holds me against his chest, whispering calm affirmations that I *will* be okay as I drench his shirt in undeserving tears over a boy who stole my heart and broke it in a matter of weeks.

Matt proved Jen right—he only wanted me because Nate did. And it looks like Nate actually wanted me for the right reasons.

I don't know what I'll do when I see Matt again, but I believe with all my heart the man holding me will be there to give me strength should I need it, or throw a punch if I allow it, or be a wall to hide behind. I don't know what will happen, maybe all three. Maybe Matt will disappear to Mount Olympus, where all the gods should be instead of walking the earth, plundering and breaking us mere mortals for sport, in affirmation of their superiority and for the simple fact that they can.

Go away, Matt, the god of virility. You got my virginity. I'm of no use to you now. Find your Eden and leave me be…

It's late when I plop down in a chair and check my phone, wondering how the game went and did my girl miss me. I should have called her, apologized for not going along. I hate the idea I left her to go to the game by herself. Yes, she went to support a guy I can hardly stand the sight of, but the reality is she was sitting in the stands alone, surrounded by people she didn't know. One of her least favorite things.

When I see her text saying she's here, I glance around, then check the rest of the house and outside. Nothing.

I've missed more than one text and both were hours ago. I should have been checking my phone all along.

Fuck. If she came, why didn't she find me?

I call her.

It goes straight to voicemail. "Baby, I'm sorry I missed your texts. I'm still here. Where are you? Please call me."

Fuck.

I call again just to be sure it didn't go to voicemail because she was calling out at the same time I was calling her. I get her voicemail, again.

She's mad and turned her phone off. I'm sure of it. I don't blame her.

Fuck this night. I never should have chosen my friends over her. The weight of that sits heavy on my chest. Stupid drunk-ass guys with big mouths and egos to match. She said she was sort of over these kinds of hangouts, but I didn't think it was this bad.

Fuck, fuck, fuck.

I snag a bottled water on my way out. It doesn't take long to park along the curb of her dorm. A little charm gets me through the lobby and to the elevator bank after visiting hours—way after.

Guilt rings heavy as I wait for the elevator.

When I make it to her door, I softly rap, hoping to only wake her and not the neighbors, if she's even a sleep.

Seconds tick by and nothing. I knock harder and whisper through the door, "Gabby, it's me. Open up."

Nothing.

Knock harder. A little louder, "Come on, baby, let me in."

Harder. Louder, "I'm sorry. Please, baby, let me in so I can apologize in person."

Grovel. Beg. Whatever it takes.

My anxiety spikes at the thought she might not be in there. She might not have made it home.

"Fuck!" I bang on the door. "Gabby!"

"She's not in there," a sleepy voice I wish I didn't know rasps from down the hall.

My gaze sweeps her way. "What?"

Jen motions to the door I'm near ready to bust down. "Gabby's not in there."

"How the fuck do you know that?"

Jen scratches her head through a yawn. "The football team showed up a few hours ago and moved her out. Took 'em maybe thirty minutes. Left the place bare. If it wasn't nailed down, they took it."

"Nate?" I seethe at the idea of her being with him instead of here in her bed where I was hoping to be.

She shakes her head. "Nope. It was Dwight, Deke, Trent and a bunch others." Her tiredness must quiet her bitch as there's not a hint of cattiness in her demeanor or tone.

I look back at my girl's door and sigh. She fucking moved out.

What'd you do, Gabby? What made you run?

Jen could be lying. I wouldn't put it past her, but then, where is Gabby and why wouldn't she return my calls or texts?

Quiet steps on carpet draw my eye to Jen as she approaches, stopping close enough to touch if I had the desire to, which I don't. Ever.

"Rumor has it there was an incident at a Kappa party. Gabby ran out in tears."

"The fuck?" I crowd her to the wall. "Who the fuck told you that?"

She shrugs. "There were a lot of stories flying while the football team moved her out. Who knows what's true, but I'm betting there's a grain of truth to some of them?"

"I wasn't at a fraternity party, and neither was Gabby," I growl, not knowing if any of what she says is true, but I do know I'm not letting Jen sniff up this tree looking for answers.

I turn and stomp out. Dread fills me with each step.

Was she there?

Did she hear those assholes?

I have to find her.

Fourteen

THEN

MORNING COMES LIKE A DRUNK SAILOR AFTER A night on the town, weaving and nauseated, and I didn't even have the fun of getting drunk. I roll to my back, groaning, and realize I didn't bump into a body. I blink into the dimly lit room, finding it empty. No Nate.

I sit up, only to ascertain it's not such a great idea. Back on my side, I spot a water bottle tucked into the corner of the mattress and bedframe. I grab it, note how cold it is and hold it against my forehead and cheek. He must not have left too long ago for it to still be cold. I alternate drinking the cool liquid and holding it against my heated skin.

Fan. I need to buy a fan.

After, I crawl out of bed and find some sustenance.

A soft click has my eyes opening. I guess I fell back asleep. Nate creeps closer until we lock eyes. "Hey, sleepyhead." He caresses my head and down my hair. "I brought food."

I grab his hand, holding it in mine, and tuck in under my cheek. "My hero," I grate, clear my throat and sigh when exhaustion makes it hard to say much more.

He bends over and kisses my cheek. "Tell me what you need."

"To feel human again."

He chuckles. "I'm pretty sure you already are, but maybe some food will help you *feel* like you are."

When I struggle to sit up, he swoops in, lifting me like I'm not 5'10" and weigh nearly as much as he does—okay, maybe not quite, but more than I'm sure he's used to—and places me on the couch.

Wait. What? "There wasn't a couch here last night, was there?"

"Nope." He opens a drawer, pulls out a t-shirt, and hands to me. "Cover up those tits, please."

I pull it over my head. "What, you don't like boobs?"

He hands me a to-go container and sets a water on the table next to me. "I love 'em." He plops down next to me with his own container. "But if you don't want me sporting a boner and staring at your poking-through-your-thin-as-shit-tank-top nips, then you need to cover them babies up."

Well, okay then.

"You were out cold. The guys and me moved the couch in early this morning from the commons room. You need a place to chill away from a bunch of horny, testosterone-laden guys who may think it's cool to have a chick on the team, but having you live under their noses may have them fantasizing about your ass as you study and relax in that *I'm kinda awesome* way you have about you."

I bump his shoulder. "You're crazy. No one thinks I'm awesome, least of all me."

He nudges my container. "I think you're awesome, Firecracker. And I don't like many people. I may look like the friendly guy, but I don't let many in. You got in. I just want to be sure you don't have any of these guys perving on you—unless you want them to. Got me?"

I swallow a bit of eggs and blink the tears away. "Yeah, I got you."

"Good. Now, eat. We need to scope out a TV we can acquire for your room."

I nearly choke when he keeps eating. He's dead serious.

"I don't need a TV."

"Well, I do. I plan on being in here a lot, and I like my creature comforts." He settles lower on the couch, legs wide, food propped under his chin. "Eat," he prompts when I just keep staring at him in disbelief. "Also, you need to tell me about Matt. He showed up here this morning. Dwight dealt with him, but I'm sure he'll be back."

I choke on my bite this time.

He calmly pats my back. "We'll get you through this, Gabby. You've got a whole team behind you now. You're one of us, and we protect our own."

"I don't want you to hurt him."

He locks his eyes with me. "You telling me the truth of what happened will determine how badly he hurts and for how long."

We're silent as we eat. I finish before him. He finishes off my food and his.

His hunger makes me miss my brothers a little. Not enough to reach out to them but enough to cause an ache that reminds me we don't have the kind of relationship I wish we did.

I do tell Nate all the dirty, shameful, embarrassing details, each word said and those not. I cry. He's steaming mad. He plans on hurting Matt. I talk him off the cliff, but only just.

The rest of the day is spent running errands, doing laundry, buying a TV for my room instead of *acquiring* one, and a team dinner and movie in the common room where we're short one couch nobody complains about. Then it's lights out for an early Monday morning practice.

I don't see Matt. I don't talk to him. I don't turn on my phone to confirm if there are missed calls and texts from him. I'd be heartbroken if there weren't any, and even more heartbroken if there are, and I have to read his texts and listen to his voicemails.

I can't avoid him forever, but maybe I can for a bit longer.

Nate holds me as I cry myself to sleep. He doesn't leave.

He doesn't leave the next night or the next or the next.

Matt god of virility: *Please, baby, just talk to me.*

Matt god of virility: *I don't know what I did, but I promise you I didn't mean it. I love you.*

Matt god of virility: *I'm feeling like a needy girl here. Just answer. It's been a week. Let me know you're okay.*

Me: *I'm physically okay. I can't see you.*

Matt god of virility: *Please, tell me what I did. Give me a chance to fix it.*

Me: *You can't fix who you are. You can't fix me.*

Matt god of virility: *Why would I want to fix you? You're perfect.*

Lies. Lies. Lies.

Me: *Liar.*

Matt god of virility: *I've never lied to you.*

Me: *I have two words for you: chubby chaser.*

Matt god of virility: . . .

Oh, fuck. She heard. She was there, and she heard what those fuckers were saying. But then she must have heard me—

I spot Nate in the distance. For a big fucking guy, he's been hard to track down. There's a handful of footballers. They walk like a unit, people moving out of their way, glancing, admiring but not approaching. I glare, looking harder. Between their shoulders I spot my dark-haired beauty. She's huddled between them, in the middle where no one can really see or get to her.

Is this why I haven't seen her? They've been hiding her all this time, walking like centurions from class to class, guard dogs on the lookout for me.

Rushing forward, dodging people in my way, I make it within a couple of yards of them before they stop. Nate and his guys zoom in on me. They're a formidable force, but they don't scare me. They may keep her hidden, but she's still mine. I see it in his eyes. He may have swooped in and saved her, but she's still all mine; otherwise, she'd be sequestered under his arm at his side, not behind him like he's a protector, but like he's a boyfriend.

"Gabby," I holler around the wall of muscle between me and her. "Please, baby, just talk to me. Don't throw away what we have."

"Had." Nate steps forward, bumping me with this chest, but I hold firm. He's not bigger than me. He outnumbers me but can't beat my determination.

"You don't know what the fuck you're talking about." Anger rises over my need to see and comfort my girl.

"Don't I?" He charges me backwards, far enough she can't hear him. "You think you can use her. Call her names. Degrade her and expect to what, slip right back into her welcoming arms?"

"I never called her any names." I push him back, getting in his face.

"Your silence was screaming your agreement with your asshole friends," he seethes.

His anger is no match for mine. "You don't know that." I motion over his head. "She doesn't know what happened. If she did, she wouldn't be with you."

He rolls back on his heels, arms crossed. "But she is *with* me."

Nose to nose, fire brewing, I threaten what I will defend to my grave, "You better not lay a fucking hand on her. She's not your type, and you know it."

He smirks and leans in, his breath skating over my face. "You think you know my type?" He licks his lips, his eyes caressing my face, sending chills of hate down my spine. "It was one kiss, Matt. Get over yourself. You're boringly straight." He shrugs. "I wanted a taste of a McIntyre. I got one. Doesn't mean I don't crave a firecracker who lights up the night like nobody's business."

"She wouldn't." She deserves devotion—what does Nate know about being faithful?

His menacing smile only grows. "She already *did*." He shoulders past me, and it's then I realize the others are gone, along with Gabby. He was distracting me while they sequestered her away.

Was it all a distraction, untruths? Is she *with* him? Them? Did I push her into the arms of other *men*? It hasn't even been two weeks. It's a fight. A misunderstanding. We aren't broken up. I'm still hers. She's still *mine*.

Isn't she?

Fifteen

THEN

"**Y**OU SURE ABOUT THIS?" NATE'S EYES MEET mine across the center console. He was so confident earlier. "I'm sorry. He pissed me off. I never should have made it sound like we're sleeping together. I'm not a bragging kind of guy. Even if we did… were… are, I'd never talk about it. Swear."

He's done nothing but apologize since his confrontation with Matt, and Matt's done nothing but send me text after text. I read each one. They swing between apologizing to angry and back.

I didn't reply. The damage is done. The hurt solidified. Nothing he can say will change or make up for that. He can't charm his way back into my heart, my panties. He's ashamed of me. *I'm* ashamed of me.

There's nowhere to go from here but forward—*without* him. But in order to do that, I need him to let me go. Stop trying to make it right. It's not possible.

Beyond the truck's windshield, the house is nearly vibrating from the party raging inside. We've returned to the scene of the crime. Jen promised she'd have Matt here just after ten. It's nearly that now.

"I'm sure." I step out before he can talk me out of it.

We meet at the hood of his truck, the engine hissing as it cools off from idling for so long. We've been here an hour. I didn't want to be late but couldn't stand the idea of being in that house longer than necessary.

On a fortifying breath, I step forward, one foot after the other. Nate falls in at my side, close but not touching. I don't want to be touched, coddled. Not now. Not when we're getting ready to do some damage I never imagined I'd willingly do. I don't deserve comfort when *he'll* have none.

Dwight meets us inside, his face nearly as somber as Nate's. "They're nearly here."

Nate takes my hand and leads through the throng of people to stop at the bar. We down a shot each, no one checking to see if we're legal. It's a college party at its finest.

I spot a few of Matt's friends lingering in the corner, babes hanging all over them, not an inch of fat on them besides their all-too-perky breasts.

I'm not hating, not really. But how would my life be different if I'd been more like them genetically? Born willowy and delicate. Waifs never went out of fashion.

"Hey." Nate drags my chin to him. "Fuck 'em. You're ten times the woman they are."

"Ten *times*, huh? Thanks for that." I'm only teasing him, trying to lighten the heavy moment.

"Fuck." He leans in, his breath tickling my ear. "You *know* I didn't mean it like that."

I pat his chest, giving him a small nod. "I know."

"Couch or wall? Pick your poison."

"Couch," Dwight grumbles, eyes shooting to his phone. "They just drove up."

Before Nate can sit, I shake him off and plant myself against the wall. He moves in close, caging me in, his brow raised. "Am I picking you up, or hiding you from the room?"

"Hiding." I'd never agree or want to be the center of attention.

Moving in closer, one arm rests on the wall over my head, teasing my hair. His other hand slides up my neck, running his thumb over my bottom lip. "You gonna hate me after this?"

"No. I could never." Me? I already hate.

He sighs, his forehead meeting mine. "Thank God."

"Incoming," Dwight mumbles as he passes into the kitchen.

"You ready?"

I bite my lip, panic setting in and stealing my confidence.

"Breathe, Firecracker." He tips my chin, eyes locked, and brushes his lips across mine. "Why you doin' this?"

"So he lets me go." I latch onto his wrist, trying to quell my trembling.

Nate's mouth presses to mine, lingers for a second and pulls back. "Why do you need him to let you go?"

My heart crushes in on itself as I whisper my painful truth, "Because he thinks I'm a fat co—"

His roar is forced into my mouth as he cuts me off with a crushing kiss. Angry and demanding, he pushes through my parted lips to plunder and consume every inch of my mouth with his tongue. His moan draws a surprising sigh from me, as I relax into his tightening hold, caught up in his passionate denial of the words leaving my mouth.

Banded in his arms, the world forgotten, the reason for our deceit falls to the background as I kiss him back, wrenching him closer with a grip in his hair and around his back. He tastes like tequila and hot summer nights, of a man who accepts me and could maybe love me if I let him off the bench.

He squeezes my ass, grinding against me. My insides clench, surprising the hell out of me. I'm wet for my best friend. How is this possible? I never for a second thought I'd be turned on again by anyone. Or even want to be. But Nate… He's not just anyone… He's more.

Each sweep of his tongue, each caress of his hands, each press of his body to mine, every deep groan tells me he accepts me… He *wants* me.

For the right reasons?

Am I doing this for the right reasons? I was ending something tonight…

Are we starting something here?

As if sensing my thoughts, he sucks my bottom lip and murmurs, "Don't fucking stop. Not yet."

No. Not yet.

I dive back in. His pleasured moan gets one in return.

"Fuck me. I knew you'd light up like a firecracker."

I don't get to respond, at least not with words. My tongue greeting his has him picking me up, urging my legs around his waist, and we're on the move. His mouth never leaves mine. My needy hands don't stop, even as the cool air tickles my skin and has goosebumps racing.

It isn't until my back hits cold, hard metal do I pull away to find us outside, wedged between him and his truck. Heavy breaths warm my skin as the heat in his eyes takes me in. "You okay?"

"Yeah." I am, right?

"Damn, I thought you two were going do it right there against the wall." Dwight rubs his crotch. "I need a honey to help me alleviate this ache you two created. Like live porn."

"Dwight," Nate growls.

Breaking his grip, I slide down his body till I'm standing. His hands rest on my hips, his back to his friend, partially hiding me. Protecting me. My head hits his shoulder, and his hand grips the back of my neck.

"I got you," he whispers only for me.

"Yeah, ugh, the deed is done. Matt saw y'all and stormed out the back door with Jen in tow. If I read the situation correctly, he's going to use *her* to lessen *his* ache."

"Dwight." Nate's frustration is evident as his grip tightens.

"I'm going." He lifts his hands, backing up. "I'm going."

"Dwight." I stop him before he gets too far. "I'm sorry for involving you, but thanks."

"Nah, baby girl, it's all good. Check y'all later." He slips into the darkness.

Nate pulls me into a full body hug, resting his head on mine. "I'm gonna feed you. Take you home. Hold you a minute because I'm gonna need it. Then I'm going to my room and jacking off like you didn't just rock my world. Got it?"

On a chuckled sigh of relief, I nod and kiss his cheek. "Got it."

Still Nate. Still friends… Still us…

Till the end.

"I'm gonna need you to suck my cock until I can't breathe." My dead eyes meet her *oh-so-hopeful* ones. "You got a problem with that?"

She drops to her knees.

I guess that's a *no*.

My head hits the back of the house, praying Gabby will come this way, see Jen with my cock down her throat and feel half as dead as I feel.

I want her to feel my pain.

I growl my discontent when her lips wrap around me and suck before taking me deep. I shudder and harden when it's Gabby's light blue gaze I see when I close my eyes.

My girl, look what you've made me do.

I won't fuck Jen. I can't bring myself to go there, but I will use her to forget Gabby. To hurt Gabby. To punish myself for falling. For failing. For letting my girl down. For not being enough.

Then I'll find a stranger and fuck her until I can't remember Gabby's face.

Until my girl's eyes no longer shine in my memory.

Until her unforgiveable betrayal no longer hurts.

Until my idiotic ego understands what it's done.

I've lost my girl.

I'll never get her back.

I don't deserve her back.

Matt McIntyre (heartbreaker): *I get it now. I'll let you go, but you need to understand this is your choice, your doing, by not letting me make it up to you. If you think I'll forget you, you're dead wrong. Gone West - I'm Never Getting Over You*

Me: . . .

Sixteen

NOW

CAN'T TAKE MY EYES OFF THE SCREEN. IT'S LIKE A pile up on the highway. You know people are injured, yet you still can't help but gawk, trying to take it all in, figure out what the hell happened. That's me.

How the hell did I get here?

It's been seven years of trying to forget her, not seeing her, not letting the memories of her loose.

Her face haunts me from the frozen picture on the screen. I've rewound the story a dozen times, and each time it's the same. The ending doesn't change. The lost look in her eyes as reporters hound her, trying to get her reaction, eats at my stomach lining. The possessive urge to get to her, protect what's mine, what fucking eons of nameless, faceless women haven't been able to erase.

It's all still there, once buried, now clawing its way to the surface, its way to *her*.

Look away.

I fucking can't.

"Hey." Jace walks in my office, his eyes on his phone. He's here to talk about the marketing campaigns I'm supposed to be reviewing and have my top two picked ready to discuss. I haven't even opened the files, much less looked at the presentations.

Stuck in the middle of my office, the place I've been for, well, however long it takes to watch a three-minute news story a dozen times, plus the amount of time it's been paused… a shit-ton long time.

In my periphery, his head pops up when I don't reply. I don't meet his eyes. His gaze bounces between me and the screen. "You saw it, then?"

"Mm huh," is about as good a response as he's going to get.

My door flies open. Victor and Michael barge in.

Anybody knock anymore? I could be busy.

I *am* busy. Gawking. At My Heart on the screen.

Jesus, get a grip.

Take the wheel.

Do fucking something.

Just make it go away.

Bring her to me.

The urge to fuck a stranger gnaws at me. My go-to MO since she broke my heart—since I broke my own damn heart.

I don't do *that* anymore.

Maybe stopping was a stupid choice.

I've made lots of stupid choices in my life. Stopping being a man-whore wasn't one of them. I know for damn sure.

"Brother?" Michael grips my shoulder. "You need something?"

Yeah, the last seven years of my life back.

The ache in my chest is surprising, considering it's been a gaping hole since I was eighteen. When she ripped my heart out through chest, and trampled on it, like my love meant nothing to her.

"I think he's in shock. He needs a whiskey." Victor heads to the hidden liquor cabinet below the TV.

"It's ten in the morning," Jace tries to logic us.

"I don't think it matters." Michael forces me to sit on the couch. "Not today." He wrenches the remote from my hand and powers off the TV.

"What the fuck?!" My eyes burn from the loss of her face so close I could touch her. "Turn it back on." I scramble for the remote.

Michael and Victor play keep away until Jace steps in, holding his hand out.

Victor slaps it in his hand. "Pansy," he grumbles.

Relief floods me when Jace turns it back on, but she's gone. I knew it, of course. It was paused. The story is over.

Jace hands me a tumbler of Macallan, three fingers full. "Sit. It'll come back on."

It's the sports channel, and this is big news. It's even bigger *local* news.

"Monica," Jace talks to my PA via the intercom on my desk phone. "Cancel Matt's meetings and hold his calls. Send emergencies my way."

"Yes, Mr. Cavanagh," Monica responds as efficiently as ever.

The three of them sit, working on their phones, while I sip my liquid courage and stare at the TV, waiting for my girl to appear.

I'm two people: the man I was *before* her and the man I am *after* her.

Before her, all I wanted was to find *the* girl I could love and build a relationship with like my parents have—devoted and unbreakable. I thought I'd found her.

After her, well, that's where the playboy comes in. She's the reason for my manwhore ways… *She* drove me to it.

For seven years.

Seven. Fucking. Years… Literally.

Nameless faces. Endless nights. Anyone and everyone. Didn't matter as long as they didn't look a thing like my Gabby. I used each and every one of them to fuck the memories of my girl silent, to crush any hope, any dream I still held of making things right with her.

I fucked.

I fucked.

Then I fucked some more.

For seven long-ass years.

Two thousand, five hundred and fifty-five days, give or take an hour or two, I was in hell, my own personal brand of hell, or so I thought.

Until… Everything came crashing down. The worst consequences came knocking… Pounding… Beating down my door, showing me what true hell was.

I nearly broke up Joe and Sam, stalled their wedding by fucking his ex-assistant, Lydia, and Jace's ex-girl Vee, whom I knew as Bonnie (I actually didn't fuck her, but I would have if she'd let me do more than eat her out). It's a long-ass complicated story.

The Cliffs Notes version? My manwhore ways got me into the situation, not giving a damn who I fucked or the consequences, until the price was too high and hurt two of my brothers, nearly beyond repair. *Nearly.*

Now, I'm celibate. Sworn off women. Not trusting myself not to fuck it up by literally *fucking it up*. Maybe this is the third version of me.

How many more do I have in me?

But as I look at the screen, begging it to show me my girl, I can't help but hope there's a fourth version of me that looks more like Matt 1.0., who still believed in love and that my soul mate was still out there waiting for me to pull my head out of my ass and make things right.

Maybe Matt 4.0 could find love again.

The ball is snapped. The holder sets it, and I kick the hell out of it just like the other countless times. As soon as it's in the air, my kicking leg still off the ground, I'm slammed, pummeled to the ground. The breath is knocked out of me, the sting so intense, my eyes water and my vision blurs, the life knocked out of my limbs.

I lie there, trying to suck in air, trying to remember why I love this game, why I put up with a bunch of dick-swinging assholes who see me as a cum catcher and nothing more.

"Don't get up, sweetheart. I like you on your back, where you belong. Such a pretty view." The asshole who tackled me, illegally, saunters off, getting a downlow high-five from his teammate. Not a flag in sight. No penalty called.

Stupid charity game. It's off season for God's sake. He never would have gotten away with that in a regular season game. Hopefully. I don't have much confidence in fair play anymore.

Fuck! I thank God when I finally steal some air, spotting one of the specialty coaches and trainers strolling over as if me being laid out isn't of any consequence to them or the franchise.

I hate this team. I've given them four years of my life I can never get back.

My contract is up at the end of year. I'm out of here. Nothing is worth this bullshit. I'll scrub toilets over playing for New York for another season.

Once I'm on my feet, I get a mix of cheers and boos. They're a finicky crowd. They love me in private, one-on-one encounters, but the mob mentality of hating a woman in football runs rampant in the stands during games and on the field. It's harder to take out a kicker—I'm not on the field as much—so when they find a chance, they take it. Hard.

Assholes, all of them.

"Coach Levy wants to see you after the game." That's all the specialty coach has to say to me. Not *great kick, you did it again*. Not *good game*. All I get the head coach wants to see me.

Terrific. Joy. Maybe he'll fire me. Ask me to work for free, which I'm nearly doing now. Not really, but it seems like it compared to all the other players in the league.

I limp off the field. My job is done. We won the stupid charity game thanks to my field goal.

You're welcome.

"What did you do?" I pace my apartment overlooking Central Park, breathing a sigh of relief for having dodged the reporters outside my building.

How do they even know where I live?

"Do what, Firecracker? You need to be more specific if a flat *I don't know* won't satisfy you."

He's teasing. He knows what I'm talking about. "Nate."

Silence.

I check my phone to see if we're still connected. We are.

"I may have mentioned you're not happy with your current gig, and wouldn't we benefit from acquiring the number one kicker in the nation who just so happens to be the only woman in the NFL?"

"Why would New York take that deal?" I'm baffled.

He's not wrong. I'm not happy here. I'm downright miserable most of the time, but it hasn't impacted my performance. I'm still able to succeed game after game. It's no secret management isn't happy to have me here. They don't approve of a female on the field, much less playing football. The mostly all-male staff, top to bottom in their organization—except for the kitchens—is proof of that.

Of course, they don't come out and say it. It's in their actions, their grumbled discontent, their unwillingness to make positive change. Granted, they acquired me from the draft my junior year. Also Nate's doing. He was a senior and wanted me with him, as if he had a say. Turned out, he did have some pull. Unfortunately, he only lasted one season in New York before being traded to Dallas.

It was a great move for him. He's flourished there. He's not going anywhere. Dallas would be stupid to get rid of him like New York did. But, truly, not all teams mesh, despite how good it looks on paper. I'm proof of that.

"I don't know, Gabs, but they did. That's all that matters. Get your shit packed. You're coming home… to me."

"That part I'm happy about."

"But not your family?"

"Nope."

"Maybe they'll come around. They've had time to let it sink in. Realize how stupid they are."

That makes me laugh. "Yeah, not a chance. Nobody is smarter than my dad and brothers. According to them."

"Then fuck 'em. Send me your flight details. I'll pick you up. And don't let them make living arrangements. You know you're living with me, wife."

"Yes, husband. And I can't wait."

I can't. Truly. I've missed him something fierce. These years apart have been painful.

"Love you, Firecracker."

"Love you too." *See you sooner than you think.*

My flight lands tomorrow, and I plan on surprising him.

Seventeen

NOW

SHOULD HAVE KNOWN HE'D LIVE IN A FANCY gated community, each house having acres of land, set back from the street, with homes larger than some of the dorms from college. Definitely larger than any house I've lived in, much less visited.

The security guard waved me through when he saw my face and recognized my name. He was all smiles as he advised, "Mr. Sinclair added you to his list. He has your remote for the gate and keycode in case you're without your remote. It'll get you in and out, but if you have any troubles, just give me a holler." He hands me his card.

"Thank you." I set the card in my cup holder with a mental note to add him to my contacts.

He must recognize the dazed look in my eyes. "Take the last left, third house on your right."

I nod, already looking past his name tag to the opening gates. "Thanks again, Andrey."

"You have a good day, Ms. Chisholm, and welcome to Dallas."

Since Nate doesn't actually live in Dallas, I assume Andrey's talking about the team.

I nod again. Thank him, *again.*

I'd like to say I'm happy to be here, but besides Nate, everything about Dallas is freaking me the hell out.

My family lives here.

I grew up here.

Matt is here. The guy who broke my heart nearly seven years ago. Besides a few times on campus over the last few years of school, I haven't seen his entirely too handsome face since the break-up. It feels like years… Decades… Forever.

It'll be okay. It's not like we run in the same circles, live in the same area, go to the same school anymore. DFW is a big place. I grew up here. Lived eighteen years before laying eyes on the man I've never been able to forget, much less get over.

Plus, that was Austin. I've never seen Matt in Dallas except on the news attending one event or another with a different woman on his arm each time. Always beautiful. Always thin. Nearly always blonde. Never once did any of his hanger-oners look a thing like me. Also, never once did he look like they meant a thing to him. A perpetual playboy.

Still, that lingering ache palpitates in my gut whenever my thoughts drift to him. You'd think I'd be over him by now. He's obviously over me—if he'd ever been into me at all.

I slow in front of Nate's house with its stone façade, dark wood, slate roof, a front door a giant could walk through, large trees, window after window after window. It's beautiful. Stunning.

I get to live here?

No garage in sight. I keep going till I turn into the driveway and spot the garage on the side of the house and a detached building that could be another three-car garage, but I know it's his weight room with guest quarters.

I park outside the garage next to two other cars, neither of which is Nate's unless he's lowered his standards. They're not in the price range he's become accustomed to. The snob.

Being in New York for the last four years, I don't even own a car. I walked or used the subway, cabs, or a car service. I'm rusty at this driving thing, and buying a car is on my immediate to-do list.

I could let myself in with the key Nate sent me, but I've never used. However, the other cars in the driveway give me pause. He obviously has company. Naked company more than likely. Naked company I'd prefer not to walk in on and see *naked*.

I send him a text and knock on the door.

Me: *Open the door!*

Let's see which one he replies to first. When nothing happens, I text again and ring the doorbell.

Me: *Seriously, put the dick away and come give your wife a hug.*

Nate: *WTF, Firecracker!*

The door flies open to a scowling bestie only in sweats, sporting a woody that could check the mail—at the curb.

"Jesus, put that away. You'll scare the neighbors." I'd say *scar me for life*, but it's too late for that. I've seen Nate in all stages of arousal. I don't fluster easily… anymore.

"What the hell, wife? You just show up, no call, no heads up so I can take the trash out, air out the place?" He grips my arm, pulling me inside, slamming the door without a thought for anyone sleeping at this early hour, and pulls me into a hug. "Fuck, I've missed your face."

"I haven't missed you at all."

"Liar. Your panties are soaked to see me."

I slap his chest and step out of his hold, eyeing his hard-on. "Could you do something about that?"

His grin is devious. "What? I'm happy to see you."

Laughing, I drop my purse and bag on the floor. "You came that way. It's got nothing to do with me."

"If I *came* this way, I wouldn't still be hard. Just be happy I covered it up before I answered the door." His smug ass yawns and rubs his chest. "I'm hungry. Breakfast?"

"I could eat." I could always eat.

Working out like we do, eating healthier, I've slimmed down, but I'll never be tiny. My 5'10" large-boned frame just won't allow it. Plus, I need muscle to do my job. I wouldn't say I'm chunky anymore. Chubby chasers need not apply.

Matt. Fuck. Why'd I go there?

"Hey." Nate tips my chin, coming in close so we're nose to nose. "You okay? Freaked out to be here near your family, and *he who shall not be named?*"

"You can say his name."

"No, I really can't." He kisses me softly, sweetly, and sighs, "I've fucking missed you, Firecracker."

"Yeah, well—" I glance over his shoulder, noting a guy and a girl coming down the hall looking tired and sex-worn out. "Incoming." I turn my back and head to where I hope the kitchen is located.

As they *talk*, I start the coffeemaker and down a glass of orange juice, leaning against the counter, waiting.

I could make breakfast.

Nah, he makes it way better. Truth.

He saunters around the corner twenty minutes later, freshly showered and no longer tenting his sweats. Did he have company while he *cleaned up?*

"Eggs and bacon?" He ignores my inquisitive look by sticking his head in the fridge.

"Sure. You know I'll eat anything."

He jerks back, smirking, his damn sexy-as-hell quirking brow testing me. "We know you don't eat *anything.*" He pulls out a frying pan. "Have you broken your fast and finally tasted cock?" His smile turns catty. "Or pussy?"

No. And no. But that's none of his business. My celibate state is my own. "Not all of us like *both.*"

"Babe, I just wish you liked *anyone's.* Snake or a kitty, pick one… Anyone's other than *his.*"

I've tried. It didn't go well.

He knows this. Why's he bringing this up? Irritation has me speaking before I can rein it in, "So, is this how it's going to be? Randoms coming and going? Strangers wandering around the house?"

He starts to flip the bacon, his muscle lax, sated. "Not if you're offering to be my favorite flavor," he throws over his shoulder, his eyes zeroing in on me as he licks his lips.

He's kidding, *and* he's serious.

We've kissed over the years. Had heated drunken moments. But one or both of us always comes to our senses before it goes too far, before we cross that line. He's my best friend, and I love him to the end of the world and back a thousand, million times.

I clear my thoughts and pour two mugs of coffee. "I'm missing a major ingredient, and you know I'm not built for sharing."

Bacon done, he leans against the counter, arms crossed, facing me. "You're a greedy girl, want all of me to yourself. I know. And I'm a greedy boy, wanting it all." He slides closer, closer, closer, pressing me to the hard surface behind me, his thumb teasing my bottom lip. "I love you, Firecracker. You know that, right?"

Damn, why'd he go all soft on me? "Nate," I sniff. He can bring the tears faster than anyone, except maybe *he who shall not be named*.

"Say it," my bi boy growls. The fact he's on top no matter who's in his bed makes his offer all the more tempting.

"I know. I love you too, husband."

He swoops in, taking my mouth in a gentle kiss, no tongue, just plump lips opening and closing over mine, pressing in and backing off, slow and easy. It's me who darts out, licking across the inside of his top lip, just a taste. It's instinct. It's want. It's a longing that never settles, the need to be wanted, desired, craved. It's him, and it's not exactly him.

He kisses along my cheek, resting there, his breath whispering across my ear, "You give me this body, Firecracker, we'll only need my cock. For you, I could. You're more than enough. Always have been. Always will be."

Jesus, I shiver, wanting so badly to be all that *he* needs and wishing he were what *I* need. It would be so easy to fall in love with my best friend. Maybe I already am. But a part of me has been lost, never to be found, stuck to the one who left me too easily, possibly loved me for what I hated about myself and was ashamed of me all at the same time.

Sad thing is, no one could ever be more ashamed of me than me.

He squeezes me, holding. Then he lets me go, slipping back to the stove, cracking eggs. "Besides, you've heard of strap-ons, right?"

I giggle through my shock. "You'd want me to peg you?"

He laughs loud and hard. "I'm impressed you even know what that is."

A shrug a shoulder. "I'm not all *that* innocent."

He pulls me to him. I hug his back. He pats my hands resting on his abdomen. "You're the most innocent a non-virgin can be, Gabs." He presses a kiss to my temple. "I love you all the more for it. But, yes, I've recently discovered I'm top versatile. Who knew?"

So, he now likes to receive and not just give. Interesting and hot. Men are such sexual creatures. Not that women aren't, but I'm attracted to men, so that's where my sexual buttons reside. Nate all turned on and grunting, giving or receiving is hot. I never thought watching two guys together would be a turn on—apparently it is. But to be a part of it, not just watching, is even hotter. At least in my head.

Breakfast ready to be devoured, our discussion moves on to tamer territories of car buying, team meeting, practice schedules, and when my stuff will arrive from New York.

I've missed my husband. It's good to be home—*him* being my home, not Dallas.

Eighteen

NOW

ACCORDING TO THE NEWS REPORTS, SHE'S BEEN here a couple of weeks, and I see her everywhere I go: in a passing car, on the street, in the local café, the lobby of MCI. Even once in my reflection, I swore I saw her behind me, but when I turned, she wasn't there. It hurts every time, to think she's so close—within reach— only to be disappointed time and time again.

If it's not in my waking world, it's in my dreams. I'd say nightmare, but truly there is nothing nightmarish about my girl except the fact that I fucked it up royally. And that, right there, haunts me every damn day.

It's driving me crazy, making me mad, insane with want and long- ing, the need to fill the hole in my soul shaped like the 5'10" beauty who didn't have room in her heart to forgive a stupid kid for being an idiot, afraid to stand up to his friends, at least when she could hear it. The truth of it all she'll never know unless I can get her to talk to me.

Do I want that? *Yes.*

Do I dare put myself out there only to be shot down again? *I don't know.*

She probably doesn't even care after all these years. That is the di- lemma. The crux of it all. Be brave and fail. Be brave and succeed.

After all my fuck ups, do I even have it in me to be brave one more time when it comes to love?

"You've got to turn that shit off." Joe walks in my penthouse suite that's nearly identical to his and Sam's in the other MCI tower.

I check the clock. It's only half past eight. "What are you doing here?"

"You missed the breakfast meeting with Dad." He points to my phone on the coffee table. "You're not answering your phone."

It rings again as he says it. I ignore that call too. I've got nothing to give right now, and the day has barely even started.

Coffee in hand, I sit back and watch the recorded sportscast showing Gabby training with special teams and running with Nate and the rest of the players. My girl is out front, Nate sticking to her side. Always at her fucking side.

Joe makes himself a steaming cup and sits down next to me. "How's she doing?"

"Good. Really damn good. She's a natural. Knew it the first time I saw her punt. I knew it before Nate or Coach ever laid eyes on her."

"Maybe you should have been a recruiter." He side-eyes me. "Did you miss your calling?"

I chuckle and sip my barely warm coffee. "Not even a little bit." I'm right where I belong. Working day in and day out beside my brothers, father, uncles, and cousins, and thousands of dedicated, high-performing employees.

McIntyre Corporate Industries was founded by my grandfather and his brothers—my great uncles. Then passed down to their sons.

My father is the CEO. Fin, my oldest brother, is VP of Accounting and Finance but will take over the CEO role when Dad is ready to retire, which Fin is hoping isn't anytime soon. He's focused on locking down his girl, Margot. Being the workaholic he is, it hasn't been easy for him to let go and delegate to make time for his girlfriend-soon-to be-wife and kids. He's working on it. Damn hard.

Both Joe and Sam, his wife, work for MCI as a VP tag-team of Products & Technology. His finesse to her technical smarts. He's really the VP. She doesn't hold that title, but don't remind him. It'll only piss him off. They share his office at his insistence. I know it's to have her around to collaborate and bounce ideas off each other, but I also recognize by brother is a caveman when it comes to all things Sam. Where he goes, she goes, and vice versa. End of story. Go ahead, complain about it, see where it gets you.

"Hey—" he points at the screen, "isn't that Nate? Wait, wait—" He stands up. "There, back left!" he shouts. "Isn't that—"

Yep, my heart thrums wildly. There's my girl, warming up in the background. I want to scream when the camera pans right and she disappears from sight.

I sigh and switch it off. I need to get my head on straight before my own father fires me. "How pissed is Dad?"

He follows me to the kitchen. "He's fine. He understands."

I turn at that. "What exactly does he understand?"

Joe rinses our cups and places them in the dishwasher. "Me, Fin, you... We've all gone a little crazy over our girls. Fin and I are over the hump, well, me more than Fin." Fucker's beaming about it too.

Asshole. Love the guy, but still, *calm the preening, brother.* "We get it. You're in love. Life is magical. Your woman shits glitter and burps fairy dust. Life is good. Don't rub it in."

He stares daggers before busting out in a deep laugh. "I was about to break you if you mentioned Samantha's magical pussy."

See, fucker said it himself. I didn't even have to.

He glares, reading my thoughts. "Just don't. Don't make me hurt you."

I hold up my hands in surrender. "I wouldn't dare." I know pussy talk is crossing the line. I can call *him* a pussy, which he's entirely too proud of because he's a *pussy for her*, and only for her, but I can't dare talk about his woman's p-word. Don't really want to, anyway.

As much as I miss the p-word—*damn, now I can't even think the word*—the only one I think about, and definitely don't want to talk to my brothers about, is Gabby's. It's been a damn long time since I've seen, much less been within ten feet of her and her glorious p… p-word. Fuck! Seriously?

I know she's more than one amazing body part. I loved every inch of her, inside and out. Her heart was pure gold, worth more than her incredible kicking leg. But at the moment, all I can think is who's been loving that body that used to be mine? Is it Nate now that she's home?

"What are you going to do about Gabby, Brother? You can't keep going on this way." Joe presses the button to call the express elevator to our corporate offices.

"What way?" I get the feeling he's talking more than just about Gabby.

"You've been hiding out. You avoid getting together with me and Sam. You talk to Jace, but if you didn't have to for your job, I'm sure you'd avoid him too. And you're avoiding all things that have pussies."

"Nah, I petted a female dog the other day. It went pretty well, if I do say so myself."

"Ass," he grumbles and punches my arm. "You know what I mean." He lets out a heavy sigh. "We put it behind us, Samantha and me. Jace doesn't hold a grudge. He knows you didn't know it was Veronica. And… you didn't even fuck her. You just—"

"Went down on her. Put my face—my mouth—*in* and *on* the most cherished spot a man can only dream of going. Jace is not forgetting that. *I* can't forget it."

"You didn't fucking know!" he tries again.

"It doesn't feel like it matters. She was his. I touched someone who wasn't mine to touch." I scrub my face. I should go back to bed. Call in sick. Run away.

"She was a bitch to Samantha. She tricked you. She conned all of us." He stops my progress out of the elevator. "You didn't fucking know, Matt. *She* knew, and she used you to hurt Samantha, to hurt me."

"If I wasn't such a slut, she wouldn't have been able to use me. I might have been looking with clearer eyes, but all I saw was a way to—"

"Forget Gabby," the sadness in his voice matches my own. He understands. He's been there, in a way.

He got messed up with a girl when Sam broke up with him after her father died, after his killer was after her. She pushed Joe away. He got drunk and ended up in bed with another woman. He was too gone to even know—let alone consent. He thought it was Sam. In his head, he was loving on his girl. Turns out it was a chick Jace sent to his room to *help him forget*. She raped him instead.

The anger and guilt over that nearly broke him and ended his friendship with Jace, but being Sam's brother, they worked through it. Sam and Joe made it through, only to have it all brought up before their wedding by Veronica's scheme to break them up. The scheme I unknowingly played a part in when I flew Veronica—whom I thought was Bonnie—and Lydia, Joe's ex temporary assistant, to Vegas for a night of debauchery I was all too willing to participate in. *Manwhore.*

"Yeah, something like that." *Exactly like that.*

Every woman since Gabby disappeared on me is to forget her, to dig the hole to bury my feelings in, to hide the hurt and disappointment in. Disappointment in her… in me.

"You not forgiving yourself is dredging it all up for us. Your hard head is making us relive it any time we're with you because the regret is written all over your face." He grips my shoulder. "Please, Brother, if not for you, for us. There's a glimmer of hope we haven't seen in ages. Forgive yourself and let it go. And either let Gabby go, or man the fuck up and go get her back. Either way, come back to us. Be a part of our group. The Six Pack misses you. *I* fucking miss you."

"I'm right here, Brother." I pat his chest and then mine.

"You're here, but you're not. We haven't seen you in years. And that's the fucking problem."

NOW

MY HEAD IS GOING TO EXPLODE, MAYBE MY HEART too. His offer is so sweet and genuine. At first, I think he's joking, but the tautness of his jaw and the tenderness in his eyes say otherwise.

He leans in and presses his lips to mine for three unsteady beats of my heart. "Breathe, Firecracker." Another kiss to my temple. "Think about it. We'll talk… later." He steps back, holding my arms out at my sides. "You look stunning." That damn sexy eyebrow of his makes an appearance, pressed and eager for a night out. "Ready?"

Not even a little bit.

A single nod is all he gets. My voice is hiding, riding on a tailwind in the back of my brain where he's blown my head off—figuratively, of course. This is my Nate, my faux husband. The man who kisses me like I matter, like I could be his everything if I'd just get my act together and realize he's the one for me. He'd never hurt me. I know that to my core.

But I also believe, I'm not *his* one. My bestie has a hankering for innies and outies, and I could never limit him no matter how much he tries to convince me or himself I'd be enough. His sexuality isn't about me—it's not that I'm not enough. It's that he needs something different. God,

114

I do love the man. I could see us together forever, raising a family, beating back the prejudice we're both facing in our careers—hand in hand, together. A united front, the center and the kicker, a match made on the line of scrimmage, gridiron tough.

Then there's that pesky part of my heart that's still holding out hope that my one and only love will find his way back to me. Make me forget all about how he broke my heart, my spirit, my confidence, and produce a miracle that allows us to mend the trust he broke so easily, so callously.

It's a fairytale. I know.

Growing up with a sick mom, being raised by my dad and four brothers, fairytales were not sanctioned in our house. It was a daily dose of reality-stale crackers for us. No *spoonful of sugar helps the medicine go down* fanciful sentiments. No coddling. No false hope. We were taught life was difficult at best, and if you were lucky, you died before it got worse.

So, give me this indulgence. The dream that Matt, the god of virility, comes riding in on his white steed to sweep the Amazonian Princess off her feet with no care for her size, marries her, raises a team-sized brood of babies, and lives happily ever after in the castle surrounded by a moat that keeps naysayers and dream demolishers away. It's ironically sad that I'm dreaming about having babies with a man who doesn't want me, thus validating both my mom and dad's predictions of my life: I'm only good for *having babies*, and *no one will ever love me the way I am.*

But Nate does. Doesn't he?

I could never be enough for him.

And I want more than just babies. I want a career. The career part has been good. It's the team part that's been sorely lacking. I'm still holding out hope that The Dallas Stallions can be different.

…But a family. Despite my father tainting that vision, I still want it. I want it all with a man who loves me like he can't imagine a life without me.

Be lovable. I can't believe, after all this time, I'm still struggling with that.

"Gabby?" Nate grasps my hand as we drive to the venue for tonight's charity event. "You okay? Did I fuck us up?"

"God, no." I stretch over the console and kiss his cheek. "I love you for asking, for thinking it's even possible… with me. I just—"

"Need time to process?"

"Yeah." I lay my head back, watching him drive. "It could be something, though, couldn't it?"

He sweeps his hand across my cheek. "It could be everything, wife."

Everything. I love the idea of that. I want to be someone's *everything.*

But would *I* be *his* everything? Could *he* be mine?

Too much to consider tonight. "Can we just have fun, not think about the future, not try to solve all our problems tonight?"

"Yeah, Firecracker, we can. Whatever you need."

What about what he needs?

Yeah, no. That's too heavy for a fun night out, all dressed up and ready to impress.

We manage to make it through the reports unscathed. Nate did most of the talking, redirecting questions about our personal lives or relationship status—with others and each other—back to the event at hand, raising money for Raven's Hope, a charity helping battered women and their family get back on their feet.

Thankfully, that's nothing I have first-hand knowledge of. My dad may be a chauvinistic ass, but he never laid a hand on my mom or me.

"I feel underdressed," I whisper as I observe women in full-length ball gowns. My dress is a simple but classic LBD—you know, the one every woman should own. Nate's in a charcoal suit, but he's not second-guessing his choice as we pass men in tuxes.

"That's the older crowd, Gabs." He motions to the back of the room. "There's our people, dressed just like us." He kisses my temple, pulling me into his side, gripping my hip. "You're a beauty no matter what room we're in. Relax."

His *I got you* is a given. He keeps me close as we mingle, moving through the grand ballroom to the bar on the outskirts. Across the room, I spot Dwight and a few other guys on the team. This isn't an official team event, but Nate said a handful of guys signed up to attend to help give publicity to the good cause. Apparently, it's a regular thing the whole team does. There are team-sponsored charities they support and host events for, but in between, it's events like this that keep their schedules busy and their faces helping those in need during the off-season.

As the other guys make their way to us, I search through the nameless faces in the room, always looking, always wondering… *Is he here?*

Even when I know he's not, my heart still seeks.

Nate caresses up my spine to rest his hand on the back of my neck, a small squeeze then light circles with his thumb. I relax into him and sip the sparkling soda he hands me as he babies a beer. Neither of us are big drinkers. If we indulge, it's at home. Public is for a public persona, and that persona should remain sober and in control at all times.

That's a hard lesson we learned from our time as younger athletes. A photographer caught us, one time, sharing an innocent kiss at a club, years ago. That picture still churns through the news circuit as if it just happened. I believe it's the reason Nate got traded to Dallas. New York didn't want to deal with a woman kicker in a relationship with their up-and-coming center. Nate will never admit it, but I'm sure the kiss is to blame. We didn't even get the chance to defend it or explain it away.

Though, truthfully, I'm not sure anyone besides the two of us could ever truly understand the depth of our friendship and what it means to us. We're each other's support system. The strength when the other is weary. The confidence when the other is unsure. The love when the other is hurting. I am just as much his right hand as he is mine. A partnership. Husband and wife in all ways except one… the sex. There's none of that happening between us. None for me, though he has plenty.

A twinge of pain at that reminder—I could never be enough for him—has me looking away, focusing on the sign about tonight's event.

Raven's Hope welcomes you in proud sponsorship with McIntyre Corporate Industries.

McIntyre… Could it possibly be another family… not Matt's?

My mulling it over is broken up by meaty hands and a friendly face. "Baby girl, looking hot tonight." Dwight hugs me tight, clasping hands with Nate behind me. "Looking good, man."

"You clean up alright yourself." Nate captures my hand and slowly brings me back to his side.

"Dog, you know I look the bomb. Don't be lyin.'" Dwight eyes our locked hands. "Damn, you two should just marry and get it over with. Serious, dude. Lock that shit down."

Nate notices the color draining from my face before he pulls in, my back to everyone, whispering, "Breathe," as he bullshits with the guys, completely ignoring Dwight's remark.

Is that the universe speaking?

I feel stabbed in the gut for doubting my place in Nate's life, yet at the same time, I feel guilty for even considering it when my heart is still owned by another.

My stupid, stupid heart. What's wrong with me? Nate is a perfectly good man. Amazing even. I'd be lucky to spend the rest of my life being loved by him—in whatever capacity that holds. But I don't think I could share him. I'm not secure enough to give all of me and watch him loving someone else too. It's selfish, I know. That's why it's hard to say no and even harder to consider a yes.

When I finally get a full breath, feeling steadier on my feet, I excuse myself to find the ladies' room. I shake off Nate's inquisitive brow, reassuring him. "I'm fine."

Navigating the room full of beautiful, seemingly carefree people, I rush through the farthest door to the lobby, only to run smack dab into a hard, suited chest and strong hands that grip my shoulders to stop my forward momentum.

"Gorgeous?" his rasp is unmistakable.

My heart races. Dear God, I must be dreaming, or I hit my head, and I'm passed out somewhere. Both are possibilities.

I draw my gaze up his broad chest, over his god-chiseled jawline to lock on those bright green eyes I've fantasized about for far too many years to be healthy. How it is he's even more handsome than I remember?

"Matt?" I think I'm going to faint.

Twenty

NOW

FUCK ME. SHE'S EVEN MORE BEAUTIFUL THAN I remember. I loosen my grip when all I want to do is pull her into my chest to ease the ache roaring inside. I slip so easily back into the role of loving her, of protecting what's mine. When she isn't, hasn't been mine for seven long-as-fuck years.

"Gabby, are you okay?" I glare over her shoulder to see if someone is chasing her with how fast she was moving. "What's wrong?"

She frowns and tries to free herself from my hold. I only let her step back enough to find her footing. "Matt? What…" Her eyes widen. "McIntyre," she blurts, like saying my last name makes all the sense in the world. "You… you're hosting this event?"

She didn't know? "We—my family's company—host this event every year for Raven's Hope." Her new team always sends players to increase the draw of those with big pockets, whose donations will provide much-needed funding to the woman's shelter and outreach programs.

Back to the issue at hand. "What's got you spooked, had you nearly running out the doors?"

She glances over her shoulder, but the door has long shut behind her. "It's… nothing." Moving with the grace I could never forget, she slips out of hold. "I was heading to the ladies' room."

I don't entirely believe her excuse, and as much as I want to, I can't stop her. Instead, I admire the swish of her hips as she disappears inside the restroom. My girl is thinner, not in an unhealthy way, but enough for me to miss the curves she had in abundance.

I don't know how long I stand there scowling at the floor, thinking of her and wondering how I ever let so much time pass without reaching out to her. It's not like I couldn't afford to go wherever she was. And it's not like I didn't know *where* she was, *who* she played for, *how* she was doing.

I knew. I kept track. Internet stalked her on more than one occasion, and may or may not have alerts set up whenever her name appears in the media.

"You're still here." She's honestly surprised.

She has no idea the lengths I'm willing to go to keep her here in front of me. "You really think I'd just walk away after not having laid eyes on you except from afar or on TV in seven years?" I draw closer because I can't hold back the need, forcing her into my chest or moving back a step.

She stands her ground. *That's my brave girl.*

Her tantalizing scent fills my nostrils. She fucking smells like home, floral and sweet. *Mine*, my soul screams, waking up from a long seven-year slumber. I thought my soul had died. Apparently, it's been hibernating, waiting on her to return.

"I don't know what to think, Matt. We didn't end on the best of terms. For all I know, you'd prefer never to see me again."

Damn, that stings.

"Hear this: I never wanted to leave you then. I can barely stand the thought of leaving you now that I've found you again."

Her laugh is humorless. "*Found me?* Don't act like you've been looking for me all these years."

My growl is instantaneous as I grip her hips, securing her to me. "In every fucking room. In every face. In every news report or sports broadcast. In every dream. In every waking nightmare, I search for you. Hoping." I run my nose along her cheek, taking a deep, satiating breath. "It never ends. The need. The want. The ache. The fucking hole in my chest. You can think I walked away, but it wasn't *me* who did the walking."

Jesus Christ. I step back, running my hands through my hair. I've got to calm down before I steal her way or fuck her right here on the lobby floor. I wouldn't apologize for either with the way her body is responding and that look in her eyes.

Am I imagining hope?

With pleading eyes, begging for leniency, I point to the door she exited a few minutes ago. "Can we get a drink? Dance? Eat something?" I need a minute to get my bearings, sweeping my hand up and down her glorious form. "You pack a powerful punch. I'm sideswiped, baby." I hold out my hand. "Please, help me find my ground before we dredge through more of our past."

The second her warm hand touches mine, hope blooms like she's the sun to my light-starved world. Her small smile screams of reprieve. "Yeah, I'm not feeling all that steady myself. Truce?"

"Thank fuck."

I'm going to kill Nate. He knew and didn't warn me. But damn, if I'm not elated to have my hand back in Matt's. The fit… is perfection. I've only ever held hands with two guys. Both I've loved hard but in entirely different ways.

One stole and broke my heart. The other mended it.

One still holds it. The other wants to… maybe.

Surprising the heck out of me, Matt walks right up to Nate and the guys. Dwight does a double-take and glares at our joined hands. I try to tug free, but Matt only tightens his hold, offering his hand to Nate and then Dwight, his jaw so tight he could crack nuts.

"Nate. Dwight. It's good you guys could make it." He then continues till he's met all the players in our little group. Others are mingling, or more than likely, flirting.

"Hey, man, we're glad to be here. Lend our support." I half expect Nate to bite Matt's head off, but he's congenial, welcoming even.

Weird. This whole thing is… *weird*.

Matt and Nate hate each other. Don't they?

Wait.

Matt said they host this event every year. Nate said his team attends this event every year. *This* isn't the first time Nate has seen Matt since we parted ways. Not only did Nate not tell me Matt would more than likely be here, the ass set this up, dragged me here, but not before he… I tug Nate's jacket. "I need to speak to you. In private," I grit through clenched teeth.

I want to knock his smug smile off his face. Not that I condone hitting. I don't. But his meddling ass needs to be knocked down a peg or fifteen. I intend to do just that but verbally, not physically. Never that.

My stomach twists at the pain in Matt's eyes as I pull away from him to tug Nate far enough away my tongue lashing won't have an audience, or God forbid, reporters.

Before we can make it out a side door, Nate redirects me to the dance floor, where he proceeds to twirl me. How dare he. I'm mad at him. And he's being all Casanova-ish. His big arms encase my body, drawing me close, like lovers do. Which we aren't, not yet… Probably not ever. I love my Nate, and he gets me going sometimes, but he's not…

"You can't even keep your eyes off him for a minute." He nuzzles the side of my face. Intimately. I sigh and relax into him. "You can't blame me for getting you here under less than full disclosure." He tips my chin, holding my eyes captive. "You still love him. I know it. You know it." His magically sexy brow motions in Matt's direction. "You need to let him know it too. Forgive him. Give him a second chance. He's not the same guy you knew in college. He's changed, especially over the last six months or so."

My head is spinning. "Didn't you just propose marriage to me only a few hours ago? What was that? A ruse as well?" I rear back, his last words registering. "Six months? How the hell would you know so much about his life?"

His hold tightens. He won't let me run. He never does. He forces me to stay and fight with him or forgive him, but escape is never an option with my bestie. "You'd be surprised how many of these types of events he and I have had to deal with running into each other."

"You never said."

His smile is endearing. "*He who shall not be named?*" His sexy brow pops. "Would you have wanted to know?"

Gah, my heart hurts at the idea of Nate keeping this from me. "So, what? You and he are best buds now? Lovers?"

His laugh is immediate as he hugs me to his chest. "I wish. No, we've come to an understanding. We both want you." Nate's gentle expression brings my attention back to him. "I have you, but not fully. I wasn't lying to you earlier. I want a future with you, but not like this, not when the most important part of you still belongs to him."

"What? My lady bits?"

"No, smartass. Your heart."

Crack. He can always break down my defenses, bringing me to the knees of truth. "I do love you, Nate. I adore you."

He kisses my nose. "I know you do, but not in the way I want. Not in the way you and I deserve." He scans over my shoulder, nodding. "Go for it, or let him go, Firecracker. It's time to move on. Seven years is too long to be stuck." He kisses my cheek and spins me away, only to release me gently into Matt's arms.

Surprised, I scramble to process what's happening here.

"He loves you." The god of virility only adds to the guilt and shame that now cloud my vision.

"I love him." I don't clarify. I'm not sure Matt deserves to know the difference.

He only nods on a hint of a smile. "I know. He's been there for you all these years. A fierce protector. A good friend."

Wow. Maybe Matt has changed. Not a hint of jealousy can be found in his words or demeanor.

"He may not be my favorite person, but I can respect what he's been for you, what he means to you." His hand twitches on my hip.

"He wants to marry me," I blurt before I process if it's a good idea to share that fact or not.

Another nod with a scowl this time. "Have coffee, lunch, with me tomorrow."

"Did you hear me?" He has to know where he stands.

"I heard you, Gorgeous." His smile seems sadder now. I don't mean this evening. I mean since college. He's more subdued. Not the charismatic guy who wants everyone to love him, knocking you over with his dimpled smile and knowing glimmer in his eyes. He's still a god in my eyes, but in his, he's fallen from grace.

What happened, Matt? Did I do that? Did I take your shines-like-the-sun personality from you?

My eyes prick at the idea that I—or anyone—hurt him enough to take away his radiant Matt-ness.

"Then why would you still want to meet up?" To win me over?

Yes, oh God. Yes, please do that.

"Because you didn't say *you* wanted to marry *him*." He presses a kiss to my forehead—on his spot—the spot that's been barren since he last did it, leaving his mark, making my heart ache even more for him.

Nate tried to kiss me there once, and I nearly broke my neck trying to duck away. I didn't even realize what I was doing until after it was done. He never tried again. He respected that forehead kisses weren't a casual thing for me. They were *everything*.

"I still have the same number. Call or text me tomorrow. Let me know when and where. I'll be there." With a squeeze of my hand, he leaves me alone on the dance floor.

I watch him exit through the same door I ran out of earlier and right into my past that could possibly be my future—him.

Maybe it wasn't such a coincidence, us meeting here tonight.

Maybe he knew I'd be here, and he came for me.

My eyes instantly find Nate's. His are already on me, waiting, knowing I'd be saturated. His chin rises, motioning to the door, asking, *ready to leave?*

I meet him halfway, my hand slipping into his.

Home. He feels like home.

But does he feel like *everything?*

Twenty-One

NOW

I SIP MY COFFEE OUT ON THE BACK PORCH overlooking the pool. My phone is sitting beside me, taunting me to text Matt, accept his offer for coffee or lunch. I want to, truly, deeply, madly. But my gut is in knots at the idea of *trying* again. Not just with Matt but with anyone.

I've dated over the years. It didn't go well. They were either too interested in my status as an athlete and what I could do for them, who they would meet, what events I could get them into, or they may have been genuine, but *I* never felt that spark, that desire to get naked and see where things led.

One time. I tried one time, and before he could get my clothes off, he told me I *needed to lose twenty pounds*.

People baffle me, guys in particular. What gave him the right to tell me that? To believe the judgment in his head was okay to say out loud. Did he really think I'd get naked faster, drop to my knees to suck his cock because he made me feel belittled and ashamed of my size? Has it worked for him in the past?

I couldn't get out of there fast enough. Of course, I didn't tell him to go fuck himself. I slunk away in shame, feeling like the fatty my mother always said I was.

No one will ever love you the way you are.

Yeah, I'm getting that.

The world at large has been in cahoots with my mom. Even after death, she still manages to remind me nearly every day, I'm not a size two worthy of her love or any man's. If it's not my size on the news or in gossip rags discussing if I have a gland problem or eating disorder when I do lose a few incidentally, it's my sexuality. Am I a lesbian? Am I bi? Because I must be if I want to play football. And Nate's favorite, am I dating Nate Sinclair? Then it goes into how he could do so much better than me. Because God forbid the Dallas Stallions' star center would fall for someone like me.

Nate and Coach Eaton are the only men who have ever made me feel completely accepted as I am.

I once thought Matt was one of those men. He proved me wrong.

Do I dare put myself out there again, open to ridicule and judgment by a man who couldn't be more physically perfect if he tried? Open myself to comparisons on social media of the exes who looked better by his side?

"Hey." Nate kisses my cheek. "What's going on?"

I bite my lip and look away, hiding my glistening eyes. It's too damn early to cry. I let out a deep exhale. I need to work out. Tomorrow's training is going to hurt if I take today off.

"Look at me, Firecracker," he demands in his gravelly morning voice.

When my eyes meet his and the looming tears fall, he's up and in my face, swiping at them before I can. "Fuck, Gabs. What's going on?"

"Nothing." I try to move away, but he locks me in his arms. Running is not allowed, remember?

"She's in your head again, isn't she?"

He always knows. "Never far."

"Fuck her. She's dead. Let her ideals die with her. Don't let her win by letting her in your head." He leans back, pulling me with him, sequestered at his side, half on his chest.

"My dad wants to see me. Have a family dinner."

"Shit. Already? You just got here."

It's been three weeks.

"I'm always afraid what he'll say, if a report talks to him or my brothers. I can almost hear them taunting, *fatty, fatty, two-by-four, can't fit through the bathroom door.*"

"Fuck, I'm going to kill them," he growls. "They wouldn't do that, would they? They'd look like assholes."

"Maybe out of spite for not coming to see them, giving them what they want."

"A proverbial punching bag?"

"Something like that. Now that I'm home, I could see reports seeking them out. When I was in New York, I was safe from the probability of that happening."

"Is that what set you off this morning?"

I wish it were. "No."

"You saw the newsfeed of you, me, and Matt this morning, didn't you?"

"Yep. I didn't even know we were being photographed except when we were walking in."

"We look good, though, the three of us. We could make a happy threesome. Think of our beautiful kids."

"What, yours and Matt's?"

He slaps my ass hard enough to sting. "Don't degrade yourself to be funny. I'm talking about the two of us having kids with you."

I lift away enough to see his face. "Is that what you want? A wife and a husband? Honest?"

He lays a quick kiss on me. "I want you, Firecracker." I see the "but" in his eyes.

"But you wouldn't turn him down if he was down for it?"

His dirty smirk is quick to fire. "Babe, why do you think he hated me so much in college?"

I sit up, facing him as it occurs to me at last. "Because you wanted him?"

He toys with my hair. "I hit on him the year before. I was a freshman, and he came to visit his brother. You know how much of a football fan Fin is. They came to a party. I was drunk, thought I saw interest in Matt's eyes. I kissed him without consent. He knocked me the fuck out."

"Oh my god! Why have you never told me this?"

He shrugs. "Not my finest moment. I thought he was in college. Turns out, he was seventeen and still in high school." He raises his hands. "I had no idea."

"You were eighteen? Still a babe yourself."

"Yeah, and still trying to figure out what I wanted."

"It's hard to picture you trying to figure out your sexuality. You always seem… so secure in who you are."

He pulls me to my feet and into a hug. "I fall in love with the person, not the body parts." He doesn't say he's in love with me. He's not, right? "No more moping. Light snack then workout." He hands me my phone. "You need to text that man. Put him out of his misery and set up a time to meet today."

I groan, still uncertain. "How can I trust anything he says?"

Nate turns before he passes through the back door. "Because he's sorry. I was an ass back then, Gabs. I don't think we know the whole story."

He disappears inside. "Anyway, trust him or don't, but put him behind you or make him your future. Just *do* something."

Closing the door behind me, I follow him to the kitchen. "And you what? Wait around for me to decide? How is that fair to you?"

He stalks me to the island, pressing in. "It's not me or him. I've got you no matter what. The only difference is if you and I," his sexy brow waves, "make babies together, make a future as true husband and wife." He captures my cheek. "I'm not there, Gabs, but I know I love you deeply. We'd make a good team. We love each other. We're a cohesive unit. We've always just fit. But I know you're not sure of my ability to commit to you—*only* you. I'm willing to try if you are. But we can't have

Matt between us." His brow dances again. "Unless, of course, he's literally *between* us."

"Pig." I smack his chest. "Always thinking with your cock."

He growls. "Don't say cock to me when you're in your skimpy boy shorts and tank top, teasing me with your amazing tits."

"You're just turned on thinking of Matt," I tease and skip around the island before he can grab me.

"Isn't everyone turned on by that man? Jesus, he's like—"

"He's Priapus, the god of virility."

Nate chuckles. "Yeah, he really is." He swats my ass. "Now go get ready. We've got thirty till we meet the guys."

"Yes, sir." I run out of the kitchen.

"You're a tease, Gabriella Elisabeth Chisholm!"

"And you love it!"

"Damned if I don't," he grumbles.

Twenty-Two

NOW

'M NERVOUS AS FUCK. I GUZZLE A WATER BECAUSE if I have another cup of coffee before she gets here, I'll be bouncing off the walls.

It took everything I had to walk away from her last night, leaving it in her hands to reach out to me or not. Sleep didn't come until the wee hours, staring at my phone until the screen blurred. I forced myself to turn it off and place it in my home office to charge, far enough away where I couldn't check it every fifteen seconds.

When I finally did open my eyes, relieved I got in four hours of sleep, better than I thought I would, I was elated to find a message waiting from my girl. I'd slept so long, I had to rush to shower and get here fifteen minutes early to scope out the best place to sit and order a coffee and water. I skip a sweet treat, hoping I can convince her to grab lunch so the date will last longer. It's nearly eleven now.

My skin buzzes seconds before she steps through the door. I pop to my feet, waving her over like a pubescent teen on his first date with the prom queen, who only agreed to coffee not a date.

Not a date. I'll have to fix that.

Her dark hair is in loose waves down her back and shoulders, longer than it was in college. Her faded jeans hug the legs and hips I've missed so fucking much. I really miss the cutoff shorts she used to wear. Damn, those toned legs go on for days. I know she's wearing a top, but it's her pensive face that has me meeting her halfway to our table and pulling her in for a hug. "Breathe, Gorgeous. I swear it'll be okay. It's just me."

It's just you. Yeah, that doesn't mean much when seeing you again is everything.

"You say that like it's not a big deal," her voice breaks at the end.

Fuck me. She's going to make me cry. And I don't fucking cry, except over losing her.

"I guess what I mean is, I'm so fucking happy to see you. You don't need to be nervous, because whatever you say, whatever you need, I'm all here for it." I guide her to our table, waving down the waitress and ordering Gabby a coffee and more water as she settles.

When I take my seat, her light blue gaze is on me, roaming my chest, my shoulders, and finally my face. I can't help the smile that breaks free, loving her eyes on me again after such a cold and desolate absence.

"Have you gotten bigger? Broader?" she blurts and then blushes.

"Yeah, I grew a few more inches and filled out more. Not as big as my younger brother Joe, but definitely bigger than I was at eighteen." *The last time you saw me.*

"You look good." Her smile is honest and open.

"It's so good to see you." I nearly reach over the table to take her hand, but pull back. I guess I can't do that, not anymore, not yet. "You look as beautiful as ever. Life agrees with you." WTF? *Life agrees with you?* Idiot.

She laughs into her mug of coffee the waitress slipped in front of her a moment ago, stirring in creamer but no sugar.

Didn't she used to drink it with sugar?

"So, tell me what you do."

I'm disappointed. I don't want to talk about mundane shit, but maybe this is what she needs: to know I'm not the stupid punk I was when she knew me. "I work at my family's tech company in marketing."

She eyes me speculatively. "You're being modest. You're vice president of marketing. You don't just *work* there."

Did she look me up at some point, the way I did her? Was she curious about me too? Or did Nate fill her in? "And you. A hotshot NFL player. The first and only *woman* playing in the NFL."

She rolls her eyes dismissively. "Whatever."

She's not proud of it? "It's quite an accomplishment." I garner her eyes, leaning forward. "Gabby, there's no one else *in the world* who can make that claim. It's all yours. Own it. You deserve it. Be proud."

"I guess. But I hope that changes. I shouldn't be the only one."

"That's a different topic completely." Now she's pissing me off. "You don't think you deserve it, didn't earn your spot?"

"I'm a showpiece. A rare gem." Her gaze flits out the window. "I never wanted the limelight, the fame. It's a lot."

"I agree with the rare gem, but you're not a trophy. Your record speaks for itself. It's not like you're sitting on the sidelines collecting a paycheck for looking pretty. You're kicking ass," I laugh, "not literally. You're the number one kicker in the nation. Male or female, you're it. The Stallions are damn lucky to have you, and New York is an idiot for letting you go."

"I'm glad they did."

"You weren't happy there?"

What has her life been like since college? I know Nate was with her in New York for a while, but he's been here for four years now. Did she have no one all this time? No one to back her up? Stand by her side if things got hard?

She shrugs. My girl is good at that. "They didn't want *me*. They wanted the publicity."

"I hope they paid you well for it."

Her eyes widen. "You don't know?"

"Know what?"

"I'm the lowest paid kicker in the league. It's pretty embarrassing, but considering I still make a ridiculous amount of money for kicking a ball, it's good. I don't need more."

What the hell? "That's not right." I pull out my phone and text Fin.

Me: *We need to buy the Dallas Stallions.*

Fin: *I'll get right on that.*

Me: *I'm serious.*

Fin: *Wait. Really? If you really are serious, I'll look into it.*

Me: *Dead fucking serious.*

"Everything okay?"

Damn. I put my phone away. "Sorry, I had an idea I shot off to my brother. It was rude. Won't happen again."

"It's fine."

"Are you happy to be home? Near your family and Nate?"

"Nate, yes. Family, not so much."

I sense a minefield. I knew there was something up with her family. She never wanted to talk about them or what was up with her mom.

"I'm supposed to get together with them this week. I'm not looking forward to it."

"I could go with you. Be a buffer," I throw out.

Is that overstepping? If is it, I don't care. I'm putting myself out there, not holding back.

To my surprise she doesn't shoot me down. "I might take you up on that offer."

I should tell him *no*, but I don't want to. If I see my family, I could use a buffer, the distraction, hoping my family would behave with company in the house. Nate is planning on going with me. That's a complication I'm not sure how to handle.

I want them both there. A wall I can hide behind if needed.

We decide to walk around after we finish our coffees. At some point, my hand ended up in his, and I have to still my heart to keep it from tripping over itself in elation.

Somehow, we've managed to kill a couple of hours, and my stomach growls just about the time he says, "Have lunch with me. There's this great place around the corner. I'm starving. And I'm not ready to say goodbye."

No, I'm not ready for that either. "Sure. Sounds good."

When we get to the restaurant, I leave him at the table to go to the restroom. While I'm in there, I text Nate.

Me: *I should be home for dinner. You?*

Nate: *I've got plans. I'll see you in the morning. Ride together for training?*

He has plans. All night plans? My stomach twists. This is Nate. He has hookups, always has. I can't expect him not to have sex and connection while I figure out my life and if Matt has any place in it. But still, the thought of Nate curbing his desires if we decide to get married doesn't sit well.

Could I ask that of him?

Could I live with a husband who needed an open relationship? Could I deal with him having sex with someone else and not feel completely inadequate—or worse, cheated on?

Would I want him to bring that home to our bed?

What if I met someone amazing who wanted me to leave Nate after everything?

Jesus, that's some heavy shit right there.

My attitude has soured by the time I make it back to our table, along with my appetite. When I order a salad with grilled chicken, I get a scowl from Matt, who orders a hamburger and sweet potato fries.

His sigh into the silence has me asking, "What's wrong?"

He's tentative, editing his thoughts.

"Just say it, Matt."

His brow furrows at the bite in my tone.

"Sorry. I'm irritated, and it has nothing to do with you. Please say whatever's on your mind."

"You're too thin." He drops that bomb like it's not going to explode in my lap.

I laugh, too hard. "You're serious?"

"I know you work hard for your job. You probably can't control it, but I miss the curves."

"You're shitting me right now." I force myself to stay seated when all I want to do is run out the door. I'm such a freakin' runner. I hate conflict.

I hate to *disappoint*. That truth stings. Deep.

Leaning forward, getting close enough to get a little tipsy on his all-Matt scent. "I thought you of all people would be happier with the slimmer me."

He shakes his head and slides closer in the rounded booth. "I know you believe I thought a certain way in college. I know there was an incident that drove a fucking seven-year wedge between us. But hear me when I say, I loved your curves and not *just* your curves." He lowers his head, close enough for our noses to touch. "Every fucking inch of you, inside and out, I loved. Never wanted you to change, not for me, not for anyone."

He steals the air from my lungs, and I fight to recover. I felt that, back then. I felt his love of my body. "But that night—"

"You want to get into that? Now? Here?"

I shake my head. "No. I really don't."

"I didn't mean to insult you just now. I don't want you to think you need to eat salads around me. If you want a hamburger or a twenty-ounce steak, get it. Eat salad if that's what you really want, but don't ever curb your appetite for me or anyone else. You're the only person you need to make happy." He leans in close, his breath tickling my ear—I remember those days when he did it to whisper dirty, dirty things for only me to hear. "But know, I loved you then, not because of your body, but because of who you were. I still fucking love you—never stopped. And I will love you at any size, any age. You have always been and will always be perfection to me, my gorgeous girl."

Yep, I'm pretty sure I've died, and this is heaven.

"You can't say stuff like that to me." As much as I want to, I can't trust him. It's too soon, right? Or is it too late?

How can it be both?

I've been angry and hurt for so long, never wanting to see his face again, yet yearning for it too. Did I miss something back then? Was I too immature to see the truth? If he really loved me like he said, then how could he let his friends talk about me like that? I never would have let anyone treat him like I was treated—how I *felt* I was treated.

He slips back to his side of the booth, leaving me bereft for his closeness.

"I'll go as slow as you need, but I won't hide my feelings or lie to you." He stretches his long arms out from his sides. "What you see is what you get, Gabby. I'm a schmoozer by nature. It's part of my job to sell people what they don't know they need. But I'm going to be straight up with you. I've no intention of losing you to Nate—not again."

"I won't give him up."

His wicked smile grows. "I'm not asking you to. But you'll be in my bed and not his."

Twenty-Three

NOW

COLLAPSE AFTER OUR TEN-MILE RUN. NOT everyone made it, but I always do. Even if it kills me, there's no way I'm letting any of these guys outrun me. God gave me powerful legs. I know how to use them. I've learned to love running over the years. It's a release I don't get anywhere else, and also a bit of an ego boost when I can outlast most of the guys on my team.

"Fuck, Firecracker. Do you think you could back off just once?" Nate falls beside me, our heads nearly touching as we stare at the bright morning sky and replenish our bodies with much-needed oxygen.

"You could have stopped at any time." Many do. Only a few make it all the way to the end. Ten miles is the max our coach lets us go before we get reprimanded for training too hard.

He chuckles. "No, I couldn't. Always at your side, babe. Always." His noodle arm hits my stomach and slides to the ground. "Even if I die trying to keep up."

"You've gotten soft. I used to be the one chasing you." He started this little competition between teammates in college.

"Yeah, well, the view is better when I'm doing the chasing."

I have to laugh at that. I don't want to know what my ass looks like when I'm running. I feel the jiggles. I don't need to see it.

He sits, urging me to stretch before our muscles lock up.

"He doesn't want me in your bed." I twist away so I don't have to see the look on his face.

"Are you in my bed? Did I miss it?"

I twist the other way and catch his gaze. "He doesn't expect me to give you up. He says he still loves me."

His brow quirks, and when mine goes up to match, he drops his on a head shake. "Did you tell him you love him too?"

"Whose bed were you in last night?" I ignore both of his questions.

He stands, offering me his hand. "Come on. I need to hydrate and shower."

"Is that code for you don't want to talk about it?" I let him lift me to my feet.

"Tell you what. When you tell Matt you love him—never stopped, haven't even touched another dick—I'll tell you whose bed I was in."

I get a sinking feeling in my gut. I stop and look back at the field as I process what he said.

He's sleeping with someone—more than sleeping with them?

"Gabby?"

I don't know how to handle this. *If* I decide to go for it with him, how do I be okay with him needing someone else? And what if that someone else is a woman, not just a man—men?

I turn away. "Yeah, I'll see you in a bit. I need to talk to Coach." I jog off even though my legs are jelly, and I'm sure I'll trip all over myself in a few more strides. I make it far enough to disappear around the corner and stop.

I'm going to lose him. I can feel it. If I don't marry him, he's going to marry someone else, and I'll lose him. Whoever he marries won't accept me in Nate's life like we have been. He's had many ex-partners and almost-partners who were jealous of our relationship. Nate told them to fuck off, but if he's serious enough to fall in love and marry, I'll be the one fucking off.

I can't lose him.

He's my rock. My best friend. My true family.

Oh fuck, I can't breathe. I bend over, against the wall, head pounding, eyes stinging. *I'm losing him.*

"You okay?" Mandy, one of our physician assistants, kneels beside me.

"I, uh…" I slide down the wall. "Actually, no." I fight my emotions. I can't cry on the football field. *There's no crying in baseball*, screams in my head.

Mandy drops next to me, arms on her knees, watching some guys messing around in the distance, throwing the ball, wishing they were quarterbacks. "What can I do?"

"Could you give me a ride?"

"What the fuck?" Nate's tone is cool as he comes to a stop in front of us. He's pissed and wants nothing more than to yell at me.

Mandy stands, brushing off her shorts. "I'll, uh, be in the parking lot, say in five minutes."

I wait until she rounds the corner. "You need to go, Nate." I struggle to my feet, brushing him off when he tries to help me.

"That's not how you and I operate." His scowl is fierce enough to make grown men cower. Thankfully, I'm not a man.

"Well, there's lots of stuff happening that's not our *norm*. You'll have to forgive me as I try to navigate this bumpy fucking road." I head toward the locker room to grab my stuff. I need to buy a fucking car, so I'm not tied to Nate getting me to and from training.

"You're running from me, really?" His shock gives me pause.

I don't want to hurt him. I want him to be happy—even if it's without me. "Some things you can't help me with."

He gets in my face, nose flaring. "Yeah, like what?!"

"You." It's a whispered admission I probably should have kept to myself.

He rears back. "Me?"

I start for the door. "I need some time. I'll see you later."

"*Me* she says. I'm the foremost authority on *me*, Gabs." He grabs my arm, and I spin to face him. "You're worrying me. Is this about what I said earlier?"

I place my hand on his chest, leaning in, desperately wanting to hug him. Make this right. Soothe the worried beast in him and the scared little girl in me. But I can't. "I love you, Nate. I always will." I slip inside, swiping at my tears.

"Fuck!" he yells from the other side of the door.

Walking out of a meeting with Jace and our teams, my phone buzzes with a text.

Gorgeous Gabby: *Would you join me at my dad's tonight?*

Damn, love that she's not only texting but reaching out to support her when she needs it.

Me: *Of course, send me the details.*

"Catch ya later." I tip my chin to Jace as I head to my office and tell my assistant to hold my calls.

Not able to resist, I call my girl.

"Hey," she sniffles.

Alarm bells go off. "What's wrong?"

"Nothing. It's just been a day."

"It's barely ten a.m. Not buying it." I start to pack up. "Where are you?" I shoot a message off to my PA, telling her to reschedule my day. The perks of being the boss—one of them.

"Home."

"I'm on my way." I nod to Monica on my way out.

"You don't know where—"

I laugh. "I do, actually. Be there in thirty. I'll bring lunch or take you to lunch. Which do you prefer?"

"Actually, I have a favor to—"

"Anything."

She giggles. "You're very agreeable."

Love the sound of her giggling. It does dirty things to my cock. "My girl called *me*. I'm over the moon. What's the favor, Gorgeous?"

"I need to buy a car."

"Done."

"You know I'm asking you to go with me so *I* can buy a car. I'm not asking *you* to buy me a car, right?"

"Still, consider it done. Do you have anything in mind?"

"No clue. I haven't had a car since my beater in college."

"I think we can do better than that. I'll pick you up. We'll grab a bite, then go car shopping."

I park in Nate's driveway, manage to get out of the car and halfway up the walkway before she has me stumbling back when she flies out the door and into my arms. Her hold is tight and immediate.

"Baby." I wrap my arms around her and kiss her head, eating up the moment. I don't know what's wrong, but something has my girl's feelings all jumbled. The fact she reached out to me has my chest puffing and the seeds of hope that took root the day we had coffee blooming and sprouting leaves. "I got you."

I'm in no rush, but when Nate pulls up in his truck, she eases out of my hold to grab her purse and shut the front door. She doesn't even look in his direction as we walk to my car. I open the passenger door for her, glance toward the garage and find Nate standing there, arms crossed and a frown on his face. I give him a chin lift and get one in return. He turns and walks inside, the garage closing before I make it to my door.

My phone buzzes.

Nate: *Take care of our girl.*

I quickly punch out a reply.

Me: *Always. You coming to her dad's?*

Nate: *Yep. Be ready. Her family are assholes.*

Me: *Great. Sounds like fun.*

I don't dwell on the confirmation that Nate knows her family and I don't. He's been with her for seven years. It's a given he knows Gabby in ways I can only hope to… Ways I need to *earn* the right to know. I have no right to be mad at him. He's been there for her when I haven't. I can only be angry at myself for that.

I climb in and set my phone in the middle console. "What are you hungry for?"

"Anything that's bad for me."

I'm laughing as I reverse out of the driveway, happy she didn't ask for fucking rabbit food. "I know just the place."

She'll be smiling by the time we're done eating. I can't have my girl sad and hurting. If she won't confide in me, I can at least give her a reprieve from the heaviness on her shoulders.

"Do they have chocolate?" Her eyes shimmer with possibility instead of melancholy.

"Oh, yeah. I gotcha covered."

Twenty-Four

NOW

LICKING THE SALT FROM MY FINGERS, I CATCH HIM eyeing me across the table, smirking like the satisfied god he is.

"Go ahead. Say it." I wave a fry in his direction before eating it in two bites.

"When's the last time you had a greasy burger?"

I can't hold back my laugh. That's not at all what I thought he'd ask. I've been waiting for him to ask why I was upset earlier. But he hasn't. "Too long. The team nutritionist in New York had me eating clean, lean, and green, which is great. But—"

"Sometimes you just need a little grease." He shoves the last of his burger in his mouth, smiling all the while.

"Yeah, and," I hold up my shake, "ice cream. Real, full-fat ice cream."

He pulls his phone out of his pocket, types, and puts it back. "I've got a surprise when we're done here."

My eyes widen. When is the last time I had a surprise? A *good* surprise? Maybe the night I ran into Matt at the charity event. I may not have thought so at the time, but I'm beginning to believe it now.

"I'm done." I wipe my mouth and hands, then pop out of my seat expectantly. "Come on, slow poke, don't make me wait."

His dimpled smile hits me in the chest. It's been too long. I've missed his face and those damn dimples. I smile back and take his proffered hand.

Outside, Matt shakes hands with a guy big enough to give Dwight a run for his money, a buzz cut, and steely gaze I'd cross the street to avoid, but since I'm with Matt…

"Gabby, this is Victor. He's a good friend and head of security at MCI."

"Hi, Victor." I shake his hand, his smile tight but not unfriendly. I'm kinda surprised he smiles at all. He seems more likely to spit out nails than smile.

"It's nice to meet you, Gabby." He hands over a set of keys.

"What is this?" I look to the keys and then to Matt and back to Victor.

Matt opens the driver's door of the sleek black SUV Victor was standing by when we came out. "It's your new car, if you like it. If not, we'll find you something else."

I gape at him. "Is he for real?" I ask Victor, who lifts his chin to Matt. "You're serious?" I ask Matt.

"Completely." He urges me forward. "Get in and see what you think."

I'm in shock as I sit behind the wheel, checking out the luxurious leather interior. It's black just like the outside. It's entirely too fancy. But dang, it's beautiful.

"Why don't you drive it a few days and see what you think? We can drop it at your place or mine before we go to your dad's."

"You just made a phone call, and boom, here's a car?"

His chuckle is sexy as all get out. "Something like that. I have the same car. I love it. It's safe, and I thought it might work for you too." He throws it out there like it's no big deal.

"I have to pay for it."

"Decide if you want it, then we'll deal with the logistics."

"This is unreal."

He and Victor just laugh at my awe.

"You have no idea what the McIntyres are capable of when they put their minds to it," Victor offers.

I'm not one hundred percent sure if it's an explanation or a warning.

Instead of focusing on that, I kiss Matt on the cheek and nod to Victor. "Thank you both. It's an amazing surprise. I'm sure I'll love it."

I'm sure I'll love you if you keep being this sweet and thoughtful.

I'm sure it's already too late. I feel my resistance crumbling.

Can I trust this feeling?

Can I trust him?

What about Nate?

We end up dropping my car off at MCI. Her eyes grow big with wonder, taking in the twin buildings in the heart of downtown Dallas as we pull into the private parking garage for the penthouses on the top two floors of each tower.

She was nervous to drive her new car, so I did. Victor drove mine back here. He tosses me back my keys with a quick look to Gabby and a chin nod of approval. I'm glad he agrees, but he's not the one who needs convincing.

"We still have a few hours before we need to leave for your family dinner. Do you want to hang out at my place? Or we could do something?" Before she answers, I head for the elevator and hold out my hand when she follows.

I've never been a hand holder. Maybe when I was younger, I thought about it when my parents did, but it just never felt right with any girl, except this one. She's the only girl I've ever held hands with. The only one I've kissed on the forehead, leaving my invisible mark—telling the world she's taken. The only one I ever wanted to do either with. Maybe because only her hand fits mine so perfectly like we were forged to fit, and well, her forehead is the perfect height, directly in front of my lips when we stand toe to toe. Perfect fit… in every way.

Her gaze is locked on our joined hands as if she's thinking the same, feeling the connection that's rippling along my skin, sinking into the depths, and awakening all those thoughts and feelings about her— about us. What we used to have, and could have again. There's no going back, but I sure as fuck want a chance to move forward *with her*.

"Don't you have to work?" Slowly she rips her gaze from our connection and up my arm to land on my face. The dazed look in her eyes gives me ideas about how we could spend the next few hours.

Jesus, nope. Celibate, remember? Fuck, fuck, fuck.

The dig of the elevator announcing our arrival at my floor reminds me she asked a question. "I'm playing hooky."

I wish I could say it's a first, but my philandering ways made me miss more than a few days of work over the years.

I'm not that man anymore.

Are you sure? You still want to fuck when things get bad, when you can't quiet the storm in your head.

She was the storm in my head I needed to quiet. I was a manwhore because of her. It was the coping mechanism I'd established the night I entered a party I didn't want to attend, only to come face to face with my girl in the arms of Nate. He kissed me, then he was kissing her. I bet he got a good laugh out of that. Fucker.

I grit my teeth as I unlock the door. I gotta get a handle on my wayward thoughts. I have a shit-ton of baggage, but she doesn't need me dumping it on her today, on the day she's invited me to meet her family.

No, she didn't invite you to meet her family. She invited you to be a distraction between her and the family she doesn't really want to see.

It might not be ideal, but I'll take it. It shows she still sees me as some kind of safety, if nothing else. That matters. Any way to get closer to her, to know more about her and where she comes from. Protect her.

"Can I get you a drink? Water? Soda? Scotch?"

She laughs at that. "Water. Arriving drunk to my dad's is probably not a smart move."

I hand her a bottled water from the fridge. "Because he'd be upset seeing his baby girl inebriated?"

She scoffs. "Hardly. Because I need to be on my toes. Never know what will come out of his or my brothers' mouths."

What the fuck?

"Are you serious? You have to be sober—be on your toes—around your family?" When she only shrugs, I take her hand and guide her out onto the deck. It's a beautiful day, but really, I need a good lungful of fresh air to stop my murderous thoughts. I rest against the railing, looking down. "That's fucked up."

"You've no idea."

My gaze slides back to her leaning against the glass, barely even outside the sliding door. "It's a beautiful view." I clock her white-knuckling her water bottle. "Come closer."

"I'm good."

She's anything but. I rest against the railing, crossing my arms, searching for her truth, and then it clicks. "You're afraid of heights."

Another shrug.

"Always?"

A quick nod.

"We can go inside." I step toward her. The last thing I want is for her to be afraid in my home or around me.

She points to the sitting area. "We could sit."

"Alright." I take a seat on the long couch, patting the space next to me. If she wants to face her fears, I'm here for her.

When she sits next to me, I pull her into my side, wrapping my arm around her shoulders. She settles in, letting out a deep sigh. The way the patio is designed, you can't see through the lower vertical railing slats unless you're right in front of them. This sitting area is to the side and hidden from prying eyes. In her case, it keeps her from seeing down and out. She can still see up, but mostly I think it's the down that scares people.

"Do you need anything?" I do mean *anything*, but most would take it as meaning food, drink, bathroom, the immediate necessities.

"I need you to tell me what happened." She doesn't have to specify for me to know what she's talking about.

My heart pangs at the thought of dredging through what I know we must if we have any hope of moving forward. Together or apart, it needs to be settled between us.

Before I can consider where to start, she continues, "Only, I don't want it to be now. Maybe tomorrow. Maybe the next. Just not today."

Relieved, I kiss her hair, wishing it were her mouth. "We need time. It's more than a passing conversation. I've got an idea."

She tilts her face toward mine, searching, always searching for what I'm not saying. "Run away together?" She's joking, but the flair in her eyes tells me there's a partial truth here too… A hope… A wish.

"You're not far off."

Her eyes widen, and her brows rise. "What?"

I chuckle at her open surprise. "I have a trip coming up. Come with me. It'll give us a few days to talk through it all, get to know who we are now."

"What kind of trip?"

If I tell her, it'll scare her off. "It's a family thing. But we'll have time to ourselves. It involves a beach and sun, if that helps persuade you."

She sits up, looking down on me. "You had me at *come with me*."

Damn, I love that. I love you. "Good. We'll do your family thing tonight and mine next weekend."

"Sounds good." She stands. "Now, where's your bathroom?"

And like that, we have plans to spend the weekend together. I don't tell her I'm tacking on a few extra days. Once I get her alone, I don't intend on letting her go.

"This way." I lead her inside, hoping it's the first of many rooms and places I get to lead her into, walk beside her through, or follow her delectable ass to the ends of the earth.

Twenty-Five

NOW

"**Y**OU'VE GOT TO BE SHITTING ME." AS MATT parks along the curb of my family home, we find my dad and brothers on the porch, beers in hand and arms crossed like the intimidating assholes they believe themselves to be.

"The welcoming committee?" Matt jokes.

"Um, I should probably apologize now for anything they'll say. Just ignore them."

"What would they possibly say?" His runs his fingers along my jaw, pulling my gaze back to him.

My head hits the headrest as I work to calm my heart. "I never know with them, and to be honest, if they weren't such hotheads, I wouldn't be here. But I'm worried since I'm playing for my home team, reporters might decide to come talk to my family. The last thing I need is more bad publicity."

He frowns. "That's the only reason you're here?"

"Pretty much." I take a deep breath when my dad's scowl deepens. *We're coming, Dad. Hold your britches.* I smile at Matt, hoping he doesn't sense my nerves. "Ready?"

He squeezes my hand before I open my door. "Gabby, don't let them walk all over you. You don't need them." His gaze flits out the window before returning to me. "By the looks of it, they're the ones who need you."

That only makes me laugh. "The only thing I'm good for in their eyes is producing babies, cleaning, and cooking. The fact that I'm not here doing it only pisses them off."

His growl has me wanting to climb over the middle console—as if I'd fit—and onto his lap. "Then let me apologize now for killing them." He kisses my cheek and getting out.

I forgot about alpha-Matt. His alpha has grown larger over the years too. This is the first I've seen him flex that muscle since we've *reconnected.*

Be still my heart and my panties.

Matt stalks to my door, holding his hand out like I need his assistance. I want to push it away, showing my dad and brothers I don't need any man to help me out, but the fierceness in Matt's gaze has me gripping it for dear life. "Show them letting a man be a gentleman doesn't make you weak, baby."

Down, panties.

He kisses my hand and links our fingers when we come to stop beside his SUV, just as Nate parks behind us. My eyes flit to Matt before returning to Nate's truck. His windows are so dark, I can hardly see his rugged face behind the wheel before he opens the door.

I didn't tell Matt that Nate was coming because I thought he wasn't. After this morning, I'd texted Nate, telling him not to worry about coming with me. I should have known he'd ignore me. The man has a protective streak a mile wide, whether we're in a tiff or not.

Nate comes around the front of his truck, stopping besides us. He kisses my cheek, whispering, "We're going to talk," before pulling way without another glance and fist-bumping Matt.

"Let's do this." Matt steps forward, his grip tight on my hand, Nate's hand low on my back.

This is either going to be the worst visit ever or the best. I'm not sure which, but my family probably has no idea what to think as the three of us approach the house.

"It's about time you paid your family a visit, Gabriella." Dad steps forward.

"G2!" My oldest and dumbest brother greets me like it's a winning nickname.

"Dad, Greg, Ry, Marc, Nick, this is Matt, and you all know Nate." I step aside, letting the men do what they do.

I'm taken aback by the large, charming smile on Matt's face as he reintroduces himself and shakes each of their hands. Kill them with kindness, I suppose.

It's a tactic. I wonder how long it'll last.

I don't even get hugs, simply nods of hello, which doesn't go unnoticed as Matt slides his eyes my way as if to ask, *what the fuck?* A small shake of my head is all he gets. There's no excuse for how they treat me.

I'm like Cinderella who snuck out to attend the ball and just never came home. My evil stepmother and sisters—my dad and brothers—didn't want me to go, but they really don't want me to come home either. I forget for a moment why I even bother.

Though I'm ready to turn around and leave, Matt's strong hand lands on my back, urging me forward and inside the cage I managed to escape.

"I hope you like cold beer and pizza," Dad says to Matt and Nate, but his sneer lands on me. "Gabby didn't think to come earlier to cook a proper dinner for our guests."

Yep, welcome home to me.

I won't cower. "You're grown men, completely capable of cooking a steak or spaghetti. Don't blame me because you didn't think ahead. *You* asked me here, remember? I thought I was the guest," I mumble the last under my breath.

Dad's face reddens. He'd smack me if he thought he could get away with it. "Such disrespect. I raised you better than that."

Actually, he didn't. He didn't raise me at all. If he wasn't working, he was drunk, drowning his sorrows over losing my mother when I was twelve. Before then, if it wasn't to get him food or a drink, he didn't really have much use for me. I wasn't one of his prized sons.

Matt steps forward. "Pizza and beer sound great. Anything we can do to help?"

"Nick, you and your sister set the table. Ry and Marc, get the pizza. Greg, beers," Dad barks orders, and we all jump to it like no time has passed. I slip out of Matt's hold and into the dining room.

When we're alone, Nick pulls me into a hug. "I'm so glad you finally came home. I've missed you."

I hug him back but pull away first. "Yeah, all those missed calls and visits really tell me how much you missed me."

"Ah, Gabriella, don't be like that. You know how he is. If he's not controlling it, it's not happening."

He lays plates around the table. I follow with napkins and silverware. "You're a grown-ass man. You need to move out and find your balls."

"Excuse me?"

I jerk around to find Dad glaring death on me. I don't back down. I found my backbone. "There's no excuse for all your grown sons still living at home. Don't you want them to get married, have kids, find lives of their own?"

"You need to hush that mouth before I shut it for you," he seethes.

"Dad!" Greg shoves through the alcove between the kitchen and dining room to stand between Dad and me. "We haven't seen G2 in years. Let's not scare her off in the first five minutes."

Jesus, I hate that nickname.

I blink and find Matt staring down at me, anger and frustration bubbling behind the concern on his face. I pat his chest just as Nate presses to my back. My protective men. Maybe they're what gave me the confidence to speak up, talk back to Dad. Neither of them would ever let anything happen to me. I might not trust Matt with my heart, but I've always trusted him with my safety. His protectiveness is only matched by Nate's. What I wouldn't give to have grown up with these two by my side. How different my life would have been.

"Mr. Chisholm," Matt speaks to Dad, but his eyes are locked on me, "if you ever threaten to lay a hand on my girl again, you and I are going to have a problem." He looks over his shoulder. I can't see Matt's face, but Dad swallows, not looking nearly as confident as he did a minute ago. "And if you ever lay a hand on her, it will be the last thing you ever do. We clear?"

"I… What?" Dad backtracks. "I would never—"

"We clear?" Matt is facing him now, his back muscles rippling with tension.

"Clear, son," Dad admits.

Twenty-Six

NOW

"YEAH, I WOULDN'T CALL HIM *SON* EITHER," NATE chuckles behind me, gripping my hand and pulling me to the other side of the table, away from my father.

I've never seen my dad cower. I glance at Nick, who's smiling at Matt in awe. My other brothers are avoiding any eye contact at all. Damn, they're like broke dogs. They need to get out from under Dad's reign.

I start to sit, but Matt urges me into the next seat so he's closest to Dad, and I'm between him and Nate.

When Greg hands me a beer, it's Nick who's there offering me a glass of ice and a Coke instead. I take the soda with a small, "Thank you."

Greg scowls and sets the extra beer on the table. I'm sure one of these seven men will drink it. There is way too much testosterone in this house. I'd forgotten how stifling it can be.

Matt lays his hand on my thigh, pulling my attention to him. His head tilts, hiding my face from my father, his eyes asking me if I'm okay.

I squeeze his hand with a small nod. I'm not great, but I'm okay.

"Nate, you've been doing really well. I assume we can expect more of the same this season?" Dad directs his question to Nate, but his eyes are on the slices of pizza he's stacking on his plate.

"Yes, sir. It's going to be a great season, especially since Gabby is here." Nate winks at me.

Matt places a piece of fully loaded—meat and veggie—pizza on my plate.

He remembered.

Then hands me a packet of parmesan.

If he keeps being this sweet and attentive, I've no hope of keeping my feelings in check.

He and Nate go for the five-meat pizza, laughing as they both grab for the same slice. Nate lets Matt have it.

"There's plenty, boys. More's in the kitchen," Dad throws out.

It's Marc this time who gets up, taking the empty boxes, replacing them with full pizzas from the oven, where Dad insists they be kept warm. He never did have a taste for cold pizza. As for me, I almost like cold pizza better the next day. *Almost.*

Digging in, I avoid looking at anyone. I don't want any questions directed my way. I find meals go smoother if they forget I'm here.

Why did I come home again? Oh, that's right, bad press. The last thing I need is my new team regretting buying me from New York. I'm finally home with Nate. I don't want to take a chance of messing that up. I need to make nice, or at the very least, fly below the radar.

Anxiety scratches in the background, waiting, knowing something is bound to happen. I'll look at someone or breathe the wrong way—or, I don't know, exist at all—and Dad will say or do something that will embarrass me and piss off the men on either side of me.

Nate's only met my family once. It went fine. I didn't dare bring him back to chance another meeting that could go less than stellar.

I never told him about my family and how they treated me, except when I told him about my mom. I think he's guessed over the years, but I'm not one for sharing my shame and seeing pity form in his eyes.

"Not that you asked, but your brother," Dad motions to Greg, "is up for lieutenant. All your brothers are shining stars in their fire houses."

I smile at them. Of course they are. Dad wouldn't have it any other way. So they work hard, always wanting to impress him. "Congrats, Greg. I've no doubt. Y'all always succeeded at anything you put your minds to." I catch Nick staring at me. "You working toward fire marshal?"

He opens his mouth to reply, but it's Dad's voice that cuts in, "Nah, he wants to stay in the action, right, Nicky?"

No, he doesn't. It's written all over his face. "Sure, Dad."

I glare at Nick before sliding my gaze to the head of the table. I shouldn't say anything, but… "Dad, have you considered your kids might aspire to be something other than what you want?" Yeah, that's not going to stir the embers burning behind his eyes.

"What would you know about what *they* want? You haven't been home for more than a meal or two in seven years," he spouts.

I grab for a second slice of pizza. "Well, you're so welcoming and all—"

"Haven't you had enough?" Dad interrupts.

"Yeah, GT, leave some for the rest of us," Greg teases. He's trying to be funny, but it hurts. It always has.

My hand falls back to my side. Old shame awakens, taking root. *Never enough and always too much.*

Nate frowns.

In huff, Matt slides a piece onto my plate. "She's only had one. She's a professional athlete. She needs to eat. How many have *you* had, sir?"

Holy shitz!

"You know your daughter is quite the star herself." Nate wipes his mouth and sits taller, staring down my father and brothers. "I don't remember you coming to any of her games to support her. In fact, I don't remember you ever even calling just to see how she is. How about Thanksgiving and Christmas? Oh, that's right, she's spent all of them with *me* because she doesn't feel welcome in this house. Do you even know when her birthday is?"

Oh, hell. This going to be bad. I tug on Nate's shirt as he stands.

He squeezes my hand. "Sorry, Firecracker." He kisses my cheek, nods to Matt. "I'll be outside." To my dad and brothers, he leaves them with his parting words, "I wish I could say it's been good to see you again, but I prefer not to lie."

Matt leans into me, worry all over his lovely face, and whispers, "Why don't you go with him? I'll be right there."

I'd like to say I stayed and stood up to my father some more. But I think I've done enough damage for one visit. I quickly escape, squeezing Nick's shoulder as I pass.

So much for appeasing my family so they stay sane if a reporter should approach them. I'm totally screwed and embarrassed as hell for me, for my family, for Matt and Nate to experience my homelife firsthand.

I'm never coming back here. I tried. It didn't work. Too many years, too many people reaming on me about my size, my profession, my dating life—as if I have one—for me to take more flak from my family.

It's a wound that's never healed, and coming home only made it worse. I thought I'd moved on, yet the festering shame bubbling inside me proves I'm stuck right where I was as a kid. I haven't moved on at all…

Not from my family.

Not from Matt.

I've been stuck all these years, just like Nate said.

I'm pitiful. I'm hopeless. I'm a fucking idiot. I'm a twenty-five-year-old professional athlete, yet I'm still that little girl hoping, praying someone will love me… just as I am.

Fuming, ready to rip the walls from this pesky excuse for a home, I wait until my girl disappears from sight and hear the front door open and close. Jaw tight, I look to Greg and her other brothers. "Why do you call her G2?"

She cringes each time the three older brothers called her that like it's a cute nickname. It might be cute to them. It's obviously not to her.

"It's nothing, just what we've called her since she was a kid," Marc explains.

"What does it stand for?"

Tight-lipped, they share a look between the three of them but remain silent.

"Gabriella Two Ton," Nick, the youngest, admits.

My blood, already at a simmer, now boils.

I don't blame Nick. He's the youngest of the men in this room. He hasn't said a disparaging thing to Gabby. I can tell she has a fondness for him. He gets a pass.

But the other four, not so much. "Shame on you for belittling your daughter and younger sister. You're supposed to lift her up, not beat her down."

"The world is a cruel place. She needs to learn where she fits," her dad raises his voice. "I don't appreciate you coming into my home and disrespecting me."

"I don't appreciate the way you treat your daughter. I came into your home offering you kindness and respect, and all you did was berate her, trying to make her feel small and unworthy, in an effort to make yourself feel big and manly." I push my chair back. "I have news for you." I turn to the older brothers. "Making a woman feel lesser than does not make you a man. It makes you a bully.

"And you, Mr. Chisholm, should be ashamed of yourself. Gabriella is a beautiful woman—inside and out. Any man would be lucky to know her, much less blessed to win her heart. You treating her like she's less than your sons is a tragedy. How many times have you told her she's eating too much or kept food from her? You should have taught your boys how to treat a woman. Is that why there is no Mrs. Chisholm? Did you run her off?"

He jumps to his feet. "How dare you!"

I stand slowly, calm on the outside, a hurricane on the inside. "No. How dare *you*. How dare you treat the woman I love with such careless disregard. How dare you burden her with the belief she is anything other than beautiful in stature and heart. How dare you dismiss her gender-breaking accomplishments as if she's not trailblazing for women to follow in her footsteps. How dare you not love your daughter the way she deserves. How dare you love her *less* because she doesn't have a dick between her legs!" I roar the last line, shaking, trying to regain my composure.

Her father is sheet-white and slumps down onto his chair.

I move around the table, speaking to Nick, "Should you want help getting out from under the thumb of your father, give me a call. I'd be happy to help." I glare at the older brothers. "If you three can grow up and stop treating a woman like her weight equals her worthiness and apologize to your sister, I could be persuaded to help you too, but only after you have groveled to her satisfaction."

Leaving behind stunned and silenced assholes, I round the corner to find my girl, sobbing silently by the door. "Fuck me." I stalk to her, picking her up, her legs wrapping around my middle as I storm out of the house. "I thought you were outside. I didn't mean for you to hear any of that. I'm sorry to upset you. I'm so sorry, baby."

She mumbles coherently enough to barely understand her, "That was amazing."

Thank fuck. I kiss her head. "Let's get you home."

Twenty-Seven

NOW

I ROLL OVER TO FIND A GORGEOUS MAN IN MY BED, but not the one I was hoping for. I blink a few times just to be sure I'm awake. I did go to bed alone. I'm pretty sure.

"Did I miss something last night?" My voice is scratchy from an emotional hangover and not enough sleep.

"I came in to check on you." My bestie smiles and cups my cheek. "You okay?"

"Yeah." I fall to my back, eyeing the ceiling on a yawn. "It went about as I expected, except for the whole my two guys defending me to my family."

He tweaks my nose and stands. "That part was pretty amazing. Matt deserves a blow job for that speech."

"You were listening?" I thought he was in his car and just jumped out to help when Matt came out with me in his arms. *Sigh*. Me in his arms. Pretty spectacular. Not my finest moment, being insulted by my family, but Nate and then Matt standing up to Dad like they did? It's everything to have their support.

"It was kinda hard to miss, especially with my ear to the door. You know, just in case y'all needed backup."

"The whole point of me going was to *not* piss off my family. I think I fell a little short." A lot short.

His laugh is immediate and eases my worry. "I'd be surprised if they talked to reporters, Firecracker, or said anything negative if they did. The old man was shaking in his boots. The McIntyres have pull, lots of it. Your dad's no idiot. He's a jerk who needs to be flogged, but he's not stupid enough to take them on. I'm sure of it."

He holds out his hand. "Up you go. Let me feed you before you diva out on me because you're tired *and* hungry."

"I'm not a diva." I take his help getting up but pout.

"You are when you're needing sustenance. And after last night, your body is drained. You need to replenish it." His head in the fridge, he says over his shoulder, "Speaking of drained. I thought lover boy would have stayed over last night."

I work on making coffee and try not to let the disappointment of Matt leaving me at my doorstep to take an uber home get to me.

Holding my head between his massive hands, his green eyes scanned my face. "I don't want to move too fast." He glanced over my shoulder. "All I want to do is hold you and be sure you're alright, but if I come in, I'm going to hold you all night. And if I hold you all night, I'll be fucking you come morning." He presses a kiss to my forehead. "We need to talk before we get physical."

He held me on the porch until his ride arrived. It was the sweetest thing anyone has ever done for me.

"Gabby?" Nate hip checks me as I stare at the machine brewing.

"Hm?"

"Stud? Why didn't he stay?"

"We need to talk *before we get physical*. His words." I grab two mugs from the cabinet and creamer from the fridge.

"And when are you going to talk?" He mixes batter in a bowl, and I look around, realizing we're having pancakes. He smiles. "Yes, I know they're your favorite. Toss me a couple of bananas. Let's make them as healthy as possible."

I gladly hand him the bananas and try to hold in my excitement. It's just food, right? Fuel. Nothing to get excited about. But… Pancakes!

"Babe, I feel like I'm having a one-sided conversation here. You're giving me a complex." He juts his bottom lip out.

"Puh-leeze, there is nothing wrong with your ego." I hand him his mug of black coffee. "He invited me on a trip this weekend. A family thing. We're going to *talk* then."

"You're going?" He seamlessly flips a pancake.

"Yeah. Why? You don't think I should?" I set the bar with napkins and silverware.

"No, not saying that. Surprised is all."

I let out a sigh. The vision of Matt's handsome face pops into my head. "Yesterday was a really good day with him, even before last night. It just seemed like the perfect opportunity to get some quality time to work through what happened and see where it leaves us."

Nate slides a plate of pancakes my direction. He chuckles when I clap out of giddiness. "In the guise of full disclosure, that little *family thing* he invited you to is Fin's wedding on their private island. The youngest brother, Joe, owns it."

"What?!" I shriek. *Owns an island.* Who does that?

"Yeah, so you might want to pack a few options for a beach-front wedding." He kisses my head as he passes. "Close your mouth, Firecracker, or I just might stick my tongue down your throat to convince you to marry me instead."

Holy guacamole.

He did not just say that. "Nate!"

"Just sayin', babe. It's a gaping hole. I could fill it with my cock if you prefer."

I chuck my napkin at him. He catches it, laughing, and wipes his mouth. "Love you too, Firecracker." He continues with his plate down the hall toward his room.

I guess we're not eating together.

We haven't talked about why I was upset yesterday. I know we need to. I have no answers. *He* didn't seem upset, so why eat alone instead of together? Is this the start of our new pattern? Living separate, disjoined lives?

My stomach churns, my pancakes not nearly as appetizing as they were five seconds ago.

Damn you, Nate, for dropping one bomb after another, and ruining my pancake morning.

"Son, should I be worried? You're bringing a stranger to Fin's wedding." Dad sits behind his large mahogany desk, his fingers steepled, his brow arched, not a hint of anger—which is new. Usually, I've done something to warrant his ire. I've been beyond good this year, since before Joe and Sam's wedding. Since I gave up sex and realized I've been tripping through life, falling into one pussy after another with no real direction except one—forget my Gabby, bury my feelings, forget I ever knew what it meant to love to the core of me and be loved in return.

Now, *forgetting* is the last thing I want to do.

It's ironic, really. Now that I have the chance to get her back, my distraction is still because of *her*. Whether she was in my life or not, she continued to rule my every move, my every motivation, and every beat of my locked-up heart. For seven fucking years.

I can't help but chuckle. "Yes, you sure as fuck should, because if I can't close this deal—" I wave in the air, at a loss to find the right words to accurately describe how devastated I'll be. I lock on his gaze. "Demolished. If I can't win her back, I'll be demolished."

His features soften as he stands, comes around his desk, and pulls me into a bear hug. "Then let's be sure that doesn't happen."

On a tight breath, I pull back when I can without tears glistening in my eyes.

Dad pats my shoulders. "I never thought…" His fist covers his mouth as he fights his own welling emotions.

Fuck, don't make me cry, Dad.

"…I'd see the day you'd find a woman to capture you so completely. I'm so proud of you, Son."

A less-than-humorous laugh escapes. "Don't be proud of me yet. I hurt her in probably the worst way I could have, given her history." I match his scowl. "And no, I didn't cheat on her."

Relief lowers his shoulders. "That's good at least."

"Yeah, except then I have to explain to her our breakup is what led me down the path you've seen me on for the past, well, long enough."

He fists his hands on his hips. "You sure you need to confess that?"

"I'm sure. I'd rather she hears it from me than read it in the media or from any number of women out there who won't be pleased to know I'm tying myself to one woman and one woman only."

He points at me, taking his seat behind his desk. "You see? That is why I'm proud of you. You own your shit, Matt. You don't shirk from the consequences of your actions. That's a great quality to have, Son. Damn proud."

I clear my throat, backing toward his door. "We good? 'Cause I have work to do and a woman to win back."

"Go with God, Son." He chuckles, pulling out his phone. I've no doubt he's either calling or texting Mom.

I've never been the shining star of my brothers, but it's nice to know I can make him proud every now and again.

Twenty-Eight

NOW

MATT PICKED ME UP IN A CHAUFFEURED BLACK sedan that drives us to the private airport to take their family's corporate jet to the wedding Matt has yet to tell me about. You'd think as a professional athlete, I'd be used to chauffeurs and private jets. New York had a private aircraft, but it was nothing like this. It looked like a normal jetliner except there was more seat and leg room. But *this* is ridiculously opulent. Chrome, dark wood, and cream leather as far as the eye can see, with reclining chairs with footrests, to couches and sitting areas with tables and TVs. Insane.

I was introduced to Matt's family. I knew Fin from college but I don't think he remembered me. So much for making an impression. His brother's girls, Margot and Sam, or Samantha. I'm not sure which I'm supposed to use. I've heard her called both. I'll have to ask Matt when we get a moment alone.

Then there are the friends, whom Matt also calls *brothers*: Victor, whom I've met; and Michael; and Sam's brother, Jace.

And let me not forget Matt's parents, Hugh and Fiona, incredibly welcoming and nice. Not at all like my family. Even Margot's parents, brother, sister, and her fiancé were warm and kind, more on the reserved side, but I got the impression they don't really know the McIntyres all that well. Their reservations could be about the whole trip and not about me.

This… is a whole new world. I should be on edge and ready to jump ship, er, plane, but sitting next to Matt on one of the couches, snacking on finger sandwiches, raw veggies and fruit with dips, and cheese, crackers, and assorted meats, I feel completely at peace. Like this is the place I was always meant to be. Maybe I was—am—right where I belong and would have been a long time ago, if only…

"You're awfully quiet, Gorgeous." He brushes my hair off my shoulder, kissing behind my ear. His grip tightens on my hip when a full body shudder has me leaning into him.

"I'm just enjoying the moment." My pale blues lock with his emerald eyes. What color eyes would our kids have?

Don't. Don't get ahead of yourself.

"I'm glad, baby. Sit back and relax, and let me tell you a story."

He proceeds to tell me how Joe met his Samantha on a trip home on Thanksgiving break from college with Jace—her brother. It was love at first sight, but she was too young, so he held back. That is until a crazy man killed her father and shot her with a single bullet that passed through her father's heart and into her shoulder when he jumped in front of her to save her life by giving his.

Wow, that's crazy and heartbreaking.

Matt cups my cheek and swipes at my tear. "Damn, Gorgeous. Didn't mean to make you cry. It's all good and way more complicated. But that's volume two." He kisses me gently, one, two seconds then pulls back. "That story is for later. But know it has a happy ending. They married this past December. Wedded bliss if I ever saw it."

He practically lies down, pulling me to rest on his chest. His voice vibrates under my ear as he speaks, "Now Fin and Margot, theirs is a friends-to-lovers tale…"

Margot was Sam's friend. Fin had the hots for Margot right away, but his little Pixie was hiding a secret that kept her from sharing her heart, giving in to what they finally couldn't resist. "Sam and Margot both graduated from different colleges a few weeks ago. Fin has been living in Austin, working remotely, until she graduated, and decides where she wants to go to medical school." His hand runs up and down my back, making my eyes close, but my ears are focused on his voice. "Rumor has it she's not sure if she still wants to be a doctor. I guess time will tell."

His voice comes in and out as I begin to drift off.

Warm lips press to my forehead. "Rest, baby. I'll tell you anything you missed later. Plenty of time to talk when we get to the island."

"You tell the best stories," I murmur into his neck.

His laugh rumbles in his chest, shaking me along with him.

It's the best feeling.

I have a girl crush. The problem is I don't know if it's on Sam or Margot. They're both pretty amazing, even though Margot hasn't been feeling that great. She says it's just stress and a sensitive stomach, but I don't think Sam is buying it.

We're resting on the beach under some sort of covering while the guys play in the water. I can't stop myself from searching out Matt every few minutes. My heart skips every time I find his eyes already on me. Sometimes he waves. Other times he winks. This time he quirks his head, a heated question burning up my legs.

Yeah, I need a distraction from all things Matt McIntyre.

I turn my attention to Margot. "You feeling any better?"

"Honestly, not really. I think I could close my eyes and sleep for a week. I can't wait to spend three weeks here relaxing just like this. Doing absolutely nothing—except my husband."

That sounds like a dream, relaxing for three weeks anywhere, but especially here on the beach with the one you love. Absolute heaven. Speaking of heaven, my gaze drifts back to the man I can't stop looking for, waiting for, longing for.

He finally told me the reason for the trip when we found ourselves alone in our cabana with one bed… just for us. *Heaven, help me.*

I catch the concern and watchful eye Sam has on her best friend. "How long have you been feeling yucky and run down?"

Margot says something about her heart being fine that I miss but tune in when Sam's frown deepens.

"I wasn't thinking that at all. Really, how long? Usually, you're full of pep and the last person to fall asleep on a trip."

"I don't know, a month or so. It's just graduation and the stress of getting engaged, married, deciding if I still want to be a doctor or not."

Matt was right. Margot going to medical school may not happen. But, dang, a doctor, how cool is that?

Sam looks to me before returning to her friend. "Margot, when was your last period?"

"What?!"

When Margot doesn't answer, Sam asks again, "Period. How long."

"Oh, shit." Is this a shot-gun wedding—or nearly, considering they're already planning to get married.

"I can't—"

"You could—"

"But—"

"Come on."

Margot and I wait on the path heading back to the cabanas while Sam runs to tell the guys… Well, I don't really know what she's telling them. I'm pretty sure it's not that she suspects Margot is pregnant.

In Sam and Joe's cabana, Margot eyes the box of pregnancy tests Sam hands her. "Why do you have these?"

Seemingly nonchalant, Sam says, "Sometimes I'm late. I always have a supply with me, just in case."

"Are y'all trying?" Margot is surprised by the thought, nearly as surprised as the possibly that she herself could be the one knocked up.

"We're not *not* trying." Sam smirks. "It's fun thinking about, and practicing is… Just, wow."

Laughter fills the room until Margot's turn to tears. "I can't be." She fights to keep herself in check.

I know the feeling, girl.

Sam and I step forward, hugging her. It seemed like the right thing to do when someone you're crushing on has a meltdown. It doesn't matter that I just met her. She's hurting. That calls for hugs. Plus, baby. Wow.

Sam urges her to the bathroom. "You won't know until you take the test. Go. We're right here with you."

I hand Margot a tissue. "You don't know me. But you're not alone." I point out the window toward her man, even though we can't see them. "And that man out there will be nothing but ecstatic to know he knocked you up. The McIntyre men are possessive Neanderthals like that."

They're shocked. "Matt is like that too?"

I laugh. "Seriously?"

"Yes. Matt seems more playboy than caveman," Sam casually offers like she didn't just drop a bomb.

Playboy? Is that how they see him? They don't see the deeply caring person who is protective and stands up to a girl's family just because it's the right thing to do? I don't know Matt the way they do. He wasn't a playboy when I knew him in college. And now, when we're together, his eyes are always on me.

Is he a playboy now? They seem so casual about it.

Sam sends Margot off to do the test. While we wait, my mind races. How much has he changed? What type of life has he had in these lost seven years between when he was my Matt till now? Has he been someone else's Matt? Has he fallen in and out of love over and over again?

My stomach sours at the idea of endless woman knowing Matt the way I do—*did*. Do I really know him at all anymore?

Everyone was so surprised to see Matt brought a date to his brother's wedding. I don't doubt the surprise of bringing someone they've never met—except Fin, though I'm not sure that counts since he didn't remember me. The surprise felt more like they couldn't believe he brought anyone at all.

But if he's really been in love with me for all these years, why don't any of his people know about me? He hid it well.

Margot ends up having really great news. Well, Sam and I are excited. Margot looks like she's going to be puke.

Me, on the other hand, having come here feeling more comfortable around Matt and hopeful for a reconciliation, now doubt that's even a rational thought considering how little I know about the man Matt is today.

I fell in love with eighteen-year-old Matt.

Who is he now?

Do I already love him?

Or do I love the *idea* of who I think he is?

Do I love a *memory* of a man who no longer exists?

Twenty-Nine

NOW

WAKING UP ALONE ON THE DAY OF MY BROTHER'S wedding is not at all how I thought my morning—night— would play out. Gabby was quiet all through dinner. The news of Margot being pregnant was the talk of the night. I was distracted, celebrating with my brothers and their girls, whom I've come to love like sisters. Sam, in particular, because I've spent more time with her.

I was there in the heart of her family's devastation, being as supportive as I could for her and Jace, who's a brother to all of us. Though, like me, he's had a hard time of late, coming to terms with his philandering ways and how his actions impacted Sam and Joe, as did mine.

We've both been idiots, self-absorbed, coping with our own hurt in ways that impacted others, though we didn't know it at the time—or maybe didn't care.

I care now. I'm completely invested in staying on the straight and narrow, being worthy of the love and trust my family puts in me. I'm committed to winning my girl back despite the lack of progress in the last twelve hours or so.

I rub at the ache inside my chest. The hole her absence left seems to have grown now that I find not only my bed but the cabana empty of one 5'10" beauty.

She disappeared last night before I'd even noticed she slipped away. Worried, I was thankful to find her in our cabana, asleep in our bed. I wasn't as thrilled to find the barrier of pillows she'd laid in the middle.

Something happened between getting off the plane and dinner last night. My guess is Margot and Sam have something to do with it. Or maybe the news of Margot being pregnant and on the eve of her wedding, set something off in my girl.

Spooked her, perhaps.

Neither of my brothers had an easy go of convincing their woman to let them love them. They each struggled, crashing and burning in their own way. In the end, they didn't give up, and now, they're nauseatingly happy.

I'm happy for them. I am.

I'm worried that my crash and burn scenario hasn't occurred yet. Yesterday, I would have thought it was the devastating way we ended in college. Today, I'm not so sure.

Scrubbing my face, I climb out of bed, stretching, and survey the room, just in case my girl is hiding. Unfortunately, she's not. I do bathroom stuff, pull on my swim trunks, and step out ready to go in search of my heart, the only person who can ease the ache and fill the gaping hole.

I make it two steps before halting, my eyes landing on Gabby stretching on the side of the porch. She's in workout clothes, more like a second skin by the way her shorts and tank are hugging her body.

Fuck, my girl's fit.

She always looked good, and though I miss those extra curves, there's no denying she has a body worth millions because of what she can do with it.

I read a news report the other day, more like a gossip site, touting their claim to know for fact the voluptuous NFL kicker is involved with a woman and two men—Nate and I being the two men. Supposedly the *woman* was the source of the story, recounting her secret love affair with the only female player to go pro in a men's league, saying how Gabby has always struggled with her weight and size and that playing football was her way of *fitting in*.

Whatever the fuck that means. Playing in a male-dominated sport to *fit in* doesn't make any sense.

The story went on to say the relationship with Nate and me is only a coverup—we're her beards, because Gabby is really a lesbian and always has been.

It all makes my blood boil. The need to smash and protect has me clenching my fists and deep breathing to keep it in check.

Looking at my girl, I can see the weight of what she has to deal with on a daily basis. Not only is she breaking new ground for women, she is being saddled with unrealistic size-zero-fits-all impossible standards. The girl just wants to play football, because she's damn good at it. She's using her God-given talent. If she's breaking barriers in the process, then good for her. But don't spout lies about her size—who gives a fuck?—and her preference in the bedroom—again, who gives a fuck?

I, of course, do because I want it to be me and only me in her bed, at her side, in her heart.

But if she did prefer the soft and pink, whose business is it?

And if she were to weigh 300 pounds, as long as she's able to do her job like many of the linemen who top that number by a lot, who has the right to criticize her for it?

Fuck if I don't want to shout it from the rooftops to lay off my girl and let her shine like the rockstar she is. Don't make her into something she's not or make her feel like she has to be something else to appease the world and their skewed opinions.

"Hey." She drops her leg from the railing and stands tall. She notices my rigid state and frowns. "Everything alright?"

Fuck, no. Everything is not alright. "What happened?" I regret the edge to my voice, but it's taking everything I have not to throw her over my shoulder and stomp inside, laying her out and loving her until she is soft and pliant, completely my girl again, and all the hate the world has thrown at her forgotten.

She squints, takes a drink of water and steps closer. "You'll have to be more specific."

I lean against the post, arms and legs crossed. "When I left you on the beach, you were nearly there, open and ready to listen with a receptive heart to the rest of my story. Then you disappeared with Sam and Margot, returning a different girl than the one who left. What the fuck happened? Did they say something? Did they hurt your feelings? Did *I* hurt your feelings?"

She visibly swallows, wiping the sweat from her forehead, face, and neck. I didn't notice her sweaty state before. I thought she was getting ready to work out. But by the looks of it, she already has.

"I think me coming was a mistake. You've always been a charmer, Matt, and I've always been susceptible to your spell."

What the fuck? Her words hit hard. She thinks I'm charming her, putting up a smoke screen to mislead or daze?

She sits on the porch steps, her long legs bent, her arms resting on her knees, looking out over the ocean in the distance. "I've tried, you know." She bites her lip and turns so I can only see the curve of her jaw. "I wanted to forget you, to wash away the memory of your touch and replace it with someone else's."

A roar rumbles in my chest.

She turns, and I nearly fall over from the devastation in her eyes.

"What happened?" I need to claim all of her hurt and pain. I'm the reason. I'm the cause.

"The world never lets you forget, you know?"

I sit beside her, and my knee brushes hers. Her legs are so long, nearly even with mine, and I'm still a good seven inches taller.

"How so?" *Come on, baby, lay it out, give me your pain and let me love it away.*

"My size. Even when everything is going smoothly, football was working out for me. I had Nate—he's been my rock, my best friend, my backbone when I needed it. Financially, I'm doing great." She side-eyes me. "Not your kind of money great, but good all the same."

"Money's not everything." I've got more than I could ever spend, and I'm lonely as hell, needing the girl next to me back in my life, being my future.

"No. It comes with its own pitfalls. So does the modicum of fame I have." She picks up a long, dead blade of beachgrass and starts to break pieces off. "In my effort to forget you, I found guys who only wanted me for what they could get from my fame. Who they could meet. What events I could get them into. None really saw me. I thought they accepted me—for my size. Turns out they didn't really care how I looked or who I was on the inside. They just wanted what they could take from me."

Take? "Did they hurt—"

"Not in the way you're thinking. I couldn't stomach letting them touch me. I learned to spot the fame chasers quickly."

I'm pissed she didn't find anyone to love her, show her how beautiful she is with their hands, mouths, and dicks… And fucking relieved she didn't. So fucked up.

"I thought there was one. He said the right things. He looked at me when we talked. He didn't care about going to parties or even games. He just wanted to be with me."

I'm going to strangle whoever this guy is for getting close—

"I was kinda attracted to him, which is saying something." Her watery gaze meets mine. "I compared every one of them to you. They always fell short. But I thought…" She swipes at her tears as I fight the urge to hold her. "Maybe I could sleep with him and just get it over with." Her chin trembles, and it's killing me. "He could be the one to wash away the imprint you left on my body, my…"

She shakes her head. "We got close. I was nearly ready to let him. Then he had to go and remind me how cruel the world can be. How you can never escape your truth. How no one will ever…" She sucks in air, her shoulders shaking. She stands, facing away, leaning against the railing. "He told me I need to lose weight. Just out of the blue. His hands up my shirt, and he felt that was the moment to remind me how imperfect I am."

"Gabby." Jesus, this fucker. I want to kill him even more than the others.

"I never found… I never tried again." She swings around, eyes swollen, nose red, and tears still streaming down her face. "You ruined me, Matt. You were the only one, but even *you* couldn't get past it. My size."

"Fuck. No, Gabby, baby. That's not true. I don't know all you heard that night, but you obviously didn't stay long enough to hear me tell those idiots off. You didn't hear me set them straight and kick them out of the party that wasn't even mine." I move, afraid to touch her but not able to stop. I press into her, my hands on her hips, my forehead on hers. "Did you never notice me on campus afterwards? I dumped them as friends. I only hung out with Fin and his friends. I never had anything to do with them again."

She sucks in a trembling breath. "But you didn't. I was there. You said, *fuck you*, but not another word. I died a little more every second I waited, hoping you'd defend me. Defend *us*."

"I did. It might have taken me a minute to realize I needed to stand up for my girl more than I needed them as friends, but I fucking swear to you, I didn't leave one of them standing, believing it was okay to talk about you or any woman that way."

"You never said—"

"You never gave me the chance, Gabby. I tried. Over and over again, I tried. But then you—" I step back, reeling from the memory, "cheated with Nate, and I lost it."

"You were with Jen."

"*After* you kissed Nate. I'd never touched her till that night. Still, I didn't fuck her."

"Well, I wasn't with Nate. It was a set up. Jen was all too eager to get you to the party so you could see Nate kissing me. I thought it would make you move on. You said you loved me, and then you… chubby fucking chaser, Matt!"

"Fuck! I hate this." I capture her cheek, stealing her gaze. "I swear I've never seen you as anything other than perfect. I love everything about you—then—and now. Your curves—I miss them—not gonna lie.

Your long-ass legs, your height, your strength, your blue eyes that see into my soul as if you've known me my whole life. I called you *gorgeous* the day we met and every day after. It wasn't a line. It was the fucking truth. I've never seen anyone more gorgeous than you. But I didn't love you because of your body."

I step back, gripping my face, squeezing, not wanting to go where I need to go. She needs to know. "You think I ruined you. *You* ruined me too. I've never gotten over you. No woman has ever been good enough. I've fucking tried to forget you, bury the lock you have on my heart, fill the hole in my soul created by you leaving me! I tried to make things right with you, but you wouldn't listen!"

Her sobs have me stomping away a few feet, needing distance. The weight of defeat nearly steals my courage. I turn and almost fall over from the sight of her heaving sobs. "I said I loved you first. Told you I was scared I'd fuck it up, do something, say something stupid. You promised to be there, to forgive me when I did. Do you remember? Then, the first time I fuck up, have a second of hesitation to give everything up for you, you bail. Just like that. You were so quick to judge me. Accuse me. You were waiting for me to fail you, so you could run."

"Matt, I didn't—"

"You did! You fucking left me! I was there. I was in it one hundred percent, but one misstep, and I'm locked out, not only by you but Nate and all his boys. They hounded me, made sure I never forgot what you *thought* I did—or didn't do. Then you fucking kiss Nate where I can see it. So you can rip my heart out all over again. Being sure I knew you didn't need me. You had a whole fucking football team at your back. I was *nothing* to you."

"Matt," my girl pleads, crossing the distance to lay her hand on my chest, and I break.

I fucking break inside, desperate for her touch, her forgiveness… My forgiveness. "You have no idea the string of events you started. You drove me away, but I couldn't forget you. God knows I tried in every faceless woman who would have me. I tried to fuck you out of my head, out of my heart, out of my motherfucking DNA. I became someone I hated, someone I didn't recognize, someone who hurt two of my brothers with my careless manwhore ways. Joe and Sam nearly didn't get married because of me!" I slap my chest. "Jace forever has to know I've been intimate with his girl."

"What?" She steps back, one step, and then two.

"I fucked up, can never make it right, can never forget what I did because of *you*."

Fuck. Fuck. Fuck. I grip my hair. Why'd I say that?

Went too fucking far, man.

She runs, and I don't fucking blame her.

I don't stop her.

If this wasn't a fucking island, I'd run too.

But as I know all too well, you can't outrun your past. You can't outrun the heartache. The regret is always there. It follows me like a dark cloud, ready to rain down and wash away any hope, any good, any chance at a tomorrow with my girl.

Thirty

NOW

HOME. FINALLY HOME. I FALL INTO BED EXHAUSTED and more broken than I was when I lost him at eighteen. I thought that hurt. I had no idea how festering adult anger could really hurt so deep, I'm not sure I'll ever be able to pull the dagger out of my heart.

He blames me.

Me.

All these years I've believed I was the victim, the one betrayed. Turns out I was the perpetrator.

I never considered it from his perspective. He didn't even know why I ran, why I moved out, why I shut him out. He obviously figured it out, but in his mind, he did the right thing.

I was the cheater.

I broke my promise to always stand by him.

I ran.

Nate has always said I'm a runner. He forces me to stay and face my conflicts with him. He doesn't let me run.

Matt tried to keep me from running, but I had a brick wall of footballers between me and him.

I pushed him away.

Me.

Fuck my life.

How many other times have I been wrong, felt like the victim when I was really the perpetrator?

Have I been looking at the world from the skewed point of view as a victim of my family's mental abuse?

I thought I was the one being run over by other people's opinions of me and my size. Have I done the same? Did I assume, even expect, to be let down and hurt by Matt? Was I just waiting for an excuse to say *I told you so* to myself? To him?

No one will ever love you the way you are, my mother's voice reminds me as it has over and over again through the years.

Mother is long dead and buried. Why am I letting her rule my life? My opinion of myself?

I have to stop this. *I* decide who I am and what's acceptable for me. Not my family.

I toss off the covers and rush to Nate's room, throwing open the door without even knocking. Thankfully, he's dressing and brushing his teeth.

"I need you to take me to my dad's."

He frowns, holding his hand under his chin to catch the drippings.

"It's time I confronted him," I step closer, "but I really need my best friend there to keep me from breaking down or letting him berate me, or worse, me from killing him."

He spits and talks to the sink, "You know what time it is, Firecracker?"

"No. Don't care." I blindly took a cab home from the airport after taking a commercial flight home. I couldn't stand the idea of flying home on their private jet, the guilt wafting off me like bad cheese. I swivel and march back to my room, throwing on clothes.

Nate meets me in the hall. "It's about fucking time, by the way."

"Yeah, well, we might need backup. The men in my family hate to be woken up."

He chuckles and arches that damn brow of his. "Now I know where you get it from."

I smack his chest. "Shut up." It's true though. I hate to be woken up. I'm a grumpy puss if you do.

My eyes fly to Nate's when we pull up at my dad's and Dwight is standing there, leaning against the side of his Ford F150.

"You said we might need back up. Dwight would be hurt if I called anyone other than him. Besides—"

"He knows a thing or two about family drama." I know enough of his story to know he'll have my back and would never share my shit with anyone.

Nate's smile is sad as he grips my hand. "No matter what happens in there, I'm proud of you, Gabby. Seriously proud."

"Let's see if I can get two words out before I start crying." I wring my hands and force them still. *I can do this.*

"Even if you do, doesn't lessen the importance of this moment. It just means you care. Women feel things deeper than us men. Maybe it's the testosterone. Maybe it's society. But don't let anyone make you feel bad for crying, Firecracker, because I know you have a storm brewing, and it's time your family feels your wrath."

Dwight gives me a big hug before I even make it out of the cab of Nate's truck. "I'm here for you, baby girl. Whatever you need."

I hug him a little tighter. "Love you."

"Ah, now don't make this big ole boy cry. Love you too." He helps me down, motioning to the dark house glowing with flickering light in the living room window. "Go do what you gotta do."

Nate follows, his hand on my back. "I'm going in but will stay silent and in the corner as long as he doesn't make a move on you. If he does, Dwight and I will be on him like we're sacking a quarterback."

I nearly laugh.

Pausing at the door, I turn, resting my palm on his chest. "Thank you for doing this. I know we need to talk when we get home. But I need you to know how much it means to me, knowing you always have my back."

He places his hand over mine. "You never have to thank me, but you're welcome."

I take a steady breath, then another, and knock.

The door flies open with a growl from my father, "What!" His scowl is all too familiar, and the disdain in his eyes has me stepping back into Nate's solid chest.

"Watch it, old man," Nate growls right back.

Dad runs his hand over his face and through his already messy brown hair. "Sorry. No good ever comes from a knock at this time of night." He steps back. "Come in if you're staying."

I step inside, knowing Nate will follow. I glance back, catching a wink from Dwight before the door shuts.

Dad reclaims his recliner; the muted TV sends an eerie light around the room. He waits a beat or two. "I can see it all over your face, Gabriella. You've got something to say. Let's hear it."

Moving into the room, too nervous to sit but unsteady on my feet, I claim the ottoman closer to the couch where I can see Dad. Nate leans on the far wall near the door.

Hands clammy, pulse racing, I clear my throat and dig deep to face the man who hurt me first and possibly did the most damage. "Why was I never enough? Why did Mom hate me so much?"

"You don't—" He moves like he's coming out of his chair, but Nate steps forward. Dad falls back, hands up. "Your mother didn't hate you."

"She didn't love me. I was never right for her. I was too tall, too big, too boyish. I was too everything for her." I hate that my voice cracks, but I push through. "You. I was never enough. Never tough enough, never boy enough. You've treated me like a second-class citizen my whole life. I was only good for *making babies*. Your words. You called me fat. You let Greg, Ry, and Marc make fun of me in this house and out. You didn't protect me. You teased me, endlessly, cruelly."

I swipe at a tear, surprised Dad is staying silent, focused on me, listening.

"I've hated myself my whole life because of you and mom, Greg, Ry, and Marc. I always felt there was something wrong with me because my own family couldn't love me. Whatever I am, it came from you and Mom. It's not like I did this to myself. I didn't choose to be a girl." I point at him. "You did that. My size comes from you. You made me tall and meaty. Yet you hated me for it. Why?"

Why. Why. Why. I cry in my head but manage to keep more tears from falling.

"I didn't hate you," he grates. "I love you."

I huff out a laugh and stand. "You have a horrible way of showing it. You let Mom… Did you know what she told me? The last words out of her mouth?"

He shakes his head, eyes glistening. He always did have a soft spot for Mom.

"She told me, *no one will ever love you the way you are.* It wasn't the first time she said it, but it was the last." My eyes land on Nate, and the murder on his face has me wanting to fall in his arms. This man right here loves me, no matter what.

"She was wrong, Dad," I crack on a shaky sob, pointing at Nate. "He loves me. And the man outside loves me too. They couldn't care less about my size. And I found a man who loves every inch of me, but my fucked-up head has ruined it, believing he could never love someone like me because my own mother told me so. Because my own family couldn't love me the way I was—am."

Dad is on his feet, moving before I can blink the tears away to focus, but Nate smacks a hand to Dad's chest. He stops, looking to Nate. "I'm not going to hurt her, son."

When I nod, Nate releases his hold on my dad and steps behind me, his hand on my back.

Though Dad is free to move forward, he doesn't. "I'm sorry, Gabriella. I never thought how deeply my words would impact you. Your mother thought she was motivating you to do something about your weight. But she was wrong. Her issues with you were more about her and how she felt about herself and her own weight struggles."

Mom struggled with her weight? I never knew. "She was perfect."

He shakes his head. "No, she wasn't. She starved herself to stay the size she was. Maybe that's why I was hard on you. I didn't want to see you struggle as an adult like she did." He moves then, pulling me into a hug I can't return. "Your mother didn't die from cancer. She died from anorexia. She starved herself to death because she was so afraid I could never love her if she gained weight."

He releases me, wiping at his face. "I let her down. I couldn't love her enough. She couldn't believe I didn't care about her size. I'm sorry our issues were taken out on you. You didn't deserve that. I'm so sorry, my butterfly."

I nearly fall over hearing my mom starved herself to death and him using my nickname from childhood. Nate presses into me, giving me his support, taking my weight.

"I don't expect you to forgive me. But it's time for change around here. I heard your man, Matt, loud and clear the other night. I won't ever treat you like that again. I promise. Your brothers already know they need to change too. That's all on me. We're working on it. We were worried about your health but were bad for your heart in other ways."

We stare at each other for a minute before I nod and head for the door, speechless. Of all the ways I thought this would go, I never thought he'd apologize or change. I don't know if he will. Time will tell. But I'm done letting my past rule my future.

Nearly out the door, Dad's "Gabriella" makes me pause. "I'm damn proud of you, Butterfly."

Thirty-One

NOW

"**F**UCK, THAT WAS ROUGH. DAMN NEAR HAD *ME* crying." Nate runs his fingers through my hair while I cry, my head on his lap as he drives us home.

Don't lecture me about seatbelts. I'm a little broken here.

His hand rests on my hip, patting, squeezing, then going back to my hair. "It'll be okay, Firecracker. You got it all out. He blew our minds. Now it's up to you if you want them in your life. But don't decide now. Give it time."

A soft pat on my butt has me lifting up, blinking, to find us in our garage.

"Sorry, I hated to wake you, but you need sleep, in a bed." He helps me down, nearly carries me inside, plopping me down on the couch then heads to the kitchen. He comes back with waters and lifts me enough to sit, my head back in his lap, his hand in my hair, petting. "What happened with you and Matt?"

I tell him. Every painful detail. I break all over again realizing what I've done.

"Fuck me," is all he says for a few minutes after I tell him.

I sit up, wipe my face, blow my nose, and drink some water. I'm going to be dehydrated if I keep crying like this. It has to end sometime, right?

"You need to talk to him." He finally looks my way.

"He blames me. He's right. I gave up on him without giving him a chance to explain. Everyone deserves that."

He nods, deep in thought. "Maybe." He finishes his water and stands. "I'm hungry. Could you eat?"

"That's it? That's all you have to say?"

"No, but I need to think on it." He stops halfway to the kitchen and turns. "I don't think he really blames you. He's mad at himself."

I climb into the bar stool overlooking the kitchen and watch him making loaded scrambled eggs.

"I can't marry you, Nate."

He laughs, sliding his eyes to me. "I know."

"Really?"

"Babe, I know you. You love that man with every fiber of your body, which is why you need to do whatever you can to make it right."

"What if he doesn't want me?"

"Then he's not the man we think he is."

It's so simple to him.

Or maybe it really is that simple.

"And what about when you find someone to marry, Nate? I don't want to lose you." I admit what I've been hiding from him.

"Is that what had you upset with me the other day?" He slides next to me, pulling me into his side. "If I decide there's someone I want to marry, besides you, they will accept you, or they're not the right person for me."

"I don't want to lose you."

"Not going anywhere, Firecracker." He kisses me and gets back to cooking our late-night breakfast.

Things have been less than stellar since returning from Fin and Margot's wedding. They're off on their honeymoon. His accounting team is covering for him, but there are some executive decisions that fall to Joe and me. Things that should be a walk in the park, but my head just isn't in it.

I'm one broken man. I fucked up royally by letting my guilt rule my mouth and temper. I said I blame her, but that's not fair. She didn't drive me to slut around. That's on me. Just like I didn't drive her to be celibate all these years. That was her choice. I've no doubt Nate would have gladly relieved her of any emotional mark I left on her body—if she'd been open to it.

But fuck me if *knowing* she hasn't slept with anyone else doesn't make me hard up to love her so fucking good, she'll never consider trying to forget me or what I do to her body again. I want to be the only one who knows how to make her moan and come like it's my job, my pleasure, my destiny. I want to show her over and over again how much I love her and how sorry I am for being an idiot, then and now.

I respond to a few emails from Fin's team, asking for guidance. Shoot off a proposal to Jace on our next product release for our cell phone's operating system developed by Sam, our app genius.

When I reach the end of what needs my immediate attention, I step away, gazing out my office windows. The view is not nearly as beautiful as the one from my penthouse, which faces the opposite direction, but it's still darn good.

I refill my coffee, wishing it was Macallan. I'm about to take a sip when Monica buzzes me on my desk line. I reach across, pressing the intercom. "Yep."

"There's a Nate Sinclair here to see you."

I take a sip of coffee, *really* wishing it was something stronger. I'm not sure I have what it takes to deal with him today.

Before Monica can ask again, I respond, "Send him in."

I check my calendar on my phone to see how much time I have before my next meeting as my office door opens, and in steps the man I once considered my arch nemesis. We've progressed to amicable partners in ensuring Gabby's every happiness.

I hope this visit doesn't jeopardize that status.

"Matt." He sticks out his hand in offering.

I give it a firm shake. "Nate." There's nothing hostile in his manure. I remain open and optimistic. "Coffee?" I point to the coffee urn. "Water?" I'd offer him something stronger, but I have a feeling if we start, we won't be stopping anytime soon.

"Coffee would be great."

I sit on the couch, my back to the windows, as he pours a cup. Once he's seated in the chair facing me, I wait a tick or two, giving him a chance to settle and have a drink before asking what the fuck he wants.

Amenable, remember?

He places his cup on the coffee table between us. "I need to apologize to you, Matt."

My brows shoot up, never expecting those words to come out of his mouth. "For?"

He scratches the scruff, tipping his head back. "Far too much, I'm afraid." Sitting forward, his hands clasped between his spread knees, his eyes land on me. "For the kiss—"

"Which one?"

He laughs. "Yeah, both I guess. But I only regret one." The asshole smirks.

"Do I want to know which one?"

"Probably not." He sits back, resting a foot on his other knee, arms wide on the armrests. "And for the part I played in keeping you and Gabby apart in college. I fed off her hurt, not even considering your side of the whole thing. All I could think was to protect what's—"

"Mine."

"Yeah, I thought of her as mine. But she never has been. She's always been yours, despite my best efforts."

"You love her?" He's loyal like a best friend, but he didn't kiss her like a mere friend.

"I do, but not in the way you're thinking." He twists his lips. "Actually, that's not true. I *could* love her in that way, if she gave us a shot."

"Are you asking me to back off?"

189

His chuckle is immediate. "Would you, if I were?"

"Fuck, no."

He nods on a smile. "That's good. No, I'm not asking you to back off. I'm asking you to forgive her, man up, and go get your girl."

"I'm working on it."

"Work faster." He stands. "She's miserable, hardly stops crying. It's breaking my damn heart. Make it right, or I'll make it right for *her*."

"You wanted to marry her." I stand toe to toe. I may not play football, but he's got nothing on me size-wise. Not anymore.

"Did I?" His one brow seems to say so much, the rest of his face punctuating his sardonic tone.

Sucking in my top lip, I consider his words. "You're the reason she's here."

"Am I?" He moves for the door. "Don't wait too long, Matt. A girl hurting is a girl ripe for the picking."

I growl, pinning him to the door. "You touch one hair…"

His smile only grows. I push him hard and back up.

He straightens his shirt, brushing at it like I got him dirty. "See what a little incentive can do?"

"You're an ass." I'm not even a bit mad at him. Not anymore.

"True. I can be. But I'm loyal as fuck, and I do love our girl, so do me a solid and lock her down. Do whatever you have to do to make it right and keep it that way."

"And if I need help?" Not that asking him for help is high on my list.

He shrugs. "You have my number. Use it. I'm there." He turns for the door.

"Hey, Nate." I wait until he meets my gaze over his shoulder. "Ever considered coaching when you're done playing ball?"

His eyes narrow. "Maybe."

I nod and pat his shoulder on my way to my desk. "Consider it. There just might be an opening for the Stallions in the near future."

He spins, arms crossed. "What are you doing?"

"I said I'm *working on it*. I've got a few things in the works that need to be finalized before I can make my move." I rap my desk. "Sit on my girl for a bit longer, would ya?"

He nods. "You sure you wouldn't be open to a husband-wife type of arrangement?"

I bark out a laugh. "You mean the two of us sharing her? No fucking chance."

"Yeah, didn't think so." His hand on the knob, his greenish-brown eyes meet mine, sincerity dancing in their hue. "I was talking about sharing you too."

Fuck me. All the air leaves my lungs.

Before I can recover, he's gone.

Jesus, this guy. He's intense. Easygoing as shit but sharp as a tack, and a sexuality that could make a straight man consider experimenting *for him.*

But not this man. I was born for only one person. Whether she was born male or female, it would have always been Gabby.

Thirty-Two

NOW

'VE SURVIVED A WEEK POST-MATT BLOWOUT. I don't know how. I swear I didn't think I'd make it past that first hour on the island when I ran away from his harsh and entirely too true words. It is my fault. All of it. I pushed him away. I was waiting for him to let me down, prove I'm unlovable as my mother had no qualms in reminding me.

New Gabby, as I called myself back then, wasn't really new at all. She was me trying to be someone else, someone everyone, including myself, could like—maybe even love. But the thing is, old Gabby's hang-ups followed me—never dealt with, healed from, or confronted. There was no way to be a new me when the foundation was faulty.

Today, remarkably, I feel more like myself. Old, new, doesn't matter, I know now my parents' hang-ups were about them and not so much about me. Yes, I was a thick kid. Maybe I ate too much. Maybe it's just in my DNA. Today, I'm happy with my body, my size. Maybe I saw my mom starving and, subconsciously driven, ate extra to avoid her fate. I could be smaller, but I'm at the right size for my food intake and fitness level. I won't always work out this hard, this long. There's a good chance

I'll gain weight. It'll be a struggle to love myself at any size. But if I can't love me, how can I ever expect anyone else to?

I always thought that was a crock. I don't know if it's really about me loving myself. I think it's really more about the mindset and the energy I put out in the world. I thought no one could love me. Matt tried. I pushed him away because I didn't believe in his or my ability to love without judgment of my size.

He couldn't love me because I wouldn't let him, and I wouldn't let him because I didn't love me.

I didn't believe I was worthy.

Now, I think I am—or at least I'm getting there. It's a work in progress and probably always will be.

They say everyone has a burden to carry. My weight is mine.

"Jesus, woman, I hate you." Nate huffs in air next to me.

I'm about to fall over, but I won't let these guys see that. Not today.

Ten miles. I pushed them through. They were begging me to stop at mile eight, but I like the number ten.

Any of them could have stopped. The trainers and coaches don't make us run a certain distance. They just want us to increase our endurance and our strength.

Either way, they're not in competition with me. I'm not in competition with them. It's about being better than we were yesterday. I'm my only competition.

I'm taking that to heart, emotionally as well. Besides missing the hell out of Matt, I'm doing better than I was the day before. That's all I can ask of myself.

"I'm working on healing, becoming a better me," I offer as explanation.

"Tell me you're there. Quit torturing us along the way." Parker—the backup quarterback—is bent over, hands on his knees, trying to catch his breath.

I don't miss the way Nate's gaze keeps falling on him. Is there something going on there? It hurts to think of Nate building a relationship that doesn't include me. But at the same time, I want to do the same with Matt. I can't have Nate focused on me when I'm focused on Matt. How fair is that? It's growing pains, our closeness morphing into something else. I hope.

"Incoming." Nate draws my attention over my shoulder to find Sam and Jace nearing the edge of the field.

My heart skips a beat. "Do you think something has happened to Matt?"

Nate urges me forward on a chuckle. "Don't be so dramatic. I'm sure lover boy is just fine." He squeezes my hand. "Besides kicking himself for screwing up y'all's weekend."

I stop my frown as we near Sam and Jace. I don't want them to think I'm frowning *at* them. "Is everything okay? Is Matt okay?"

Sam swats at Jace. "See, told you we should've called first."

He flinches but only smiles.

"He's fine. I mean physically." She nudges Jace.

"Do you think we can talk?" he asks.

Nate touches the small of my back. "I'll see ya later." He gives a quick *hey* to Sam and Jace and walks away, leaving me alone with Matt's family and no idea what's happening.

"Um," I look down at my current state, "I'm a sweaty mess. Could you wait while I take a quick shower? Fifteen minutes, tops."

"Yes. Sure." Sam points to the bleachers. "Alright if we sit there?"

"Of course, but there's a lounge if you'd rather wait inside," I offer.

Her gaze floats over the field. "It's such a beautiful day. We'll wait here."

"Okay." I back away. "I'll hurry." I turn and jog, my legs hating me with every step.

"No rush, Gabby," Jace hollers after me.

I rush anyway, hurrying through my shower, saving my hair for later, and dress quickly. They're important bigwigs, They've got better things to do than wait for me on a football field.

When I turn the corner, the two of them are laughing. Jace has sluffed his suit jacket and rolled up his sleeves, showing off his muscular arms and tats. Sam's face is upturned to the sun; she's leaning back, feet on the bench in front of them, eyes closed. Her hair looks redder than his in the sunlight, but there's no missing the two are siblings. Same nose, same blue eyes, same bone structure, but where she's feminine, he's all masculine and brawn with a sadness in his eyes much like I've seen in Matt's these last few weeks. A sadness that wasn't there when we were eighteen.

That reminder makes my heart ache for the part I played in putting the sadness there.

My step falters. Is that why they're here? To talk about the regrets Matt has involving these two and Joe. I'm not sure I want to have that conversation.

Jace zooms in on me.

Too late. I've been spotted. "Hey." I offer them bottled waters I snagged from the fridge.

"Thanks."

"Thank you." Sam pats the seat next to her.

Jace pops the lid off his bottle and switches with Sam. I smile. What a simple kindness. A brother looking out for his sister.

I straddle the lower bench so I can see them better. I open my water, wondering if *my* brothers would ever consider opening it for me without me asking. Not that I need them to, but the idea that they would even think of me and *want* to do it because they can, not because I can't.

"Listen, we just wanted to come and talk—"

"I'm sorry," Sam blurts.

"What?" Jace frowns at his sister.

"For what?" I ask.

Sam brushes off her brother. "For anything I might have said to upset you when it was just you, me, and Margot. I didn't know who you were to him… That you had a history. I…" she throws her hands up, "… had no idea he'd loved and lost someone. I don't know *that* Matt. I spoke out of turn and probably set you back."

"It wasn't—"

"What made you take a different plane home than us?"

My face heats, regretting what happened on the island and my selfish choice to not fly home with them. I look away and find Nate standing outside the locker room door, scanning us—me. He tips his head, brow arched, asking, *you okay, Firecracker?*

I give him a silent *I'm okay* with a tip of my head and a small wave.

He nods his acknowledgment and heads toward the parking lot. That same ache of him walking away and me building a life that he's not really apart of flares.

"You and Nate are close." Jace pulls my attention as his gaze follows Nate.

"He's my best friend. He's been my rock when I didn't have anyone." I can't have them thinking bad of Nate, or that he has anything to do with why Matt and I broke up the first time, or why the second time didn't work out.

"That's good. Everyone needs that special person who will be there for them no matter what." His words speak a truth that seems to hit him hard. He breaks eye contact and studies something in the distance I'm pretty sure he's not really seeing.

Jace forever has to know I've been intimate with his girl. Matt's words come floating back. Is that what I'm seeing in Jace, the sadness, the loss over what Matt did?

"Matt feels horrible how things were left with you two," Sam's voice brings me back to her. "We know Matt mentioned the stuff that went down before my wedding. We just wanted you to know, we don't blame him." She eyes Jace, but his attention is elsewhere, or he doesn't agree with her.

The tightness of Jace's jaw and the lines in his furrowed brow tell a different story. "You sure about that?" I ask. Maybe he hasn't forgiven Matt.

Sam tips her shoulder into Jace, who looks between the two of us and lets out a punch of air. "Look. I'll be as honest as I can, but this whole situation is rough and not something I want to delve into. If anyone's to blame, it's me. My relationship with Veronica is what set all of this in motion." He points to his sister. "Her setting up you and Joe, trying to break you up and using Matt to do it. None of that would have happened if it weren't for me cutting her off."

"You cut her off because she was nasty and mean to me." Sam's voice rises, but then she takes a second to calm down, focusing on me. "It's a whole convoluted mess, and if you decide you want to be a part of our family—and don't be mistaken, related or not, we are a family—then come over, we'll have drinks, and I'll tell you the whole soap opera, swear-it's-true version.

"In the meantime, just know Matt was tricked. He didn't know he was being set up. He didn't know Bonnie was really Jace's Veronica. Matt was just being Matt," she grimaces, "Sorry, I know you don't want to hear that. But he's changed since all of that went down. He's a different guy. I'll be honest, though, not necessarily for the better. Him not sleeping around is great. Him beating himself up for something he got caught in the middle of is not okay. He won't forgive himself."

She elbows Jace. He scowls but turns his eyes on me. "You've narrowed in on the fact I'm not okay with the Veronica situation and her hurting my family."

"She was hurting," Sam interjects.

"Not an excuse to ruin other people's lives," he growls, takes a breath, and smiles at me. "It's not easy. None of this is easy. I don't blame Matt. Do I want to kill him, knowing he's touched what was mine? Yes, sometimes I do. Then I remember she really isn't mine, and he had no idea she was anything to me." He stands, takes a few steps, running his fingers through his dark, thick locks, then turns back to us. "There's a lot to unravel here, Gabby. The bottom line is we don't blame Matt."

He squats in front of me, close enough to see the depth of emotions in his blue gaze. "He loves you. He never stopped. When he makes his move, and have no doubt he will, just give him a chance. Please don't hold over him what none of us do. That's really all we came to say."

"I like you, Gabby. You fit us. Please give him a chance to make things right," Sam pleads.

"Have you considered the fact that he might not want to make things right? He blames me for what happened to y'all."

"Pssh, that's hooey. He was upset. He doesn't blame you." She's so sure.

"He doesn't." Jace plops down on his ass next to me. "He told me he fucked up, spoke out of anger and hurt. He's been waiting seven years to show you how much you hurt him, Gabby. You'll have to forgive him for taking it a little too far. Seven years is a long time to hold all that in, then shove all the other stuff that happened with Veronica on top, and it was a powder keg waiting to blow."

"So, what do I do now?"

Sam's smile is radiant. "You wait, but be ready. He's coming, and he's coming big."

Thirty-Three

NOW

PACE MY OFFICE, WAITING ON FIN TO CALL, AND for his PA, Angela, to drop off the papers he promised me would be here a few hours ago.

After shooting off a text to Nate to be sure my girl's holding up okay, I pour another cup of coffee—though, I probably shouldn't. I'm amped up enough as it is.

Joe comes waltzing in a few minutes later. "Any news?" He plops down on my couch. He looks relaxed, but his hands are twitchy. Probably jonesing for his wife. Those two are never far apart.

"No." I toss him a water. He's been cutting back on his coffee in-take, no reason to tempt him. With that thought, I dump my coffee in the sink in my private bathroom and grab a water for myself.

"Thanks for letting me in on the deal. It means a lot."

I hold up my hand, feeling guilty I didn't ask him in the first place. "It's the way it should be. The brothers together. Who knows, we may be starting a whole new conglomerate on our way to world domination."

That gets a chuckle that's quickly cut off when Sam walks in.

"Sweetness." His gaze eats her up.

I point between the two of them. "No fucking on my couch."

Joe secures her on his lap, nuzzling her ear, granting her giggle, before giving me his eyes. "You mean ever or right now?"

"Ever, fuckwad." I hand Sam a water and take the chair closest to them. Their happiness is hard to take sometimes, especially right now when I'm so close but still so fucking far. "Could you two," I wave at them, "I don't know… lower the volume on your love parade?" If I scowl any harder, my forehead will be over my mouth.

"Ah, Matty," Sam snickers. "It'll be okay, the love parade is coming for you."

"It's taking its own sweet time," I grumble, swallow the rest of my water, and chuck it in the trash across the room. I was feeling good about this, but as time grows short, so does my patience and certainty.

Just as my line buzzes, Jace, Michael, and Victor stroll in. "Is there a party I don't know about?"

They just laugh and take a seat as I pick up.

"I have Fin on the line for you," Monica advises.

When the call clicks over, I shush everyone. God forbid I do this without them as witness.

"Fin."

"Yeah, Brother. Sorry it all took a little longer than anticipated. You know, everyone's on island time. Angela should be to your office any second. She has the power of attorney so you can sign for me. We're flying out today and will be there before the deadline, in case you need me."

Angela walks in, falters when she sees my full house, and smiles softly before bringing the folder to me.

"I have the papers. You don't need to cut your trip short. We've got it handled." I open the file and peruse its contents.

"Pixie and I want to be there. It's not every day my brother gets the girl he's loved since he was barely an adult. The island's not going anywhere. Next trip, the six of us are coming alone." Muted voices, then, "I gotta go take care of some Pixie business before our flight."

"Yeah, I don't want to know what that means." I chuckle, falling into my desk chair.

"Nah, but you will. Just wait. Your girl's the same. We McIntyres know how to pick them. We like 'em hard to catch, making us work for it, appreciate it with every fiber of our being, then we remind them over and over again why they said *yes*."

Now, I'm picturing Fin doing his wife *over and over again*. "Thanks for that visual."

"You're welcome." A long pause. "Hey."

"Yeah?"

"Everything is going to be fine, Matt. Trust me. Trust in *her*."

"I'm trying. I want it to be Friday already."

"You don't have to wait. You can go to her today."

"Yeah, I do. I have a point to make. She needs to know where I stand."

"And we'll be right there with you."

"Counting on it, Brother."

"See you soon." The line disconnects, but not before I hear Margot giggling in the background.

Pixie business. Yeah, I didn't need to hear that.

Dad walks in with our personal lawyer, not our corporate one. "You got it, Son?"

"I do."

"Joseph." Dad waves him over and only shakes his head on a smirk when Joe kisses Sam before setting her on the couch when he stands. "I swear you two are attached at the hip."

"It's not the *hip*, Dad."

Dad just laughs, patting Joe on the shoulder as they draw closer. "TMI, Son. TMI."

Joe shakes it off.

We all know he and Sam do it like rabbits, *everywhere*. We try to ignore it and just pray they aren't doing it in the immediate vicinity of where we eat, live, and work. We all know never to use our keys to get into their apartment. No one wants to walk in on the caveman givin' it to his nerdy girl. Ask Michael. He still swears he's going to go blind from the one time he let himself in to drop off a delivery, believing they'd already left for the office. They hadn't. Enough said.

Around my desk, Joe at my side, directed by our lawyer, witnessed by our dad, and overseen by the rest of our family, minus Mom, Fin, and Margot, we sign the contract, initiate the money transfer, and officially become the owners of an NFL football team.

NOW

"**Y**OU'RE BEING WEIRD." I SCURRY OUT OF HIS hold as he tries to get me to sit, and sidestep into the kitchen. "Do you need to get laid or something?"

"Are you offering, Firecracker?"

What the… I lean over the counter to catch him sprawled on the couch. His eyes fly to mine. "Yes, Nate, after seven years, I'm finally ready to have sex with you." I toss him a soda and sit down next to him. "You wanna do it here or your bed?"

"Here's fine." He pats his lap. "Hop on, babe."

I freeze, considering it, not actually having sex, but crawling on his lap to see how far he'll take it. "Would you die if I actually did?"

"It'd be a dream come true." He tips my chin and kisses me gently. Something flashes across his face before he steals it away. My eyes prick with emotions from the sincerity that remains. "I've always wanted you, Gabby. You never believed you would be enough. But you would be." He slings his arm around my shoulder, pulling me in as he sinks lower and turns on the TV. "Now, we'll have to be happy with salacious texts and stolen moments."

I have no idea what he's talking about. "Are you kicking me out?"

His face grows solemn, his eyes on the screen. "Nah, would never kick you out. My home will always be your home."

He's been off all week, more touchy-feely than normal one minute and rushing out the door the next.

We have a rare day off, though training is supposed to be optional in the off-season, but most of us still work out four to five days a week. Coaches expect it, even though it's *optional*. Training camp starts at the end of July.

Rumor has it there's a big announcement coming, but no one knows what it's about. Some think we're being sold; others think training camp will be someplace new this year. I'm the newbie. I don't know what to think. All I know is this is the first season I've looked forward to in a long time, and it's all because of the man by my side.

Nate tunes into the streaming channel for the Dallas Stallions. Typically, it's for press conferences, according to Nate. The team logo is on the screen, no live feed yet.

"What are we watching?"

"There's a press conference today, then a team meeting tomorrow."

I groan, "On Saturday? Why didn't I get notified?" Alarm has me ratcheting off the couch. "Did I get traded again?"

"Fuck, you scared me." He grabs my hand. "Sit. You didn't get traded."

"You don't know that." I study his face, stoic, sentimental demeanor, and nervousness. "You know, don't you? That's why you've been weird this week." I pace away. "I can't go to another team that hates me. I've had to work so hard to be accepted here. I can't do that all over again somewhere else! Go through all the scrutiny again? I'll quit." I turn and smash into his chest.

He grips my hip and shoulder. "Gabs, calm down. You can't quit. You're under contract." He presses his warm hand to my cheek. "It doesn't matter because you're not going anywhere. It's just a mix-up in the office. I'll send an email and find out." He hugs me to his chest.

I settle in deeper. *That's my bestie. Always looking out for me.*

204

"Firecracker. I couldn't have picked a more suitable nickname." He tugs me back to the couch.

"I thought you called me that because you think I'm smoking hot." I wink and try not to cringe from the boast.

"That too, but mainly for your ability to go off, hot and ready." He kisses my head as we realign our position on the couch.

A moment later, the screen flicks to life. "It's the press room at the stadium," Nate fills me in.

There's commotion as reporters settle in seats. We can only see a few rows and mainly the backs of their heads. The camera must be on the ceiling like a projector. Up front, there's a long table with mics set along the edge, one for each seat.

The lady I recognize as the team's public relations rep steps up to a microphone and advises that the press conference will begin momentarily and to hold their questions until after the announcements. She reassures the grumbling room there will be time for questions at the end.

"That's Rita. You met her your first day."

"She looked familiar, but I forgot her name."

Nate's phone buzzes three times in a row. He checks it, types back, and then sets it face down on the end table next to him. His knee starts to bounce.

"What's wrong?"

"Nothing."

A commotion on the screen has him tipping his head toward the TV. "It's starting."

I sit up, feeling like I should be upright and not lounging on Nate's chest for this.

A line of suits enters the room. It takes me a second to recognize the owner, coach, and then… "What the…" My gaze bounces between Nate and the familiar faces on the screen. "What?!" I point to the screen, try to stand, but Nate grabs my waist, holding me down.

"Just watch, Firecracker. Let it unfold the way he intended."

I lean back. *He intended.* "You knew?" My eyes don't leave the screen as Fin, Joe, and Matt take their seats next to the coach, owner, and Rita, the PR lady.

"He asked me to be sure you watched the press conference. I don't know anything for certain, but—"

"You suspect you know what's going on."

"I only know he's been working on this for a while, and it's why he stayed away." He squeezes my shoulder. "Breathe, Gabs. It's going to be okay."

"I hope you're right." I lay my head on his chest, needing the comfort.

The owner of the team speaks first, thanking everyone for coming and reiterates they are to hold their questions till the end. *"I've been the proud owner of the Stallions for many years. I'm proud of the organization we've built. Through the good and the bad, we've stuck together. But I'm getting older, as many of you like to point out, and when an offer to buy—"*

"No!" Ohmygod! He didn't. "He bought our team, didn't he?"

The now former owner continues, *"—I'm happy to announce Matt, Fin, and Joe McIntyre are the new owners of the Dallas Stallions."*

"Holy shit," I whisper.

"Fuck me. He did it." Nate squeezes my leg as he sits up. I join him, knee to knee, shoulder to shoulder. "He fucking did it." He beams at me. "You'll never be traded again, Firecracker. Welcome to the Dallas Stallions for life, or until you decide you don't want to play anymore."

Holy smoly. He bought a football team. Did he do it for me? Is this the big move Jace and Sam were warning me about? I can't even… Can I be with Matt if he's the owner and still play ball? Do I want to? Both? Either? Fuck me. I wish I was there in person to look into his eyes and ask what this means. "You're not going anywhere either, even if you want to. If I stay, you stay."

He bumps me softly. "Not going anywhere, Gabs. I told you we'd be best friends for life, and I meant it. I finally got you back, not letting you go now."

"You're going to make me cry."

He nods to the TV. "I don't think it's me who's going to make you cry. Your boy is up."

Fin spoke first, but I've not a clue what he said besides introducing himself and his brothers.

Then it was Matt's turn. "*We want the Stallions' organization to know we don't plan on jumping in and making changes right away. We want to observe, find ways to improve what needs improving, and leave what's working alone. We want our organization to be at the forefront of change in a primarily male-dominated sport from the executives down to the players. We want an atmosphere of equality, where we offer equal opportunity and reward for everyone.*

"*We'll be reviewing player contracts and where improvements need to be made to ensure equality between players, male or female. Equal pay for a job well done. Now, that doesn't mean everyone gets paid the same. But it does mean the number one kicker in the nation shouldn't also be the lowest paid kicker in the nation, who also happens to be the only female player in the NFL. Our players' pay will equal how they perform on the field and keep to the guidelines of their contracts. We will not discriminate between male and female players. Just as we won't discriminate between male and female executives, coaches, trainers, even janitors. If you do a good job, your pay will reflect that.*

"*We still have a code of conduct that all players and employees need to adhere to. We're not changing that. What we are changing is an end to slanderous rumors about players' habits in the bedroom. If it doesn't affect their performance on the field, then it's nobody's business. If the code of conduct is broken, then it's team business, and not the public's business. We do not discriminate on the basis of race, color, religion, national origin, sex, or sexual orientation.*

"*I am not saying this is necessarily happening in this organization. I am stating that going forward, we will ensure it doesn't. We will be an example, a beacon, for welcoming new talent on the field and at every level in the Stallions' organization, regardless of sex or identity.*

"*We will expect this ideology from every employee. If you don't like it,*" he points to the side, *"then there's the door. No hard feelings. If you're like-minded, then we're glad you're here. We hope you stay.*

"With that said, every reporter who steps into this room, on the field, in the corporate offices, training facility, and locker room will be expected to report the truth where it is relevant to the game. If you can't do that, then," he points to the door, *"don't let it hit you on the ass on your way out. Personal lives are not up for discussion unless the player brings it up.*

"One last item before I hand it over to my brothers for questions. This issue is specific to our team because we have the only female player in the NFL, but it applies in every walk of life, in every industry. Stop shaming Gabriella Chisholm, or any woman, for her size. It's a demeaning tactic that distracts us from the actual issue. If you're talking about Gabby's size and sexual orientation, then you're not talking about women in the NFL, which means we're not moving forward, but going backward. This will not be tolerated inside this organization or out. Be warned."

Matt thanks everyone for their time and steps out of the room, leaving Fin and Joe to answer questions. And, boy, are there questions.

"Wow." I fall back on the couch.

Nate falls next to me, squeezing my hand. "That's quite a guy you got there. Was that a big enough gesture for you?"

"Holy—"

He chuckles. "Yeah, he's *that* and a bag of chips."

Thirty-Five

NOW

TEXT NATE TO LET HIM KNOW I'M ON MY WAY. I hated to leave Fin and Joe to answer questions, but I didn't say anything they didn't agree with or weren't aware of. I love football, but I've avoided it for years because of Gabby. Now, she's the reason I'm interested again, the reason I even considered becoming an owner in the first place.

What she's been going through, what Nate has been going through and countless others, it isn't right. In the corporate world, who you're fucking isn't anybody's business. As long as you don't break their code of conduct, what happens in the bedroom stays in the bedroom. Someone's sexual orientation shouldn't be a topic of discussion, not in the shaming way it's being portrayed in the media. If they want to speculate who they're dating, that's different, but making it seem like they are unfit to play in the NFL because they love the soft and pink or the long and hard is not acceptable.

I don't truly believe we can control the world's opinion, but I do know I can help my girl and her best friend and anyone else in the organization who's being unfairly treated because of who they are or aren't sleeping with. We have the means to make a difference in one organization. Maybe it will have a ripple effect, and the tides will change in favor of equal opportunity for all. In the meantime, we will be soaking up all the talent.

Bottom line, though, my girl was being hurt, and it was within my power, reach, and bank account to help. So, I did—*we* did. Plus, the tax write-offs from owning a sports team would quickly pay for the team itself, and then some.

It's not just a heartwarming move.

My brothers would do no different for their girls. Sam's work was being overlooked when she was an intern, not once, but over and over again because the head programmer was threatened by her brain, and perhaps even more so by the fact she wore a skirt. The reason didn't matter. Joe nearly ripped his department apart until they understood talent subterfuge was not going to be tolerated. He did it for the wellbeing of our company, but he mainly did it for *her*.

Fin changed the way he worked, learned to delegate, and moved to Austin to live with Margot until she graduated. He didn't want to be away from her. They'd already wasted years in an on-and-off, hot-and-cold kind of situation. He didn't think he had room for her in his life, until he *made* room. He flipped his world upside down, with our support, and he doesn't regret it, not for a second.

My gesture is much the same. I hope. We'll see.

I pull my Maybach into the driveway of Nate's house. Before I even make it around my car, my girl is running toward me full steam.

"Matt," she cries, "what did you do?" She slams into me, all arms and legs, squeezing the fuck out of me.

Thank fuck. Even if she's mad I bought her team, she's still happy as fuck to see me. I booster her up, a hand on her ass, my face buried in her neck, and fist her hair, holding her like I never intend to let her go—which I don't. "I bought your team because, fuck, I didn't like the way you were being treated. If you're mad, I'm sorry, but I'm not sorry I did it. It was the only way I knew I could make it better for you. I won't apologize for that."

"Not mad." She peppers my face with wet kisses from her lips and her tears.

Christ, she's a mess, and I love it. "Come home with me for the weekend. I need my girl. I need to explain some things, but first I need to love the fuck out of you."

She nods, releasing her hold, and I let her slide down my body, pressing my rock-hard need against her. She sucks in air, making me want to do it again, but with no clothes on.

"I packed you a bag." Nate moves closer. He came out after she did, watching from the doorway. He looks like I'm stealing his best friend. I guess I am.

"When?" She tears her eyes from me to talk to him. I feel cold from the loss and saddle up to her back.

"Earlier. It should be enough for the weekend. I have a feeling you won't really be needing any of it except maybe your toothbrush. Though I'm sure he'd lend you his." He hands me the bag.

She kisses his cheek and grips his neck as he bends to hug her tighter. "You're always the best, one step ahead of me, clearing the way. I love you." Her voice cracking twists my gut. Does she think she's losing him? Does he think that too?

"Love you too, Firecracker." He pats her butt. "Go on. I'll see you at the meeting tomorrow. Maybe we can have lunch." He catches my gaze over her shoulder. His pain is evident and then gone when he kisses her cheek.

"Why don't you get in the car?" I sweep her tears away. "I want to talk to Nate for a sec." I remote-start the car. Can't have my girl getting hot.

We both watch her climb in. She looks back, her gaze bouncing between us, smiles softly, and closes the door.

"Thank you for your help." I offer him my hand.

"What? No kiss?" He chuckles when I glare.

"Fucker." I can't help but like the guy. I hated him for what happened before either of us knew Gabby. Then I hated him for wanting what was mine. Then I hated him for getting to see and love what was mine every day I didn't get to.

"You take care of her. She's all Amazon Warrior on the outside and soft goo on the inside. Don't forget that." He turns so all I can see is his profile, his jaw tight, and I swear I see his eyes glistening.

"Never." I clench his shoulder. "Hey, I'm not taking her from you."

"Aren't you?" His gaze snaps back to mine.

I sigh and drop my arm. "I suppose in some way, yes. But you're her best friend. I don't expect or want to take that away from her—or you. I know what you did for her. What you did to get her traded to Dallas. You started all this. The trade to the Stallions, the proposal, the charity event… It was all you. You selflessly gave her what she wanted, needed, with no regard for yourself."

What she needed was me—and him.

The guy I hated brought my girl back to me, not for me, but for *her*.

He chuckles and swipes at his eyes. "I got her back. Or at least closer. It wasn't all selfless." His smile slips. "I would have married her, Matt. I would have loved her till the end of my days, given her babies. We would have had a good life."

I've no doubt he believes that. "But would you have been happy?"

His shoulders rise and slowly fall. "She feels like my other half. She always has. I would have made sure she was happy, even if I wasn't."

It happens before I even make a conscious thought: I hug him, hard. "Then she's not your one if you wouldn't have been happy too. He or she—or they—are still out there. Have faith." I pat his back and step away. "In the meantime, you're stuck with me and her. I have no intention of keeping you away. In fact, I want to pull you closer."

His eyes light up.

I hold out my hand. "No, I'm not asking you to be in a throuple with us. Your dick isn't getting anywhere near her or me."

The fucker laughs.

"But you should come hang out with us, get to know the guys—our family—and their girls. We have a standing Tuesday night happy hour, which will probably turn into a potluck once Margot has the baby, and Sam won't be far behind, the way her and my brother fuck like it's a sport."

"Really?"

"You're her family, Nate. You gave up millions on your contract to get her here. You worked your scheming magic to get her and me in the same town, same room, and you helped get us to today. You're loyal as fuck to her. In my world, that means you're family to me too. And if you're interested, we'll have a long working relationship as well. You'll have a new contract to review and hopefully sign on Monday. You'll get your money back, plus some, and an offer to be a coach when you're ready." I wave my hand. "Hell, Nate, you can pretty much take any job you want, just don't stop being my girl's best friend."

"And if I decide to leave?"

I didn't expect that. Maybe he's hurting too much to stay. "Then we'll be really fucking sad, and I'll hold my girl while she cries her eyes out over missing you. But if that's what you need, I won't hold you back and will help you get whatever job you want, even if I have to create one."

"Damn, you sure you won't marry me too?"

His easy way about him, it seems like a throwaway tease, but there's a glimmer of hope in his eyes. I hate to dash it away, but it's never going to happen.

"Yeah, asshole, I'm sure." I back up. "Thanks again, Nate. See you tomorrow and on Tuesday. No excuses."

Thirty-Six

NOW

HAND IN HAND, MATT LEADS ME INTO HIS HOME. It's still as impressive as ever, and just as daunting. What do I know about living in a penthouse, surrounded by the place he works, his family's multi-billion-dollar tech company, and his brothers who live in the towers as well in their own penthouses? It seems like a dream. My place in New York was a tiny one-bedroom flat. I could have afforded more, but I didn't want to waste my money. I didn't want or need more, not there. I never planned on staying once Nate left. It was more my prison than a home.

Relief hits me like a pile of bricks.

"Hey." Matt frowns, and I want to soothe it away. "What's wrong? You just squeezed the hell out of my hand."

"Oh." I try to release him, but he only holds me tighter until I stop fighting, then he runs his lips across my knuckles. "It just kinda hit me. I'm home, and I don't have to leave. I've been afraid to settle in, worried I'd get traded again. The Stallions have been nice enough, but I can't say they gave off warm fuzzies or happy-to-have-me vibes."

"Well, now you don't have to worry about any of that. You can stay

214

with the Stallions or go somewhere else, do something else. It's your choice. The control is in your hands."

"You mean, your hands."

He steps into me, backing me up until I hit the back of the couch. "My hands are your hands. All that I have is yours. You only need ask."

He's so close. I close my eyes for a moment, breathing him in when he runs his nose along mine.

"I never blamed you. I'm sorry I said that. We opened a door on a shitload of hurt. I lashed out, but I didn't mean it. I made my choices. I have to live with the consequences. One of them being that I pushed you away when all I really wanted was to pull you closer. Forgive me." He squeezes my hips.

I sigh and lean into his hold. "Forgiven. I'm sorry too. You were right. I ran. I didn't give you a chance to give your side of what happened. I'm sorry I doubted you." I grip the back of his neck. His forehead meets mine. "I was really doubting me."

He nods. "I know. And I know we have lots to talk about." He kisses the corner of my mouth, then slides to the other side, kissing. "I need to love you now. Talk later."

"I need you to know something." I bite my lip, running my hand down his arm. He steps back, waiting, but I move with him, not wanting the distance. "I never stopped loving you. I may have doubted your love for me, but I never doubted mine. I promise if you give us another chance, I won't run again. I'll stay and fight with you, for you, for us."

"Fuck." He ends the distance between us. His urgent kiss turns tender before he pulls back. "That's all I want. Another chance. Let me love you, Gabriella, today, tomorrow, always."

"Yes. Forever, yes." I'd cry if I wasn't so turned on.

With the speed of a *stallion*, he gets us to his room, on his bed, and naked in no time flat. Worshiping words of praise across my skin, he kisses down my neck and back till I steal his mouth, needing my lips on his.

Tongue deep as it can go, I moan and arch up when his fingers find my core, slipping in slowly.

"Fuck. This pussy is going to be the end of me." To my dismay his slips off me to settle at my side, his gaze between my legs, watching, licking his lips. "I need to taste you. It's been too long."

I want that too, just not… I grip his shoulder, garnering his eyes. "I need you. Now."

"Fuck, baby, your words." He speeds up, his finger going deep until he finds my spot. "There's my girl."

My toes curl, and I can't stop the whimper as it slides up my throat.

"Gotta make you come, Gabby, get you ready for me. I know you haven't…" he cuts off and looks away, pain morphing his face.

I cup his cheek and bring him back to me. I'm taken aback by the shimmer in his eyes. "What's wrong? Tell me." My own tears form. Does he not want me?

He shakes his head, moves closer, his forehead pressed to my neck. "I love that you haven't been with anyone else, but at the same time, it rips my heart out to think you've been alone and unloved all these years." His pained noise has me hugging him to me.

"I don't regret it," I cry into his neck, then force his head up. "Need your eyes." His tear-stained cheeks nearly do me in. My man, so tough, and so sensitive too. "I'd rather have a lifetime of no sex than have another man touch me who's not you."

His growl reverberates in the room, and I clench around his fingers that have stilled but are still deep inside. "No one is ever touching what's *mine*."

Clench.

"Only yours, Matthew."

He starts to move again, rubbing my G-spot, kissing my neck. When he finally licks and sucks on my nipple, I nearly come off the bed. "Fucking mine," he breathes over the wet peak.

Oh God, yes, please!

Clench. Clench. Clench.

I undulate under his touch, grinding, lifting, needing. "Please."

"Yes, fuck, just like that, Gorgeous. Give it to me. I need to feel my girl come." He latches on my breast and doesn't let up.

I grip his back with one hand and the headboard with the other, leverage to grind against him and to keep me from flying off the bed.

It builds.

It's been so long. This feeling is immense. He undoes me, flooded with memories of how we used to be. How well he loved my body, sent me sailing, rising to new peaks I didn't even know existed. My chest heaves and tears fall.

I've missed him so much.

I've missed *us* so terribly much.

"Gabby?"

"Don't you fucking stop," I grind through near sobs.

He doesn't. "Baby, please don't cry."

"Can't help it." I urge his mouth to mine. "Miss you so much," I sob.

He steals it, sucks it right out of my mouth as he kisses me hard, coaxing my mouth wider so he can go deeper. Tongues lashing, moans colliding, my body stretching for his, clenching, drawing him deeper, trembling and needing his every touch.

Too many years.

My body has known no other pleasure than that given by the man before me. I tried over the years, but it didn't work. My body didn't want anyone else's touch or mine. Only *his*.

He's a siren song, tuned to my frequency, that flips the switch and has me humming to the tune only he produces. It rumbles in my legs, taking my breath and arching my back. It rises and rises, blurring my vision, controlling my limbs, and echoes my pleasure around the room.

"Please." I pant.

"Got you." He kisses my breast, a quick lick. "Always got you, Gabriella." Then he latches on and bites, pulls, sucks, and licks again on glorious repeat as he strokes my insides.

Trembling. Trembling. I fall apart.

Rising and rising. I grip him so hard. Hard. Hard.

Wave after wave. He strums my tune.

It's a serenade. A song of love. A tune for two.

Ruptured. Torn apart. His mouth puts me back together.

Kissing and kissing until I can breathe and see his godly handsome face, full of love and worry in equal measure.

"Love you, my man."

He lets out a heavy sigh. "Baby, you scared me."

"No more than I scare myself with how much I need you." I urge him over me, caressing his face, shoulders, and hair. "Need you to do that again, only this time with your cock."

Thirty-Seven

NOW

LOST IN HER MOUTH, HER MOANS AND NEEDY sighs, her hands and legs pulling and pulling at me, I finally slip into the only heaven I've ever known.

I'm slammed back to eighteen-year-old Matt's head, chanting *don't fucking come* on repeat. Because this girl, right here, has been my one and only bliss. No one before her, no one after her, until this moment, has mattered.

Only a few pumps and my girl's in sync, moaning my name, making me fight the urge to fill her, ending this too soon. Seven years and it's like a day hasn't passed. My sweet girl below me, giving me the gift of her body, her heart, her trust.

"I'll never hurt you again, Gabriella." I kiss her jaw, nuzzle behind her ear, making her shake and squeeze me so fucking good.

"I know," she mewls, nipping at my shoulder.

Fuck. I shudder, thrust deeper, groaning, "Love that." She does it again and runs her nails up my back. My hips punch forward as my abdominal muscles tremble.

Fuck. Fuck. Fuck. Don't fucking come.

She sighs and gasps, clenching around me so fucking good.

"Love you, baby." I kiss a trail down to her breast, rise up, knees wide, hips grinding deep so I can suck on her nipples. Missed these lovely ladies. Gotta show them how much.

"Yes." She arches back.

Fuck, that feels good. I do it again, so she does it again.

"Fuck. Fuck. Fuck." I pound into her. "Not gonna last," I growl.

I rub her clit with my thumb, balanced on one arm over her head, nose to nose. "Need you to come."

Her mouth opens and closes, licking her lips, her tongue teasing me.

"Fuck, I want that tongue on me. On my cock." Balls squeezing. *Fuck.*

She moans and nods, but she's too far gone for words.

"My girl gonna come for me?"

She groans and clenches around me, tighter and tighter. "Yes, fuck, just like that."

Pounding faster, harder. Rubbing her little nub I want to suck, a tremble up my spine has a growl rippling between us. Not gonna… "Fuck. Now, baby. Now."

"Matt!" she screams, gripping me so tight in her arms and her pussy, my sweet girl comes.

"Fuck, yes!" I let go, head thrown back, I piston my release into her, coating her walls, bare pussy sucking me deep, taking it all, and all, and all.

I shudder as another wave releases, thinking about my cum being the *only* cum to ever be in her pussy. Ever.

Fucking mine.

I settle over her, cock still home, wrap her in my arms and kiss her tenderly until we're both calmer. I brush her cheeks, needing to know how she is. She fucking broke down while we were… "You okay, baby?"

She nods, wraps her legs around me and squeezes. I close my eyes and press in. Fuck that feels good.

"Yeah, I'm great. You?"

I swivel my hips slowly, rubbing against her clit, her juices and mine mingling between us, the only sound besides us.

"Never better." I press my mouth to hers. Her tongue comes out to lick my top lip the way she does, and the way my cock loves, as it starts to swell, coming alive for his girl.

I know we need to talk, but I really need to love her one more time. This time slow and easy until she's moaning my name and coating my cock with her pleasure. Yep, totally hard now.

She gasps.

I smile.

"You're hard?"

"Yeah, baby, not done loving you." I kiss her. "Can you take me again?" She's going to be sore. She's barely not a virgin even after all this time. The last time we were together—the last time she had sex—was the day after she gave me her virginity. Sex is still new to her soft and pink.

I need to be gentle, I remind myself.

"Yes, please."

"So fucking polite." I nibble her ear. "Gonna need to dirty that mouth."

"With your cock?" she asks so innocently.

We never did get to oral sex. Well, she didn't. I did.

"When you're ready, but, no, that's not what I mean." I run my lips over her ear. "Tell me what you want."

Her hips lift into me. "You're already giving me what I want." Her head falls back, and her eyes flutter when she does it again. "Feels so good, Matthew." She grips her breasts, and fuck if I don't get harder. "Touch me. Make me come, then fill me up. I love feeling you come inside me."

"Fuck, baby." My cock jerks. "Love those words. Don't ever stop telling me what you need when you need it."

If she had a response, it was lost on my tongue as I suck it out of her, love her slowly, deeply, and maybe a little more roughly when she starts begging to come.

Love her hard.

Love her easy.

Love her heart, her mind, her body.

Love my girl. Never letting her go.

The sight of Matt in his kitchen cooking does something to me. I want to rub all over him like a cat, leaving my scent, making sure he and everyone else knows he's mine.

He is mine, right?

He turns, his surprise morphing into a dimpled smile, full wattage, and then falls. "What's wrong?"

I twist the end of the t-shirt I stole from his closet. Nate packed me clothes, but I prefer Matt's. I only wish he'd worn it so it smelled like him.

"Baby?" he presses, cupping my cheek. "Just say it."

"Are we… together? Or are we hanging out, dating to see where this goes?"

"Ha!" He chuckles and presses a kiss to my forehead, leaving his mark. "Never letting you go, Gorgeous. You and I were written in the stars." He points to the kitchen bar. "You need to read that."

He dismisses my question so easily, but still… "So, I'm your girlfriend?"

After turning the stove off, he approaches me slowly. "Yeah, Gabby, you're my girlfriend, and I'm your boyfriend, and as soon as you let me, you're going to be my wife."

Wife. Nate called me his *wife*, and I loved it, but this feels different. More. "Exclusive?"

He shakes his head, gripping me around my hips. "You still don't get it. I'll spell it out for you, baby." He cups my mound. "Fuck, didn't consider you'd be bare under my t-shirt." He rests his forehead on mine. "I've missed the fuck out of you, Gabby. I've no intention of going slow.

In case you've missed it, this right here," he pats my pussy, making me tremble, "is just as much mine as is your heart."

His other hand presses mine to his hardening cock. "My cock is yours and only yours, as is my heart. It's always been yours. So, yeah, to answer your question, we're exclusive, in a relationship, and if I have my way, you'll be moved in by the end of the weekend."

"It's Friday," I offer in case he forgot, a little stunned. "But Nate—"

"Will have to learn to live without you in his house, but not his life. We talked. I'm not asking you to give him up. He's your family. That makes him my family. Buying the company was also for him. He's an amazing player, but he's hounded by rumors around his sexuality. I don't care who he screws as long as it's not you or me."

A giggle escapes. "He'd like that."

He groans, "Yeah, I know. I set him straight on that too. Family. Not lovers." He pulls me in, squeezing my ass. "We good? Clear?"

I nod. "Hey, Matt?"

He chuckles. "Yeah, Gorgeous?"

"Love you."

"Ah, baby, love you too." His kiss is slow and so yummy, but ends way too soon. He swats my ass. "You need to read that." He taps the counter. "Let me finish dinner."

Holy shitz. I nearly pass out when I read the contract and payout. "You can't be serious."

"Serious. You deserve it. The numbers came from Fin and Joe. We're in agreement. All you have to do is sign your new contract, but have your lawyer and agent read over it first. I sent them a copy."

His driver's license sits next to the contract. "Why is this here?"

"I noticed something interesting." He leans against the counter, waiting.

"Nice pic. Are you trying to tell me I need to get my Texas driver's license?"

He only grins. So, I look again. His DL number, address, birthday… "Your birthday is June twenty-fourth?"

His smile grows. "Yep. What hospital were you born in?"

"Baylor Dallas, though I think it's been renamed." I flip his driver's license and stare at the date again. "Same year."

He takes it from me and tosses it on his wallet, sitting not too far off, and stands between my legs. "It's gotta mean something, Gabby. You and I were born the same year, in the same hospital, on the same day. We were in the nursery together. We've known each other our whole lives, we just didn't meet until we were eighteen." He captures the side of my face and neck, his fingers slipping into my hair. "I wasn't ready for you at eighteen. I tried, but I wasn't man enough to keep you. I'm man enough now. Say you'll move in, give us a new beginning, starting fresh from here."

I want that, so much. "Yes. Forever, yes."

"Damn, love that. Love you."

My reply gets swallowed by his mouth, sweetly taking mine on a journey I've waited so long for. I wasn't ready for him at eighteen either. I didn't love myself enough to let him love me back. I was working on it, but I wasn't there. I'm *still* working on it. I'm not the *old* Gabby or the *new* one. I'm just me. Gabriella Elizabeth Chisholm, soon to be McIntyre, hopefully sooner than later.

But I'm not rushing this. I'm going to take everything he gives me one day at a time and give it back tenfold.

He never stopped loving me.

I never stopped loving him.

We tried to move on. Neither of us could. We crashed and burned in our own ways.

Ways that hurt our souls, making us miss the other even more.

We have the rest of our lives to make it up to each other, one glorious dimpled smile, one kiss, one shared breath at a time.

"I'm going to love you forever," I breathe across his lips.

His eyes glisten as he holds me steady. "Forever will never be enough, but I'll take it."

The End

Can't get enough? Want to know what's next for Matt and Gabby? Keep reading for their Epilogue and a chance to get exclusive BONUS Scenes for newsletter subscribers.

Jace's story, *Until You Save Me*, is next. Add it to your TBR.

In the meantime, if you're a fan of alphaholes and sports romances, then meet the men of my *Black Ops MMA* Series. They're tough, determined, and sometimes too alpha for their own good. NO MERCY is Book 1 in the series. Gabriel "No Mercy" Stone is tough, alpha and loves his woman fiercely (once he pulls his head out of his ass. Ha!). When it comes to protecting his Angel, he has no mercy.

Want romance with an otherworldly connection? Then check out Theo and Lauren's epic romance in The Road to Redemption. When Life put them together, the Universe noticed. What they didn't know is that they were made for each other. Literally.

This is a dream for me to be able to share my love of writing with you. If you liked this book, please consider leaving a review on Amazon and/or on Goodreads.

Personal recommendations to your friends and loved ones is a great compliment too.
Please share, follow, join my newsletter, and help spread the word—let everyone know how much you love Matt and Gabby.

Epilogue One

TWO DAYS LATER

To say I've loved this woman my whole life isn't entirely accurate, but it feels true. Maybe my whole *adult* life is more precise, but doesn't feel big enough. It's like saying the Grand Canyon is big—it is, yet it is far, far more than just big.

I believed my life could be broken up into two parts: *before* her and *after* her. Now I know there's a third part to my life: *with* her. I'm not the same man I was at eighteen. I'm both happy and sad about that.

The *before*-Matt at eighteen was a romantic, an idealist, looking for my other half to walk through life with.

The *after*-Matt, still at eighteen, gave up on love and the ideal of making a meaningful connection that didn't involve my cock. I didn't walk through life. I fucked my way through it.

I'm happy to see that version of me is long gone, though if the last forty-eight hours is a predictor, then maybe I am still fucking my way through life, only this time, *with* my girl. My *only* girl. Not a sad bone in my body about that.

My Heart stretches, pushing her glorious ass into me. I press forward, gripping her hip, letting her know I could go again when she's ready. She leans forward, pressing her face into her pillow, then rolls to

227

her stomach, turning her lazy smile on me, as she rises on her elbows, her hair a magnificent mess around her face, shoulders, and back.

Damn, I'm one lucky asshole. I kiss her nose and relish her nuzzling into me like a cat. I can almost hear her purr.

She settles on her side, facing me, her smile fading as she runs a finger down the curve of my face, then her whole hand over my shoulder and down my arm, to my hand resting between us on the bed. The echo of her touch warms my blood and teases my cock. I don't move though. It's in her eyes, the somberness on her face, the words on the tip of her tongue she needs to share.

Her gaze flashes to mine before she squeezes my hand. "My mom died when I was twelve."

Oh, damn. Okay, we're going there. I cup her cheek, touch her bottom lip with my thumb and press a kiss there. "I'm so sorry."

She shakes it off. "It wasn't… She didn't…" She punches out a breath and tries again, "I didn't have a good relationship with her, or really any of my family except Nicky, but he became a casualty of my need to escape my family's harsh opinion of me."

I frown and slip back to holding her hand, not wanting to derail whatever she's ready to share.

"I was always a big kid, not just in height but size. A fact the world wouldn't let me forget and a message my family insisted I hear. I was never good enough. I never fit in. My brothers teased me and called me names, except Nicky. But he was the youngest boy and didn't or couldn't do anything to stop them. My dad, well," she shrugs and meets my eyes, "you saw how he is. My mom, though, she went the extra mile to be sure I knew she felt my weight was an embarrassment. Her words were always the harshest, the ones that cut the deepest."

I slide closer, entwining our legs, gripping her waist, needing her to know I'm here. "I love every fucking inch of you."

Her watery smile has me needing to love her so fucking hard she'll forget every cruel word ever said to her or about her.

She nods, sucking her lips in, tears slipping free and sliding sideways onto her pillow. "I love that you do." She swipes at her face. "But you're going to have to be patient with me as I learn to accept and believe it."

"I'll tell you every day. As much as you need to hear it." I kiss her, a bit hard, a bit demanding, needing to impart the depth of my love. "I'll love the hell out of your body, Gabriella, no matter the size. But you know I love your curves." I grip her ass and press her to my hard cock, already begging to go home again. "I can't wait to get you pregnant so there's even more of you to love."

She laughs. "I thought Joe was the caveman,"

"Nope." I lift her leg and press home, just enough to make her sigh. A full body tremor has her holding on, pulling me closer. "You bring out the caveman in me, Gorgeous. I wanted to throw you over my shoulder the first time I saw you walking out of the dorm. You didn't even see me, didn't even know I existed, and all I wanted to do was steal you away, mark you, make you mine, and never let you go." I kiss her forehead. *Mine.* "I've only ever felt that way about you. My soul knew the second it recognized its other half. I'm the reason Jen got you on the dorm flag football team. She asked me to help coach. I wanted to meet you. It seemed like the perfect solution."

"Stallion," she whispers in reverence, but it's not me who should be revered, who needs to hear how easy she is to love. It's no hardship.

I push in farther, kiss her softly, then slide in and out slow enough she won't forget I'm there, but not fast enough to get us off. This is about more than just making love. "Tell me. Let me demolish the weight of their words."

My sweet girl arches, trying to get me deeper, her words faltering with every up stroke. "My mom's last words to me were," she gasps and grips my arm when I shove in hard and deep, *"no one will ever love you the way you are."*

Fuck me. I grip her harder than she needs. Thank God her mother is not alive, or she'd feel the full wrath of my anger and disappointment. What kind of mother says that? What kind of father allows it? "She was so fucking wrong." I capture her cheek and pump faster.

"My dad once told me he was glad I was overweight because guys would leave me alone because…"

Because *no one would ever love her the way she is…*

Yeah, totally ending him. Fucking asshole.

She grips the back of my neck, urging me to kiss away the pain.

I've got you, baby.

I suck her bottom lip then the top, rolling so I'm completely on top, grinding deeper, urging her legs up around my waist. "Don't let their narrow-minded prejudice rule you. They were wrong." I hold the side of her beautiful face, keeping her watery gaze on me. "I love you, Gabby. Always have. Always will."

She lunges, pressing her mouth to mine, sucking my tongue as she grips my ass and moves with me.

Tingles ripple along my skin. "Fuck. Just like that," I breathe into our kiss.

"Matthew," she purrs.

"They can't hurt you anymore, baby. I got you. You're mine to protect, hold, and cherish." She gasps as her body squeezes me. "Fuck, love that. Squeeze me, baby."

With her sequestered in my arms, I piston through every stranglehold of her pussy. Our mouths and bodies lock, pulling and giving, tangled and entwined, dancing to the rhythm of our hearts, our souls, our broken pieces melding into each other, becoming one, becoming whole.

Fuck me. It's never been this good.

Fuck. Fuck. Fuck. Don't fucking come.

The feel of her, soft yet strong, supple and powerful, letting me inside her body again after all these years—physically and emotionally. I am undone.

I'll worship at her feet, praise her existence, and protect her with all that I am. All I have. All I will ever be.

I am hers.

And I'm not even a little scared.

Her hold over me is all consuming, and I'm good with that.

"Ohmygod!" my girl moans and sighs, trembling below me.

I hold her tighter, grind harder, taking her. Taking her. Taking her.

"Holy—" Her head falls back, breaking our kiss, shaking.

I am bereft, lost without her mouth on me. "Baby." I slide my hand up her neck and bring her luscious lips to mine so I can feast. "Give it to me."

She cries as I consume her, ride her orgasm, dwelling in deep and letting her pussy feast on me in return, sucking, sucking, sucking my orgasm from me, waves of pleasure racing through me, rising, rising, rising to meet hers.

"Oh my God." She shakes, panting against my lips, her body continuing to spasm, pulling me deeper, teasing me, quenching me, satiating the beast that needs to mark her, keep her, protect her.

"My Gorgeous girl." I kiss her tenderly, still moving inside her. I don't ever want to stop. "I get it now." I kiss her nose, cheek, shoulder, as I roll to my back, holding her in place to rest on top of me.

"What do you get?" So completely lax, she doesn't even try to hold her weight off me. I press a hand to her ass to be sure she stays right where she is.

"My brothers and their girls, they're insatiable. They fuck like they're trying to break a world record. But it's not just sex. I get it now," I kiss her head, "it's so much more—"

"It's everything," My Heart finishes my thought.

"Exactly."

Epilogue Two

ONE WEEK LATER

NEVER WENT HOME. MATT BROUGHT ME TO HIS place on Friday after the news conference, and I never left. Not complaining. There's no place I'd rather be. He had movers pack my stuff at Nate's, bring it over, and unpack it Saturday morning while we were at The Stallions' team meeting with the new owners. Matt's assistant oversaw it all. I didn't have to lift a finger.

Is this my life? Pinch me. Really.

My larger items that shipped from New York are still in storage. I haven't decided what to do with them. Matt wants me to move them in here and redo the place as I like, but really there's nothing I have that I love all that much. *If* I decide to redecorate, I'd rather do it together, make it *ours*.

Given that I start training camp at the end of next month, redecorating is not high on my to-do list. I think that's more of a next off-season item. I want to get a feel for his place, um, *our* place, before making any changes. Plus, there's nothing to dislike about his furniture or style, except maybe some softer colors, lighter tones.

He has all the amenities I could ever want in his penthouse—darn it, *our* penthouse—and in the tower I could ever want. He has his own gym in the penthouse, but then there's a fully loaded gym two floors down. And who wouldn't love a rooftop pool that's heated for year-round? Only Matt and I, Fin and Margot live in this tower. For now, Joe and Sam have the pool in the opposite tower all to themselves. How insane is that?

The brothers are in the process of convincing Victor, Michael, and Jace to move in here. They currently live across the street in a high-rise condo. Sam is even trying to get Sebastian, her doctor friend, to move in here, or at least across the street with the guys. I've experienced the McIntyres when they get something in their heads. They don't take no for an answer. I'm honestly surprised they haven't just moved in their band of brothers like Matt did me and Joe did Sam. I think Margot is the only one who knew she was moving in when she did.

Not complaining. Honest. I love my take-charge alpha. I wouldn't want him any other way. Others may know him as the affable playboy, but I know the real man: the deeply emotional and caring protector, who would flip the world upside down for me.

Someday he'll be the father of my children—not too soon, but not too far away either. I'm not getting any younger, but at nearly twenty-six, I've finally gotten my feet under me, the man of my dreams at my side, and the career I never wanted until I did. I'd like to live in that space for a while before bringing littles into the mix.

Plus, once I get pregnant, my football playing days are over. I could never chance hurting our baby once I become pregnant, and there's no such thing as a nine-month maternity leave *before* you even deliver. It's a new world of a female player in the NFL, but the topic of having babies will never help the cause. So, I'll play as long as I can and hope there will be more women to carry the torch once I set mine down.

Equality can only take us so far. Though we should be treated to equal pay and equal opportunity, the bottom line is men and women are inherently different. Men can't have babies. They don't carry them for ten months and then need time to physically recover from pregnancy and delivery while bonding with their child. They can't feed their babies from their bodies like women can—if they choose to.

When it comes to equality, it doesn't mean we want to negate what makes a woman special or neglect the bonding time the men deserve as well. Will we ever get there? I don't know, but I hope my little contribution will help and not hinder the women coming in behind me.

"What are you doing, baby?" Matt's shadow envelops me before his lips press to my neck.

"Just writing down a few ideas." I minimize the screen, not quite ready to share. "I thought I might take up blogging about my experience as a female in a male-dominated sport."

"Really?" He leans on the edge of the desk he set up for me in his—*our*—office.

His expression is blank. I can't read him. Is he interested or leery of the idea? "I'd never do it without the okay of you and your brothers."

"You don't need our approval as the team owners, as long as you don't slander the team. But as your man, I love the idea. Though, I think a vlog would be better. We could set up a video channel. Or," he snaps his fingers, "a podcast. Oh, man!" He's up and pacing the room, "I love that idea. We could start out small and then grow to be even more diverse. We could develop a satellite radio station."

I press my hand to his chest. "Calm your jets, Stallion—"

"Stallion?" Funny-excited-marketing Matt morphs into sexy-alpha-ready-to-rut Matt.

Alpha Matt does something to my girly places, turning me into a cat in heat who just wants her tomcat to do her right. I rub against him, even though I know we don't have time for such things.

"Gabriella," he warns.

Which only sends shivers down my spine and my need to bend over to show him what he does to me. "You can be quick." I squeeze my breasts, nipples hardening from the contact.

"Jesus, you're a naughty siren, My Heart." He swats my ass. "Close the door and lock it."

He doesn't have to tell me twice.

"My brothers aren't going to walk in and see what I'm getting ready to do to you," he grumbles as he slips his shirt over his head.

I nearly melt when the tip of his cock presses out the top of his low-slung track pants.

"Stop staring at my cock and get over here, woman."

Yes, yes, and please, yes.

When I'm within reaching distance, he snags my hand and yanks me to him. He teases his mouth across mine. I grind against him and want to swallow him whole when he groans, "You need me, Gorgeous?"

"Yes, Stallion. Fuck me hard over your desk." I blush, having no idea where that even came from. The more he loves me, the more I feel accepted. The more I come alive.

"Jesus Christ." He nips at my neck. "Naked. Now, baby."

I suck in my lips, biting down as I unbutton my flowy summer dress. It only takes a few buttons before it's sliding down my body to puddle on the floor.

He groans at the sight of my new white lacy bra and panties set. I might have shopped a little this week besides training with Nate and the team. I moan and grab my breasts when he frees his cock and strokes it hard, squeezing the tip.

One thorough kiss, and I'm naked, pressed to his desk, my leg hitched around his hip as his fingers slip inside. I unabashedly ride his hand, the suction sound and his growls of approval spurring me on. He fucks my mouth just as vigorously as I chase my release harder, faster, my heart beating so hard, I fear I'll never catch my breath, or live past the massive orgasm that's ringing in my ears, sliding around my legs and up to my core.

"You're drenched, baby. Give it to me. You're almost there."

He bends me further, his arm banded around my waist, holding me as his other hand obliterates me from the inside out, sending me sailing when he tugs on my nipple, licking and sucking until I scream his name and a string of unfettered cuss words.

Before I can even recover, I'm flipped over, my chest flat on his desk, his hands on my hips as he surges forward in one long, delicious slide that fills me to the brim and has me squirming to accommodate his size.

"Shh, give it second," he groans, nipping at my neck, caressing up my back. "You're still getting used to me, aren't you, My Heart, my girl?"

If you consider we broke up the day after losing my virginity seven years ago and the nine days I've been with him since we've gotten back together, I'm still new to sex in general. Not a day goes by that he doesn't show me something new and exciting that gets me off faster and harder than I ever thought possible. I'm still tight, and he has to work himself in if I'm not relaxed by a few orgasms first. And those are some of the best orgasms. His eyes, his focus completely on me, loving me inside and out, every inch, every time.

He slides his hand around to cup my mound, teasing my folds before rubbing my clit slowly as he rains kisses along my back, shoulder and neck. He pushes in farther, then eases out. With each rub and each outward stroke, I need him deeper, harder.

When I'm clawing at his desk, he finally picks up the pace, linking our hands braced on the desk as his other works my clit.

"That's it, Gorgeous, take me." His words shiver up my spine, and he groans, nipping and kissing everywhere he can reach, until he stands. One hand gripping my hip, the other still on my clit, he thrusts harder, faster.

I moan when he pulls back and gasp when he slams deep, over and over. On tiptoe, I flex my pelvis till he's hitting that "Ohmygod!" spot. I swear I pee and feel moisture dripping through our connection. But I can barely catch my breath, much less take a moment to be embarrassed, because I really want to do it again.

"Fuck! You just… Fuck." He slams me harder, pinches my clit.

I scream, echoing my release around the room as he growls his in response.

A few more thrashing stabs of his cock and he collapses on me, continuing to rub my clit. "Again."

I whimper into his forehead resting on my shoulder.

He shallow pumps into me, hitting that spot that makes my legs shake, rubbing my clit and whispering dirty, filthy things into the air between us until I come again, gushing between us, and he fills me and fills me and fills me.

I clean us up in my office's attached half-bath. I thought the one in here was a waste all these years. Now, I'm seeing it in a whole new light. Joe texted me a few minutes ago, giving me a heads up that the six pack, plus some, have arrived. I curse myself for not taking her to our bedroom instead of staying in our office. Only the door separates us from my family.

I've no doubt they heard us. My girl's not quiet. I've heard Fin and Margot going at it in his office—same layout, same acoustics. At the time, I turned and walked out, telling him to call me when they were done. I never did get that call. I ended up eating a microwavable dinner instead of eating with them as planned.

Such is the life of a single guy, which I'm not anymore. Thank God.

I help her button up her dress and kiss her softly. "We've got company," I warn her.

Her eyes widen, and her chest flushes. "Who?"

I clear my throat and shrug, hoping my nonchalance will rub off on her. "Everyone."

"No, no, no, no." My girl backs up as far from the door as possible, pointing. "I can't go out there."

"Yes, you can. It's no big deal. You know my brothers do it like rabbits. You're bound to walk in on them eventually." I tip her chin to me. "Would you want them to avoid you?"

"Yes." She nods and knocks my hand away.

"No, you wouldn't." I know her. She'd downplay it, making it no big deal. I run kisses up her neck. "Come on, Gabby, we can't avoid them forever. A minute of discomfort, then it's done. Like ripping off a Band-Aid."

A few more kisses till my girl is relaxed again. I clasp her hand and open the door, praying the assholes aren't too hard on her.

The second we step into the living room, catcalls and whoops erupt. My brothers, Fin and Joe; Michael; Victor; Jace; Sebastian and even Nate are holding up paper signs with numbers written on them: 10, 10, 10, 9.5, 10, 10, 12.5.

Sam and Margot are on the couch, trying not to laugh.

"Assholes," I groan and pull Gabby into my side, where she buries her face in my neck. "Not funny." Okay, it's a little funny. I point to Victor. "What the fuck, 9.5?"

He only shrugs. "I've heard better." More likely he's had better, the kinky fuck. He has a thing for sex clubs, and he likes to share his women. Not judging. His sex barometer is not set to my level, obviously. Otherwise, he would have known that was the best sex of my life, and Gabby and I have barely scratched the surface. She squirted. *Twice.* That requires some investigation. Long. Hard. And *frequent* investigation.

Gabby glances at Nate. "12.5?" She laughs.

"Hot as hell, Firecracker." He grins, stealing her from my side. "Miss you, bestie. But you're apparently doing quite well." He winks at me and kisses her cheek before stepping back when she swats at him, heat creeping up her cheeks.

Gorgeous, baby. My fucking woman, stealing my breath without even trying.

"Did you meet everyone?" I ask Nate.

"Yep, Sebastian is the only one I hadn't seen or met before." His gaze flies to Sam's friend across the room laughing at something she says to Joe. Sebastian adores her. He's a good friend to all of us now, but those two have a special connection, not unlike Gabby and Nate.

I study the situation a little closer, noting the interest in Nate's attentiveness. I wonder…

Gabby presses to my side. "I haven't met Sebastian," she reminds me.

"I'll introduce you." Nate goes for her hand.

"I got it." There's no debate. Nate flashes me a smile and steps back, following us to the group, where I make the introductions and watch as Sebastian and Nate's eyes flit back to each other over and over as the night progresses.

Interesting.

Nate goes both ways. Maybe Sebastian likes the soft and pink and the long and hard too. He's never brought anyone to our get-togethers. I always assumed he was hetero because of his interest in Sam, but then I look at Nate. If I didn't know otherwise, I would assume Nate was hetero too.

I'm learning not to judge a book by its cover.

I've asked the world not to judge my girl by her chosen profession. Just because she plays football and is built like an Amazonian Goddess, doesn't mean she's a lesbian. She loves the *long and hard,* and I give her *soft and pink* all it can take… and more.

Mom and Dad arrived just before we ate. Thankfully they missed the sexual eavesdropping. Now that we've finished, my nerves spike. I take a pull on the Macallan Fin hands me.

"Ready?" He quirks a brow.

"Yep. Do or die, Brother."

He laughs. Let's hope it doesn't come to that." He slaps my shoulder, squeezing, keeping me in place. "I'm proud of you, Brother. You've been through some shit. Don't let it darken your future. Let it go." He motions to the room. "They have. Don't let Jace's guilt over what happened to Veronica and her brother at the hand of their father confuse you. Jace's issues aren't with you." He squeezes again. "Tell me you hear me. Your girl deserves all of you. Don't hold back from her because of your past."

I clap his shoulder in return. "I'm not fucking this up, Fin. I know I'm lucky to have found her again. Lightning struck twice. I'm no idiot. I've got this. I've got *her.*"

A quick hug and he's gone, leaving me to search out my girl in the mass of my family, who's taken her in like the long-lost sister, daughter, friend she is. I can't hide my smile when her gaze lifts to mine. Her brow arches, head tilting, seeing straight to my soul.

Come to me, Gorgeous, I beckon her.

Like the siren she is, she floats to me, all sexy legs and confident strides. You'd never know it to look at her that her confidence is shaky, built on the lies of narrow-minded people who couldn't look beyond their own shortcomings to love her unconditionally. She told me about her mom and how she really died, and the confrontation with her dad. I'm so proud of her for facing her fears, her abusers.

I don't know if I can trust anything her family says, but I'll try to remain open-minded—for her. Only for her.

But if she says *kill.* They. Are. Dead. No questions asked, no qualms about it.

"Hey." She presses to my chest.

"My Heart." I grip her hips, holding her in place and lay a kiss on her forehead. "I need to ask your forgiveness."

"For?" She's more amused than concerned.

"I embarrassed you once already, and I'm afraid I may embarrass you once more, but it can't be helped."

"What—"

"Trust me?"

"Always," she replies without hesitation.

I kiss her quickly but hold a second longer, gathering my thoughts, my courage. "I love you, Gabriella."

She holds my face between her hands. "You're scaring me, Stallion. What's wrong?"

I turn to kiss the inside of one wrist and then the other. "Not a damn thing, baby. Just showing you my heart."

After another too-brief kiss, I guide her to the windows overlooking downtown Dallas and face my family—soon to be *her* family.

Clasping her hands, I face My Heart and give her mine. "I loved you from the first moment I saw you, Gabby. You stole my breath and my heart. I was too dumb to keep you. I wasn't ready…" I look down, the weight of those words tightening my throat, making it hard to continue. Regret is a bitch.

"Hey." She tilts down, catching my eyes. "I wasn't ready for you either. We both made mistakes, but here we are, right where we belong, wiser and prepared to give what it takes to make it this time."

"Jesus, baby." I press my forehead to hers. "Love you so fucking much," I whisper only for her. I swallow, giving it a second or two before I pull back and bend to my knee.

"Matt," she gasps, tearing up.

"Marry me, Gabriella. Let me make up the last seven years of our lives by giving you the rest of mine. Spend forever with me as my wife, my better half." I manage to pull the ring out of my pocket and slip it on her left ring finger. "Say yes, baby."

"Yes!" She shrieks and jumps on me the second I stand. "Forever. Yes."

"Thank Christ." I hug her tight and steal her mouth, ignoring the cheers from our family.

When Nate practically rips her from my arms, I let her go, knowing they're all here for a reason.

I get misty when my mom tears up hugging my girl. "You have to start joining our mother-daughter lunch I have with Sam and Margot. I was going to invite you tonight anyway, but now it's in an official capacity." She hugs her again. "I always knew it would take a remarkable woman to capture my Matty. I just didn't know he'd already met her."

Gabby wipes at her eyes. "He's the remarkable one, Mrs. McIntyre."

Mom pats her hand. "And that is why you two will make it. You both feel honored to be loved by the other. Don't lose that. It's a gift. Treat it as such."

"I will, I promise," I interject, kissing Mom and then my fiancée.

Fiancée. Love that.

Love her.

Do I tell her we leave in a week to marry on Joe's island, or do I wait?

She pulls me aside, nervously playing with the skirt of her dress, her gaze flitting over my shoulder. "Do you think—"

"Hey." I turn her so her focus is only on me. "Don't be tentative with me. Whatever you want, it's yours." Her beaming smile loosens the last of my nerves. "Tell me."

"I want to go back to the island. It's an amazing place, and I feel we ruined our time there. I want a mulligan."

"Damn, you couldn't be more perfect if you tried." I nod to the room behind her. "We're leaving in a week, well, not quite. We leave on Friday. Marry on Saturday. Spend Sunday with the family. They leave on Monday, and we have the place to ourselves for the next twenty days. We'll get back in time for you to get ready for training camp."

My girl is nearly bouncing in place. "You're serious?"

"Completely. You okay with that?" I sink my hand into her hair, keeping her steady, on me.

"Damn, you couldn't be more perfect if you tried," she gives me back my words. "I love you, Matthew. My stallion."

"Love you, Gabriella. My heart, my girl." I lean in and whisper, "My fiancée." Her trembled gasp has me wanting to kick everyone out.

"Thirty minutes. Then you're making everyone leave. Deal?" She tries to give me a quirking brow, but she can't carry it off like Nate or me.

I kiss the corner of her mouth. "Deal, baby. Then in thirty-one minutes, I'm eating you for dessert."

She leans in, her lips grazing my cheek. "Then maybe you can dirty my mouth with your cock."

"Out! Everyone, get the fuck out. Now!" I growl.

Epilogue Three

THREE MONTHS LATER

IT'S OPENING DAY. THE FIRST GAME OF THE SEASON. I'm nervous as shit as I pace my private woman-only state-of-the-art locker room. Our new powerhouse owners, Matt, Fin, and Joe, had it built for me. It was already a room across the main hall from the guys' locker room, but this one was for visiting talent. Now, it's my own, equipped with showers, bathroom facilities, and a row of padded bench seats with backs in front of custom lockers with a place for my helmet, uniform, pads, a refrigerator, and a safe for personal effects—at *each* station.

They built it with the intention of having more female players, so it isn't just make-do for me. It's a room built for the future of football in this organization, a dream, a goal to open the doors, offer the opportunity to all women. It's daunting and hopeful. But for now, it's just for me, and it's lonely as fuck.

In college I had a room off the guy's locker room. I could hear them, feel a part of the team. Yell through a fucking grate. Nate would let me know when it was safe to come out, though often I didn't wait. I didn't care if I saw swinging dicks. It was part of the job, and if a dick was going to scare me off, then I had no business playing with a bunch of animals who prized the organ between their legs. It's like going into a strip club and not expecting to see boobs. The squeamish need not apply.

A knock on the door has me locking on the video screen above the door showing who's standing on the other side. My husband's dimpled grin hits me full on, staring into the camera. Then he *winks*, like he knows I'm watching, which I am, of course.

He has a keycard to get in, but it's protocol to wait until he's let in by me or by the security guard stationed outside after I give the all-okay.

It takes five steps and a single breath before I grasp the handle to let in the man of my waking dreams. Asleep, I could never dream a better life or love than the one he's given me. I would never dare believe I would be so blessed.

"Mrs. McIntyre." He kisses my cheek, stepping into me, his knowing gaze seeking mine. "You doing okay?"

"Yeah." I shrug.

His eyes fall to my shoulders and down.

"It's a little lonely in here by myself," I admit.

When his caressing perusal of me in my uniform finally reaches my face, heat and want hit me like a blowtorch, singeing my skin.

"You're too fucking hot to be in there with the guys. You'll get 'em all hard, and that," he grabs my ass and pulls me flush against his hardened cock, "would have to be painful in those pants."

"Be serious." I pat his chest and push back. I don't need his type of distraction.

He follows me as I take a sip of my water. "I am serious. I've seen you in uniform during the preseason games, but…" He shakes his head in surprise. "You're knocking me on my ass today."

I yelp when he swats my ass, but then he frowns scoping out the room. "You need a couch."

"You've been talking to Nate."

"He was right to get you a couch in your dorm room. You need someplace in here to sit other than the bench seat at your locker." He turns, eyeing the perfect spot. "It would never work in with the guys. They'd tear it up in a week. But it's only you—for now. You need a couch." He pulls me into his chest. My shoulder pads prevent me from getting as close as I'd like. He eyes my braided hair that will soon be covered in a skullcap. "Don't be nervous. You've got this. My girl doesn't let nerves impact her performance."

Usually not, but he's the owner now. This impacts more than just the team.

"Hey." He pinches my chin, bringing my gaze back to him. "It's just you, the ball, Nate, and some of the guys out there. Don't make it bigger in your mind. It's the same kick you'd give when you played flag football, the same you did for UT and New York. It's no different here."

I press my head to his. "Just me and the ball," I repeat.

He kisses my forehead, lingering, letting me breathe in his calmness. "Just you and the ball." Another kiss. "Come on. They're ready for you."

We get halfway across the hall to the main locker room before he stops and turns, his concerned gaze locking on me. "You know you've nothing to prove to me or my brothers."

I suck in air. He always knows. Fear of letting him and his brothers down is a large part of my anxiety.

He steps into me, tries to grip my hips but only finds pads, then slides up to my rib pads. Frustrated, he sighs, "Jesus, you're locked up like Fort Knox."

"My face, neck, and shins are all yours." I try to lighten his frustration and my nerves.

He frowns at my neck. I can see the *your neck should be protected too* running through his brain. Clasping my hand, the one not holding my helmet, he leans in, his words only for me, "I'm so fucking proud of you." His eyes track mine as I blush from his praise. "What it took to get here, to this level, and stay here, don't diminish that. You're here because of your skills and hard work, not because of me," he points to his chest and then to the locker room door, "or Nate." He waits.

I shuffle closer, not sure what he wants me to say—*yes, yes, I'm amazing*—is not quite my style, never mind the fact that I don't *feel* amazing. I'm just me, doing what I do, the best I can. But today. Today feels bigger, more momentous.

"You succeed every time you suit up and walk on to that field." He kisses me softly. "It's just you and the ball. Don't make it more than that."

I'm sure Coach would disagree, but I get what he's saying and love him even more for it. I kiss him quickly. "Love you, Stallion."

"Love you, Wife. Go get 'em."

I disappear inside the guy's locker room.

He doesn't follow. His place is in the owner's box. He agreed to let the coaches do their job without his interference. Plus, I know he's trying to keep the fact that I'm married to the owner low key—for me—not for him.

It's not a secret. I just don't want to flaunt it in the locker room on game day… Or really any day.

Those that hate me for being a woman in a man's game don't need the reminder I'm untouchable as the owner's wife.

I relax into that thought, not because I plan on being a fuckup, but it's a comforting reminder that he and his brothers have my back. A moment ago, it drove my nervousness. Now, it makes my nerves fade away.

As much as I want to follow her into the locker room, I know that room is the coach's sanctuary and where she needs to be a member of the team and not my wife.

Hands in my pockets, I start up the hall, slowing when I find my brothers waiting.

"We thought we might have to drag you away," Joe taunts, slapping my shoulder.

"Everything alright?" Fin's concerned gaze falls on me, then to the empty hall behind me.

They were watching.

That knowledge burns in my chest. I've always been the fuckup of the three of us. I never shined as bright as them. The middle child syndrome. Such a fucking cliché. But it doesn't make it less true.

They have my back and, more significantly, my girl's back. I can never express how much that means to me.

"Good. She's nervous. Tried to ease her worry."

"She's a rock star," from Joe.

"She's got this," from Fin.

"Yeah, she does," I offer as much for her as me. I believe in her.

But as we near the owner's box, my twisted gut and racing heart are hard to ignore. I'm nervous for her, for us. I want this franchise to succeed. Though we haven't been owners long enough to earn the win or a loss, it feels important in so many ways.

"Ah, my sons have finally joined us." Dad hugs each of us as we enter the suite. Mom isn't far behind. Sam and Margot zoom to their men.

I join Sebastian, Michael, and Victor at the window surveying the hoopla below.

Is Sebastian waiting to spot Nate like I am Gabby? I don't know any details, and I'd never ask either of them, but I do know those two have become friends over the months, beyond our weekly happy hours. Nate's eyes still find his when we're all together, yet it's more a look of longing than a confidence in owning the other's heart, attention, desire. Unrequited, perhaps.

I never thought I'd give a shit about Nate's happiness, but my wife's love of the guy and his devotion to her have me caring about him and his damn heart. Or maybe, I just want the guy locked down so he's not pining over Gabby, and fuck, maybe a bit over me too. I recognize yearning when I see it. I want him to find love in whatever form he needs to be fulfilled and content.

I swipe a hand over my face and order a drink from the passing attendant. I'm going to need a little liquid courage to make it through this game.

No matter how nervous I am, I have to remember the cameras are on us, taking in our every reaction, looking for a sign of regret, disappointment, or nerves. My brothers beside me, I paste on a smile when I see our faces on the jumbotron screens over center field, the largest in the NFL.

"Smile, Brothers. We're on camera."

We clink our glasses and toast for the onlookers.

"Jesus, is this what it's going to be like?" Joe mumbles under his breath and charming smile.

"Easy, Brother," Fin encourages as he winks at me. "It'll be worth it. We own a fucking football team. How incredible is that?"

"Unbelievable," I answer. "We can close the windows and use the block-out glass whenever we want," I remind Joe.

"Thank god. I want Sam on my lap, but not for these fuckers to ogle, or the viewers watching at home."

Fin and I chuckle. Of course, he wants privacy to cuddle up on his wife. Typical. I laugh, but in all honesty, I'm jealous these two have their wives here to hold, not that I'm not damn proud of My Heart or begrudge her career choice. After all, we're owners because of her. We owe her a debt of gratitude I'll gladly pay over and over again for the rest of our lives.

Nudging my shoulder, Fin motions out the window. The Stallions are getting ready to take the field. "Here comes your wife."

Damn, if I don't love hearing those words.

We all move to stand closer, taking a collaborative breath, watching as the teams take the field.

My wife, wearing jersey number one, is easy to spot. Though I didn't need her number to know which one is my girl. Fuck if I'm not still hard for her in her jersey. I need to have an extra made to keep at home just to watch her walk around in nothing else and peel her out of it before she takes me deep.

Fuck. Fuck. Fuck. Head in the game.

My Heart looks up to our box. Whether she can see me or not, I feel the warmth of her gaze. "You got this, Gorgeous," I murmur only for her.

Beside her is Nate, wearing number fifty-five. It was his father's jersey number when he played for the University of Washington before a back injury ended his football career. He passed away before seeing Nate play his first game in the pros.

So much loss between Nate and Gabby. It reminds me I'm one lucky fucker. My family rocks. They supported me through all my fucked-up shit, but I know they're relieved I've found my girl and settled down. I'm only a manwhore for one girl, and she's a 5'10" perfect beauty inside and out, in all her sizes, in all our phases in life, she's my forever *one*, my girl, My Heart, my gorgeous kicker.

Joe nudges me. "Wake the fuck up. Your woman is on point."

Fuck. I missed the anthem, the coin toss—I guess we lost, or we deferred to receive until after halftime, because we're set up for a kick off and my wife is lining up.

"Jesus. Fuck, I'm nervous," I admit to my brothers on either side of me.

Fin takes my drink, setting it aside, and they press into my sides, hands on my shoulders. "Breathe, Brother. She's an old pro at this."

"Yeah. Yeah, she…"

Gabby sways to her back foot, and then she's off; steady and strong, she makes her way to the ball that's just sitting there in the tee, waiting for her to kick the hell out of it. And she does that and some.

"Christ, that's a beauty," from Fin.

Joe chuckles and pats my back. "Like a rock star."

The ball soars high and far, landing in the opposing endzone, where a Raider misses it, but recovers it after it bounces a few times. He only makes it ten yards before he's tackled.

My wife runs off the field, her head tilting my direction. I swear she kisses her fingers and raises them to me. But then the proof is on the jumbotron. Her beautiful, confident smile is on the screen, her gaze on me. I place my hand over my heart nearly thumping out of my chest. My world complete. Whether we win this game or the season, I've won in life because I won my Gabby back. I own her heart just as she owns mine.

Nothing. Nothing could be better than that.

The kicker and her stallion. I think we'll ride off into the sunset… together. Always together, never apart. She said she'd love me forever. I'll take it and more—so much more.

WANT MORE MATT AND GABBY?
Sign up for my Newsletter and receive free BONUS SCENES!
dl.bookfunnel.com/vgw2tc5of1

Author's Note

I knew Matt had a story to tell. I knew he met Gabby in college, and he broke her heart by doing something stupid. Those are the only facts I knew for sure when I started writing **Until You Forgive**.

The idea of Gabby being a kicker in a male-dominated sport came to life because of my daughter. She's been begging for years to play football. We put her off with soccer and softball, but she kept dreaming of playing tackle football.

She really, *really* wanted to tackle someone.

She got her wish. She started her first season of football on her seventh-grade football team, playing for her school. She's the starting Offensive Left Guard. She's got a leg on her, though, and we're hoping she'll get to be kicker next year. The guys may outgrow her, but a kicker could go far… Maybe even pro.

How cool would that be?

I thank Matt and Gabby for letting me into their hearts, their pasts, and their pain. Matt was always the playboy in my head. When I started writing the **Until You** series, I never dreamed he would have started out as the starry-eyed romantic, searching for his other half. He showed me, didn't he?

WANT MORE MATT AND GABBY?
Sign up for my Newsletter and receive a free **BONUS SCENES**!
dl.bookfunnel.com/vgw2tc5of1

Stay tuned for Jace and Veronica's story in **Until You Save Me.**
dmckdavis.com/all-books/series/until-you/until-you-save-me

Don't miss out, add it to your **TBR**!
www.goodreads.com/book/show/59618203-until-you-save-me

Acknowledgments

If you're reading this, then you are one of the people I want to thank. Thank you for picking up my book, reading my words, and making it not only to the end but to the acknowledgments. Every section, word, thought that goes into my books is meant for you. So, thank you!

If you've ever read one of my books, commented on a post, read a newsletter, or supported me in some other way—I am deeply grateful and thank you from the bottom of my heart.

My husband and my kids are my life, my support system. I couldn't do this without them. A special shout out to my daughter for inspiring me just by being the fiercest woman I know (and yes, she's only twelve). I love you 3,000 and 1!

Thanks to the readers, bloggers, followers, Diva members, and other incredible authors who support me in amazing, thoughtful, and giving ways.

Thank you to my amazing editor, Tamara, who makes my words sing by getting the story on the page the way I envision it in my head. It's a tough job, and she's always up for the challenge.

Thanks to Krista for giving my stories the fine-tuning they need. She's more than just my proofreader. She's my third and fourth set of eyes (that just sounds weird. Ha!).

And last, but definitely not least, to the readers, I thank you for buying my books, reading my stories, and coming back for more. It still amazes me I get to do this for a living, and you are the reason why. I am blessed because of you.

Don't stop. Keep reading! And don't forget to leave a review.
Blessing, Dana

About the Author

D.M. Davis is a Contemporary and New Adult Romance Author.

She is a Texas native, wife, and mother. Her background is Project Management, technical writing, and application development. D.M. has been a lifelong reader and wrote poetry in her early life, but has found her true passion in writing about love and the intricate relationships between men and women.

She writes of broken hearts and second chances, of dreamers looking for more than they have and daring to reach for it.

D.M. believes it is never too late to make a change in your own life, to become the person you always wanted to be, but were afraid you were not worth the effort.

You are worth it. Take a chance on you. You never know what's possible if you don't try. Believe in yourself as you believe in others, and see what life has to offer.

Please visit her website, https://dmckdavis.com, for more details, and keep in touch by signing up for her newsletter, and joining her on Facebook, Instagram, Twitter, and Tiktok.

Additional Books by
D.M. DAVIS

UNTIL YOU SERIES
Book 1 - Until You Set Me Free
Book 2 - Until You Are Mine
Book 3 - Until You Say I Do
Book 3.5 - Until You eBook Boxset
Book 4 – Until You Believe
Book 5 – Until You Forgive
Book 6 – Until You Save Me

FINDING GRACE SERIES
Book 1 - The Road to Redemption
Book 2 – The Price of Atonement

BLACK OPS MMA SERIES
Book 1—No Mercy
Book 2—Rowdy
Book 3 - Captain
Book 4 - Cowboy

STANDALONES
Warm Me Softly
Doctor Heartbreak

Join My Reader Group

www.facebook.com/groups/dmdavisreadergroup

Stalk Me

Visit www.dmckdavis.com for more details about my books.

Keep in touch by signing up for my Newsletter.

Connect on social media:
Facebook: www.facebook.com/dmdavisauthor
Instagram: www.instagram.com/dmdavisauthor
Tiktok: www.tiktok.com/@dmdavisauthor
Twitter: twitter.com/dmdavisauthor
Reader's Group: www.facebook.com/groups/dmdavisreadergroup

Follow me:
BookBub: www.bookbub.com/authors/d-m-davis
Goodreads: www.goodreads.com/dmckdavis

Printed in Great Britain
by Amazon